For Corwin

I know.

STAR WARS™
REBEL RISING

Written by

BETH REVIS

EGMONT

EGMONT
We bring stories to life

First published in Great Britain 2017
by Egmont UK Limited, The Yellow Building,
1 Nicholas Road, London W11 4AN

Cover Illustration by Brian Rood
Designed by Leigh Zieske

© & ™ 2017 Lucasfilm Ltd.

ISBN 978 1 4052 8507 0

65771/1

Printed in UK

To find more great Star Wars books, visit
www.egmont.co.uk/starwars

All rights reserved. No part of this book may be reproduced, stored
in a retrieval system, or transmitted, in any form or by any means,
electronic, mechanical, photocopying, recording or otherwise, without
written permission of the publisher and copyright holders.

Stay safe online. Any website addresses listed in this book are correct at the time
of going to print. However, Egmont is not responsible for content hosted by third
parties. Please be aware that online content can be subject to change and websites
can contain content that is unsuitable for children. We advise that all children are
supervised when using the internet.

MONTH 01_

The stormtrooper chuckled as Jyn Erso fell to her knees. She raised her shackled wrists. "You can take these off now," she said. "Where am I going to run?"

She gestured to the long hallway and the dim glow from the illuminators above each cell door.

"It's more fun this way," the stormtrooper said, lifting Jyn to her feet by the binders on her wrists. The metal bands cut into her skin and grated against the sensitive bones beneath, but Jyn barely flinched. She didn't want to give him the satisfaction.

"They're always so . . ." The warden, a tall thin man dressed in black, waved his hand as if searching for the right word. "They're always so *noble* when they first arrive, don't you think?"

The stormtrooper made a noncommittal noise as he prodded Jyn, forcing her farther down the dark hallway toward her cell.

The warden chuckled at his own joke, then apologized. "I'm sorry, it just amuses me so. I can always spot a fresh one. They stand straighter." His strides lengthened, and he passed Jyn and the stormtrooper, then turned in front of them, halting their progress. The warden grabbed Jyn's chin, forcing her to face him, but Jyn jerked away defiantly. He chuckled again. "The fresh ones still have a little fight in them," he said, wrinkling his nose at the word *little*.

When Jyn didn't rise to the bait, his face soured. "This way, prisoner." He turned on his heel and walked quickly down the hall. Jyn stared ahead, trying to keep her tired feet straight so she wouldn't stumble again and further prolong the ordeal.

"They picked you up . . . where?" the warden asked casually.

Jyn didn't answer.

The warden spun around and slapped her across the face, hard. "I asked you a question, Six-Two-Nine-Five-A."

"I was captured on a ship in the Five Points system," she said through gritted teeth.

"Captured . . . and arrested." The warden sounded

proud of himself, even though he'd had nothing to do with it. "And now you're here." He swept his arm out but didn't move. One of the cells was dark and empty. The stormtrooper nudged Jyn forward, and she stumbled into the tiny room. When she raised her wrists this time, he deactivated the binders. The light on the band blinked from red to green, and Jyn's wrists fell from the heavy metal with relief.

"I'm sure you'll enjoy our little operation at L-E-G-Eight-One-Seven," the warden said. He pronounced the abbreviation of the prison system branch in a rush, turning the letters LEG into *elegy*. Jyn felt it was an appropriate title. "Welcome to Wobani." He grinned at the words, well aware of the reputation the planet held.

"Your crimes, though not the worst the Empire has encountered, are not to be tolerated. You have done a disservice to the galaxy, and to repay your debt to society, you will work." The warden punched in a code on the biometric datapad by Jyn's door, and the metal bars slid into place, trapping her inside the cell. "You will not like the work," the warden added, his tone still mild and pleasant. "And you will not like your new home here. But that's what you get when you commit crimes against the Empire. Welcome to the worst days of your life."

The warden looked down his nose at Jyn through the bars. He smirked slightly. No doubt he was used to criminals breaking down at this practiced little speech, but Jyn just gaped at him.

The worst days of her life?

The warden could do no more than scowl as Jyn laughed in his face.

CHAPTER ONE_

Jyn Erso hid in the dark.

She was not afraid of the dark. She used to be, yes, but not anymore. She knew this dark. She had been in it for hours.

Ever since she had seen her mother slaughtered.

The cave was cramped, but not as cramped as it was supposed to be. She and Mama and Papa had practiced these drills, and when they had pretended the Empire was coming and it was time to hide, they had hidden together.

Jyn was alone now.

She had a satchel with her, a few possessions she'd crammed into the bag when her mama had told her it was time. Abommy the Gig wasn't there. She'd left him under her bed, where he'd protected her from the monsters she was old enough to know didn't exist. She wished she had him now; she wished she could stroke his soft synthetic fur that smelled of Papa's clove aftershave.

Jyn shook her head. No. A toy wouldn't bring her comfort now. It was a stupid thing to wish for. She couldn't be such a baby.

Jyn clutched the necklace her mother had given her moments before she died. She squeezed her eyes shut. She wondered if death hurt. She supposed it must.

It was *so* dark.

Jyn lit a lantern. The shadows danced along the rocky interior of the cave.

They reminded her of the troopers dressed in black.

"Papa will come," she told herself, the sound of her voice tinny and fragile in the darkness.

Mama had said, "Trust the Force." Jyn tried. She tried to believe. To hope.

The hatch above her rattled. Jyn sucked in a scream of fear as the door opened and a man's face peered down.

A sob escaped her. *Saw!* He had come to save her!

But not Mama. He was too late for Mama.

"Come, my child," he said. "We have a long ride ahead of us." He reached his hand down into the cave, helping her up.

Jyn looked into Saw's face, hesitating for just a moment to take his hand. The last time she'd seen him, he'd brought her and her family to Lah'mu, to make a fresh start after they'd left Coruscant. Mama and Papa had drilled into Jyn the different scenarios that might happen if—when—the Empire found them.

"And this," Mama would say, showing her how to operate the comm tower. "If the worst happens and you need help but Papa and I aren't around, you press this button here, and Saw Gerrera will come."

And every time, Jyn would reach out for the button, eager to hit it right then. "He never visits!" she'd say as Mama pulled her back, chiding her daughter that he was to be summoned in emergencies only.

Now Saw's jaw was set in a grim line. There was no smile on his lips, no joviality in his eyes like the last time she'd seen him. A long scar cut through his left eye, making the lid droopy. His eyes bulged slightly, his lips turned downward. The rain streaked his bald head. He looked angry.

Jyn reached up and slipped her small pale hand through his dark calloused one. He squeezed her fingers gently, and she gripped his back, holding on as if she were drowning and he was the rope pulling her back to shore.

"We have to go," Saw said.

Jyn swallowed her fear, her sorrow. She nodded.

The air smelled clean, fresh after the cool rain, as she and Saw ran back through the field toward Jyn's house. It seemed extraordinarily odd that the world was sleeping around them, beautiful and still, but Mama was . . .

"There were troopers," Jyn said, tugging on Saw's hand. She bit her lower lip as she silently chastised herself. She should have counted how many soldiers had come to the farm. There was the man in white, the man Papa worked with sometimes. And the black-armored troopers. And . . .

She should have paid better attention. But it had all happened so *fast*.

"No one else is here," Saw said.

Her home and the farm equipment—a comm tower, irrigation units, a droid harvester—were the tallest objects in a sea of gently waving skycorn. A shirt fluttered up, caught by the breeze, soaring like a ghost against the night sky before wafting back down.

Jyn was pretty sure the shirt was her father's, the one that was frayed at the cuffs and always smelled like him, a mixture of cloves and dirt and grease and something else, something cold and hard. But before she could grab the shirt and wrap it around her, the wind picked up and blew it away.

The closer they got to Jyn's house, the more laundry flapped in the breeze, scattering throughout the grasslands and disappearing in the night. And then she saw the laundry basket, and the depression in the grass, stained with blood.

Hope surged in Jyn's heart. Her mama's body wasn't there.

But she knew, deep down she *knew* it wasn't because Mama had survived. No one could survive a blaster shot to the chest like that.

Jyn bit the inside of her cheek, tasting the metallic tang of blood. But she didn't say a word.

Saw moved with purpose, flinging open the door to the farmhouse. Jyn followed silently, a waft of bitter smoke making her nose crinkle. The troopers had started a fire that still sputtered in the kitchen, singeing the bright wall a sooty black.

Saw knew where to look—the work cabinet, the hidden nooks and crannies, the floorboards under the carpet. It was all empty.

He cursed. "They took it all," he growled.

And they took him, Jyn thought in dull shock. *They took Papa.*

Her eyes watered, but not from the smoke. Even though it had been Saw who'd come to save her, not Papa, she'd still hoped that maybe he would be there. Hiding. Waiting. For her.

But he wasn't. He was gone.

Broken crockery littered the floor. Jyn knew her father had tried to destroy his work before he'd told her to run. There would be nothing left. Papa wouldn't let there be anything left.

Saw narrowed his eyes and whirled on Jyn. "Your pa have any secret hiding places? Something the Empire wouldn't know about?"

Their home was ransacked, and while Mama had been able to destroy some of Papa's research, the

Empire had come too quickly. She pointed to where the safe was hidden in her parents' room, but it was empty. The log case was missing, and Papa's file bank was gone. She peeked into her own room. The black-clad troopers had even upturned her bed and shredded her dolls, looking for more of Papa's work. She wasn't sure if they'd found anything. But it didn't matter anyway; everything was in Papa's brain. And they had him now.

"We need to jump planet," Saw said gruffly. "Think, Jyn. Anything else of your father's work that may be here?"

"No," she said in a small voice.

"Then we're going."

Jyn started to move toward her room, but Saw put a heavy hand on her shoulder, stopping her.

Jyn swallowed, one hand moving to clutch the crystal necklace her mother had given her. She had left everything once, when her family had abandoned Coruscant. She could do it again. At least she had her satchel.

Jyn left the house first, and she heard something metallic and heavy drop on the wooden floorboard in the farmhouse before Saw closed the door. He grabbed her elbow and pulled her along; she almost had to run to keep up with his long strides. They were only about fifty meters away when the house exploded. Jyn stumbled at the sound and felt a whoosh of heat wash over her. What was left of the last place she called home burned, the yellow-orange flames licking at the pale grass and threatening to start a field fire.

Saw didn't stop walking. He didn't even look back at the fire or at Jyn. His shuttle was waiting for them, and Saw bounded up the boarding ramp. Jyn paused, glancing back at the smoke.

There was nothing left for her there.

CHAPTER TWO_

Jyn sat beside Saw in the cockpit of his ship. She stared straight out the window, watching as they soared through the clouds of Lah'mu. The ring that circled the planet in a constant white rainbow arched overhead, and then they broke atmosphere. The sky turned black, speckled with white stars, a glow of light from the reflected sunlight on the planet's belt just visible.

Jyn gasped.

Saw glanced where she was looking and nodded grimly. A Star Destroyer hung in the blackness of space, the sun illuminating the underbelly of the ship.

They'd sent a Star Destroyer for her father.

Papa is on that ship, Jyn realized, her eyes widening. He was somewhere, somewhere *there*, just out of reach but so close.

Saw was busy at the controls. His ship was so tiny compared with the Star Destroyer, a flea next to a giant, but his mumbling curses informed Jyn that he was worried about being spotted. Within seconds, they were well past the Destroyer, and in minutes, they'd lurched into hyperspace. The blue-gray stream of lights out the window made Jyn blink, hard, her sight blurring not just with the light but with the unshed tears that were building in her eyes.

"Hey, kid," Saw said, swiveling his chair so he could see Jyn fully. "I . . ."

He stopped. Jyn knew he was going to say he was sorry, but there was something in his eyes that made her realize he knew just how futile those words were.

She stared at his face, wondering at her memories of him being funny and kind. His dark skin made the puckered scars near his left eye stand out. He looked angry. Except for his eyes.

"I don't want to talk about it," Jyn said, pulling her knees up to her chin and wrapping her arms around her legs.

Saw's expression grew hard. "Too bad," he said, "because I need to know why the Empire came after your father like that."

"You knew why my parents went into hiding," Jyn said.

"I knew bits. But I had no idea they'd send a Star Destroyer after him."

Jyn had to admit she was a little surprised, too. She knew her father was important and that he'd worked as a scientist for the Empire before fleeing Coruscant and going into hiding on Lah'mu. She knew some of what he did. Mama and Papa had said never to tell anyone about Papa's research, but she could trust Saw. Mama had.

"He studied crystals," Jyn said, pulling the necklace her mother had given her from under her shirt. She slipped it over her head and handed it to Saw when he held out his hand.

He turned it over in his palm and held it up to the light, squinting at the clear crystal. It was, Jyn knew, a kyber crystal. Not a very good one, not worth a lot of money. Papa had worked with very good kyber crystals when he worked with the Empire. He liked rocks.

"I know about the crystals," Saw said, handing the necklace back to Jyn. "But your father must have been working on something else, something more concrete. Something they want. The Empire doesn't just come down like that for crystals."

"That's all he worked on," she insisted.

"That you know of," Saw said darkly. "Did he say anything when the Empire came? Anything at all— maybe he told you something that could be a clue."

Jyn closed her eyes. She could still hear her father's voice. *Jyn, whatever I do,* he'd said, *I do it to protect you.*

And then he had gone with the man who killed Mama.

"No," Jyn told Saw.

Saw turned to the window and stared at the blue-gray

light of hyperspace. "There's something more here," he said, mostly to himself. "Since Coruscant, Galen has been working on something big, I know it. We have to figure out what it was."

Jyn felt tears burn in her eyes. Her father had been working on a broken harvester droid the night before the Empire came. Not some big secret. But she knew Saw was right. Mama and Papa talked about it, late at night when they thought Jyn was asleep. Research and crystals and fears. She wished she'd paid better attention. She wished she could at least understand *why* all this was happening.

She forced herself to remember the way things used to be. On Coruscant, when her father had openly worked for the Empire. She had been littler then, and easily distracted, but even she knew that her parents weren't happy. When they'd moved to Lah'mu, things seemed better. More relaxed. Mama taught her every day, math and science and literature and history. Papa worked in the fields, and at night he continued his research, but it wasn't like on Coruscant. He didn't work until he collapsed, mumbling to himself, ignoring her. Things were better.

But there had still been that undercurrent of fear. It spiked occasionally, when the comm tower picked up static, or when Mama and Papa insisted they have a safety drill. They invented scenarios of bad things that could happen and told Jyn what to do. Papa liked to pretend it was a game, but Jyn knew better.

There wasn't a scenario for if Mama died, Jyn thought. They had a lot of plans, but none of them ended with Jyn alone. They would hide, run, survive. Together. Mama had never thought about what would happen if she died and Jyn hurtled away from home through hyperspace.

But when she looked at Saw, she knew that wasn't true. He was her parents' plan if the worst happened. They hadn't wanted to tell her that; they hadn't wanted her to think about just how bad things could get, but Jyn knew it to be true.

Saw was her last hope.

His eyes were red-lined, and he sighed heavily as he ran a hand over his smooth head. As if he could feel her eyes on him, he glanced down at Jyn, and he tried to shoot her a reassuring smile. But then he said, "I don't know what to do with you, kid," and any comfort she'd felt disappeared.

◆◆◆

The farther they went from Lah'mu, the more surreal the journey felt to Jyn. She half expected this all to be some sort of mistake, and when they finally stopped flying, they'd be back home, everything normal again.

But when they dropped out of hyperspace a few

days later, it wasn't beautiful green-and-blue Lah'mu that was waiting for her. It was an asteroid belt.

Saw sat up straighter, and Jyn watched as his attention zeroed in on the viewport. "We're coming up on Smuggler's Run," he said. "Strap in."

At first, it was just a few stray asteroids, but soon they were in the thick of it, the shuttle lurching up and down, left and right as Saw expertly navigated the ship through the onslaught.

"I like Wrea," Saw said. "The belt keeps people away. It's quiet."

Wrea. The planet they were going to. Jyn's body slammed against the safety harness as Saw swerved around another asteroid. It suited him, to live on a planet so difficult to reach.

When they cleared the asteroids, Jyn saw Wrea. It was smaller than Lah'mu, and bluer. *Water,* she thought. With little land masses of green and white and brown scattered over the surface, the islands big and long like fingers clawing their way through the ocean.

Saw flew the shuttle straight down, landing in a small clearing surrounded by craggy rocks. Wrea was cold, and the air smelled like salt, but she couldn't see the ocean. She could only see rocks and tangled scrub brush. As they approached a broken comm tower, Jyn realized there was more to it than just the base. A door was carved into the rock, a heavy blaster-proof door that Saw accessed with a biometric lock. The metal squeaked when it slid open. Lights cascaded down a long hallway bored directly into the stone.

Jyn lingered in the doorway, looking around at the small rocky island. At the top of a hill that seemed as if it were made of one giant boulder was a comm tower. Or at least part of one. The other half lay broken and rusted at the base.

"Not used since the Clone Wars," Saw said, walking past Jyn and into the outpost. "The natives aren't exactly friendly, but they stay off this island."

"What are the natives?" Jyn asked, jogging to keep up. The door whisked shut behind her, closing her in the dank stone hallway.

"Wreans," Saw said, winking. When Jyn didn't respond, he peered at her, noting her nervousness. "They're water creatures, and they stick to the deep. You're safe."

Jyn nodded, swallowing. She didn't believe him, though. She didn't believe in "safe" at all.

CHAPTER THREE_

The outpost was bigger than it appeared from the outside. Built directly into the rock, it had three doors on either side of the main hallway, which ended in a common room larger than Saw's shuttle. He stood in the hallway a moment, as if considering his options, then he opened the door immediately to his right. It was an old office and had obviously been used for storage. "This do?" he asked. Jyn wasn't sure what he meant, so she just nodded.

He led her down the hallway. Jyn looked at the other closed doors curiously, but he didn't pause. The large common room seemed to be half cave, with a stone ceiling curving up. Jyn didn't like it at all. It was too much like the cave she'd hidden in.

A long table stood in the center, and cabinets had been built into the wall. Saw set Jyn down at the table and opened a can of nutritive milk for her. From her seat, she watched as he went back to the hall, to the first room, and started clearing stuff away. He worked quickly, his beefy arms straining as he lugged a desk into the hallway, then several crates.

"You should get a droid," Jyn called down the hallway when Saw stopped to swipe at his sweating brow. Back on Coruscant, Jyn had had a Mac-Vee droid who took care of her sometimes and kept the apartment clean. Papa liked to complain that he wasn't nearly as efficient as Mac-Vee had been, so Mama had to help him with the dishes.

"I dislike droids," Saw said in a low voice before turning and stomping down the hallway.

Jyn scurried after Saw, following him into the first room on the right. Inside were a half-dozen beds, each with a thin mattress and a blue blanket. Saw handed her a blanket and pillow from one of the beds, and Jyn thought that meant she would be sleeping there, but instead Saw picked up the mattress from the frame and carried it down the hall to the little office by the front door. He plopped the mattress on the floor, and when Jyn just stood there, he took the blanket and pillow from her arms and put them on top of the mattress.

Saw had cleared out most of the other furniture and the crates that had cluttered the little room, but he'd left a small table and an old datapad. As he straightened the mattress on the floor and draped the blanket over the end, it finally dawned on Jyn that this was her room. A dusty, tiny room with a mattress on the floor.

She wasn't even worthy of the larger room down the hall that was already set up with beds. No. This was her room.

It was so pitiful that Jyn wanted to cry. This was nothing like her room in Coruscant, sleek and filled with the highest-tech toys available. It wasn't even like her bedroom on Lah'mu, cramped but homey and filled with the little dolls Mama had made for her. But when Jyn turned to see Saw's face, she swallowed her dismay. He looked so . . . so *anxious* for her approval that all she could do was whisper her thanks.

<hr/>

When Jyn awoke the next morning, everything seemed too dark. There were no windows. The air smelled funny—musty, not crisp. Her heart thudded as she tried to wrap her mind around the disorientation of waking up in a place that wasn't home.

Jyn rubbed her eyes. They were dry and scratchy, and then she remembered that she'd been crying. And then she remembered why. Her stomach churned, acid rising in her throat. She couldn't push back the memories of the previous day. The sound of Mama's body falling, lifeless, to the ground. The waiting, waiting, waiting for someone to save her while she hid in the cave.

But that wasn't true. She hadn't been waiting for

someone. She'd been waiting for Papa. *He* was the one who was supposed to have saved her. Not Saw. A flare of rage washed over her, surprising in its intensity. She had never felt anger like this before. And even though she knew in her heart that it wasn't fair to blame Papa for not being able to save her, she held on to the emotion. It was better than the sorrow that threatened to drown her.

There was no sign of Saw when she opened the door to her room and peeked into the hallway. Her stomach ached with hunger. She wondered if she should knock on the closed doors and find Saw, but instead she made her way to the common room and found another can of nutritive milk from the same cabinet Saw had opened earlier. She sipped it alone at the table.

Idly, she looked over the different things Saw had left there. He was a little messy; the empty can of nutritive milk she'd drunk the night before was still on the table, as well as other trash. But one side of the long table was used for Saw's work. It reminded Jyn of the way her father worked—organized chaos, he called it. There were transparent sheets of star charts and schematics of Imperial ships jumbled together. But it seemed as if Saw had swept most of that aside. There was a datapad in a mostly cleared area, and Jyn saw notes Saw had been making about crystals. He'd marked down certain planets, some of which Jyn knew her father had researched as well. Jyn touched a holo-cube on the table, and her father's face lit up, floating in front of her.

Jyn looked around guiltily; she didn't want Saw to think she was a snoop.

But Saw was nowhere to be seen.

He's in one of those rooms, she thought, looking at the half-dozen closed doors.

Or maybe outside.

She slurped the milk from the bottom of the can.

He didn't leave me.

She set the can on the table.

I'm not alone. I'm not.

It was very, very quiet.

"Saw?" Jyn said in a small voice. She didn't want to wake him if he was sleeping. "Saw?" she said again, louder.

No doors opened.

She pushed her chair back from the table, metal grating on stone. Could he have taken his shuttle and flown away, leaving her there with nothing but ration cubes and whatever Wreans were?

Jyn's heart raced, and she went from door to door down the hallway, no longer caring if she disturbed Saw. An angry Saw was better than no Saw. Most of the doors were locked, and the few that weren't contained nothing but cobwebs and broken furniture, obviously piled up when Saw was clearing the outpost for his own purposes. Jyn was starting to get more panicked, and she was actually trembling by the time she reached the door that led outside. It zipped open, and although she didn't see Saw, she heard him.

Jyn crept around the boulder to where the comm tower was laying on its side. Saw had hung up various droids—a mishmash of tall, skinny metallic bodies—by their necks all along the rusty struts, and he alternated between using his blaster and attacking the dead droids in hand-to-hand combat. Saw was big and old and scarred, but when he fought, he came alive in a way Jyn hadn't thought possible.

He lunged at one droid, slamming into it so hard its body shuddered on the metal scaffolding. He spun out quickly, leveling his aim at a droid hanging farther down and firing his blaster. Without waiting to see if his shot hit—it did—he ducked down and rolled away, ending near some rocks that he used for coverage as he fired three more shots into three more droids. Their bodies clanked on the metal tower, their empty shells dancing with the force of the shots.

"Saw?" Jyn asked.

Saw stood up, sweat streaking his bald head, rolling along the ridge of the scar on his face. He stood there, waiting for her to speak.

It wasn't until that very moment that Jyn realized

why, when the Empire was coming and the troopers were closing in, her mother had commed Saw. It wasn't because he was their friend, although that had been part of her reasoning. It was because of this.

"Can you teach me how to fight like that?" Jyn asked.

"Darling," he said, grinning, "that's the plan."

There were, apparently, a lot of droid bodies on Wrea.

"Clone Wars," Saw said by way of explanation, but Jyn knew it was more than that. The battle droids and BX-series commandos were from the old war, but there were some new models as well—a prototype enforcer droid all in black, a shiny C-B3 that'd been modified hastily, and even an IG-RM war droid that looked fairly new. All of them were broken, their cybernetics cracked or removed entirely. The droids were nothing but shells, but Saw had notes scratched into each metallic body, quick little comments about weaknesses or uses of the droids, environments where they thrived or failed. And targets—Saw had taken bright orange paint and slopped it on each droid's body to mark where best to strike or shoot.

At first, Saw just tied the droids up along the inside of the fallen comm tower. He had Jyn run the gauntlet, striking as many droids as possible. Soon after, he started to make it more complicated, using ropes to swing the droids around, throwing rocks and sticks at her to simulate battle strikes. Sometimes he would don a hollow droid head like a helmet and attack her himself.

"I thought you said the Empire doesn't use droids as much anymore," Jyn said one night as they chugged nutritives. She pulled the can away from her lips and glared at it. She could have made something tastier, but Saw didn't like the hassle of food.

Saw grunted. "The Empire learned how to fight in a war against droids," he said. "Droids and clones. It helped them to forget that war is about people."

Jyn set her can down on the table. She was still hungry; she had been hungry ever since the day her mother died, and nutritive milk never filled her the way real food did. Nothing but grassroot stew and roasted skycorn and warm crusty bread and nerf-milk cheese would help the emptiness in her belly, and she wasn't going to get any of that anytime soon. If ever again.

"Droids are sometimes harder to fight than people," Saw continued, his voice contemplative. "They can be like hive insects, sharing the same mind, the same commands, able to work both individually and as a unit. You can't think about taking out just one at a time; you have to think about how to wipe out the masses as well." He leaned toward Jyn, jabbing one stubby finger at her, his chair squeaking in protest. "Or you have to take out the one giving the commands. Kill them all, or kill the head." He shrugged. "Same difference."

Jyn fiddled with her empty milk can. She liked spending her days learning to fight. When she was sparring, she didn't have time to think about how much she missed her life from before. But she was also worried. She knew she wouldn't be with Saw for the rest of her life.

"I should be learning," she said softly.

Saw looked confused. "Learning? Am I not teaching you?"

"Not math and history and science," Jyn said. "I should . . ." Her voice trailed off. "Mama used to teach me." She thought about the lessons they had shared, the way Lyra had turned baking into chemistry class, or the way Galen had taught her about crystalline spectrometers.

An emotion Jyn didn't recognize flashed over Saw's face. Before she could ask him about it, he pushed away from the table and went down the hall toward her room. He came out a moment later with the old datapad.

Jyn had never even bothered to turn it on in all the days she'd been with Saw. But he touched the side now, and it lit up as he passed it to her. She turned it over in her hands, looking at the features. A low-light holoprojector and a networking card that would connect her to the HoloNet.

"I'm teaching you everything I can," Saw said. "Anything else you want to know, you have to teach yourself."

Her gaze drifted from the datapad in her hands to the scarred, rough knuckles of his.

"Okay," she said. "Can I go to my room now?"

Saw blinked in surprise. "Of course. You can go anywhere you want. This is your home."

Jyn made sure her bedroom door was closed before curling up on the mattress on the floor. It was so quiet and dark. Before her mother had sent Jyn to the cave to wait for Saw, Lyra had given Jyn the kyber crystal necklace and told her, "Trust the Force." Then she'd said, "I'll be there." Jyn had taken that to be her mother's promise that she would find her in the cave, but for a moment, Jyn wondered if it meant something different, if she had been saying she'd be in the Force.

Jyn sat in the center of her bed, her legs crossed, and closed her eyes. She focused on the silence and stillness of her little room. She willed herself to feel the Force. If there was anyone who could help her now, could help her reach her father, it was Mama.

She waited for the Force to prove that it was real.

It did not.

Jyn pulled the blanket over her head, then reached

for the datapad. She booted up the Imperial HoloNet broadcast. The dim blue light filled her room, and she turned the sound on low, certain Saw wouldn't want her to be listening to the enemy. With every new story, Jyn wondered if she'd hear something about her father. Surely Galen Erso's capture would be newsworthy? She just wanted to see him again.

But there was nothing.

CHAPTER FOUR_

The next day, there were no droids hanging from the fallen comm tower. Instead, about a dozen stormtroopers hung by their necks.

Jyn's stomach lurched as she approached. The stormtroopers' armor was still gleaming white and black, but it was scuffed and there were reddish-brown stains on some of it. The wind blew, and the bodies shifted on their makeshift gallows, clanging against the metal tower. The sound was hollow and reverberated and was somehow . . . somehow wrong?

Saw moved behind her. Jyn turned, and he offered her a blaster.

Jyn looked from the blaster to the stormtroopers and back again. She moved to flick the setting from kill to stun, as her mother had taught her. Saw wrapped his hand around hers, forcing her finger to keep it set to kill. "Never do that," he said in a gentle voice. "If you're going to shoot a blaster, you always shoot to kill. Always."

Jyn swallowed. The stormtroopers hanging on the

comm tower weren't moving; they must have already been dead.

This is a training exercise, she thought. *Nothing else.*

"Take aim," Saw said.

Jyn held the blaster in front of her with her right hand. It shook, so she raised her left hand, gripping her right wrist to steady the blaster. Breathe in. Aim. Breathe out.

Shoot.

The stormtrooper's body danced against the metal comm tower, swinging out like a puppet whose strings had twitched.

"Good girl," Saw said. He took the blaster from Jyn and handed her a pair of crudely carved clubs about the length of her forearm. Hand-to-hand combat.

On Coruscant, her mother had signed her up for kinesthetic and gymnastic lessons. "Because you always have so much energy!" Mama had said with a laugh. But maybe that hadn't been the whole reason.

Jyn tested the weight of the clubs. She thought about how much force to apply against the flesh inside the armor.

"Go," Saw ordered.

Jyn took a deep breath and slowly approached the closest stormtrooper, the one she had shot. It was easier, somehow, to think of beating the dead body of the stormtrooper she'd already shot once. She reared back with all her weight and slammed the club into its abdomen. The stormtrooper swung wide, and Jyn fell to the ground. She had struck with the expectation of hitting a body in armor; instead she realized that the stormtrooper armor was empty. Jyn squinted at the other stormtroopers strung up on the tower and noticed how easily they moved in the wind. None of them were people, just the outer shell of armor.

"Again," Saw said in an even voice as Jyn stood back up and brushed herself off.

Her arm ached from how she had fallen, and she dropped the truncheons with a soft thud at her feet. "I can just use a blaster," she said. "I don't have to do all this."

Saw made his way slowly to Jyn, then knelt on one knee in front of her so he was looking right into her eyes. "I have seen freedom fighters survive in battles against blasters and laser cannons," he said, not even blinking. "And I have seen rebels take down armies with nothing more than rocks and sticks."

He picked up the truncheons and pressed them into Jyn's hands.

"Again," he said, standing up and stepping back as Jyn assumed her fighting stance.

Jyn forced herself to picture the troopers who had killed her mother, to remember the fear she had felt when they chased her, the rage when they took her

father. She felt those memories inside her like a burning ember in her belly, and she only let the clubs fall
from her numb fingers when she was certain her fire
wouldn't dim.

◈

Jyn soon learned why Saw had bunkers with beds in
them. The first ship landed on their little island the
next month, and soon after, another. People greeted
Saw like an old friend, stared at Jyn curiously, and
filed into the rooms with beds as if they'd stayed there
many times before.

They brought their own food.

"Only Saw could live on that crap," one of the new
arrivals, a Twi'lek named Xosad Hozem, said as he
unloaded groceries into the cabinets. "You're a cute
little thing," he added to Jyn, curiosity in his voice.

"Go to your room," Saw said, and Jyn fled.

The others were loud. They talked a lot. They drank
a lot. But they were mostly friendly. There was Xosad,
the Twi'lek Saw knew from "the good old days," and a
crew of young men he'd brought with him—two more
Twi'leks and a Togruta. Reece Tallent was a human,
about twenty or so, Jyn guessed, with dark brown hair
and nice blue eyes. He had a similar accent to Saw's,
and Jyn wondered if they were from the same planet.
A woman came often as well, closer to Saw's age, with

black skin that seemed to sparkle blue in the light and hair that grew straight up from her head. She was so beautiful that Jyn couldn't help staring at her, and she spoke her name with a lilting, musical voice: Idryssa Barruck. She carried a pair of machetes on her back, thick heavy weapons that didn't seem to fit her lithe gracefulness.

Idryssa also brought clothes for Jyn. Saw had been giving her old things—oversized shirts Jyn wore as dresses, pants she cinched in with a leather belt. Idryssa brought Jyn real clothes and had a private conversation with her about hygiene and health. Jyn suspected Saw had invited Idryssa in part just to talk to her, and she appreciated both the kindness and the fact that he never brought it up.

After getting to know Idryssa better, Jyn was brave enough to go into the big common room while everyone else was there. Saw noticed her first and nodded that it was okay for her to pillage the cabinets for food.

"My men have been to Christophsis, and there's nothing there," Xosad was saying. The Togruta nodded in agreement.

"The Empire had done some mining there, but they were gone when we looked, and it didn't seem like they were coming back," he said.

"Ilum is another story," Idryssa said.

Jyn paused as she reached for a wrapped pastry in

the cabinet, a rare treat in Saw's outpost. She recognized that name, Ilum. Her father had spoken of it before, but he had told her it was a secret world, used by the Jedi. Jyn could see her father clearly, standing in their apartment on Coruscant, talking about how the Jedi had kept such a valuable planet to themselves for so long and how the Empire was now protecting it. Jyn would have forgotten about the conversation had it not been for the disapproving scowl of her mother as she shook her head at Papa's words.

Jyn wasn't surprised that Saw knew about Ilum; he had been following Papa's work since he'd helped them move to Lah'mu. But these other people seemed to know just as much.

Reece spread out a star chart on the table. "It's obvious the Empire's interested in these areas," he said, pointing to the map in a way Jyn couldn't see. She crept closer. Everyone was focused on Reece. "And my contact thinks he saw Galen here."

Jyn sucked in a breath, and Saw spun around to look at her, his eyes widening in a warning. Jyn clamped her mouth shut. Saw jerked his head, but Jyn stood her ground, refusing to move.

"What other information can you give us?" Idryssa asked Saw. She shifted, the blue highlights in her skin sparkling under the radiated lamps built into the stone ceiling.

Saw's mouth worked as if he wanted to swallow his answer, but he finally said, "I know he worked with crystals for the Empire, and whatever his research was, it was *very* important to them."

Across from him, Xosad nodded and shared a knowing glance with Saw.

"Galen Erso is a known supporter of the Empire," Reece said dismissively. "He's a respected scientist, but I don't see how crystals—"

"Crystals are more powerful than you may think," Idryssa said in a quiet voice. "Do not forget that the Jedi used them."

Reece made a snorting noise. "Jedi," he scoffed. "Bringing them up doesn't exactly prove your point. If they had 'powerful' crystals, they wouldn't all be dead."

A known supporter of the Empire? Jyn wondered. *Papa?* She shook her head. He had worked with the Empire, yes, but he had fled from it, and he *didn't* want to go back.

"That's a good point, though," Saw said, tapping his chin. "The Empire wouldn't want a scientist of Galen's caliber just for knowledge's sake. There has to be a reason for their support of his research."

Reece leaned back in his chair. "No, there doesn't," he said dismissively. "Saw, buddy, you're reading too much into this. Galen Erso is a shill. He's sucked up to the right people in the Empire, and he is living the high life on Coruscant. His research is meaningless."

"That's not true!" Jyn shouted.

Every single person turned to her.

"Jyn's right," Saw said loudly. "His research is key to understanding what the Empire is planning next." Jyn opened her mouth to protest—she was angry at the way Reece had dismissed her father—but Saw clamped a hand on her shoulder and steered her back to her room.

"That's not true," she hissed at him again as soon as her bedroom door shut. "Papa wouldn't work for the Empire like that. He's a good man! They *kidnapped* him," she said.

Saw looked doubtful.

"They *did*." Jyn's voice was rising, and Saw shushed her. She could feel angry tears fighting their way into her eyes. The injustice of it—to have someone like Reece talk about her father like that, as if he were a bad man!

"Jyn, it's not looking good," Saw said in a low voice. "I've been tracking the Empire's movements. I've tried to figure out what it was your father was working on that made the Empire show up on Lah'mu. And your father . . ."

"I *saw* him," Jyn said, stomping her foot. "He didn't want to go. He wanted to stay with me. He *did*."

Saw gave her a sad, pitying look, then stood and left her alone in the dark room.

CHAPTER FIVE_

Jyn glared at Reece whenever she saw him. She wished he would get off her island.

But she had learned her lesson. If she stayed quiet, Saw would let her listen in while the others were talking.

"There are more blockades around certain planets," Xosad said the next day.

"Any connection between the planets?" Saw asked.

"Not that we can see," one of Xosad's crew piped up. "But it's hard to get to some of them. We need clearance codes."

"Forging them takes work and patience," another crew member said. He dropped a code replicator on the table.

When the others shifted to different talk, about a growing partisan group based on Corlus, Jyn snuck to the table where the code replicator sat. She'd seen them tinkering with it before, and it fascinated her. She pressed one of the buttons tentatively, then picked up the replicator. It was about the same size as a data-pad but thicker and heavier.

"The little mouse is in the cheese," Reece said dryly, looking down his nose at Jyn. She dropped the code replicator.

"Let her play," the crew member said. "She can't hurt anything."

Jyn stuck her tongue out at Reece, took the replicator, and retreated to the corner of the room.

Clearance codes for ships were already loaded in as masters, but each individual code could not be exactly copied or the Empire would know it was a fake. Instead, the code replicator helped simulate the complicated algorithm the Empire used to develop ship transponder and clearance codes. It was like a puzzle, and while it was tedious, Jyn's mind retreated into the symbols and numbers.

Once, when Jyn had had trouble sleeping after first moving to Lah'mu, Papa had told her to recite the multiplication tables or list prime numbers in her mind until she fell asleep. Working on the code replicator didn't put her to sleep—it was too challenging—but it was just as relaxing. There was a steady lull to the numbers.

"Heh, look at her go," Xosad said when the group broke up to prepare dinner.

Saw stood over her shoulder, and Jyn held up the code replicator for him to look at. He cocked an eyebrow. "Not bad," he said, scanning the data. "We'll make a forger out of you yet."

Xosad started opening jars of some sort of vegetable and mashing them into a pot to make a sauce. "So, I contacted my man on Coruscant," he said casually to Saw.

Saw's eyes went to Jyn's immediately, and he shook his head just a little. "And?"

"Galen Erso is definitely there."

"He is?" Jyn breathed, hope in her voice.

"Excuse us," Saw said. Jyn didn't want to leave, but Saw's fingers dug into her shoulder until she winced. As she followed him back to her room, she couldn't help noticing the way Reece watched her, his chin jutting out and his eyes narrowing with suspicion.

"That's Papa they're talking about," Jyn said as soon as her bedroom door was closed. She hated the whine in her voice.

Saw sighed in defeat. "And you have a right to know what they're saying about him," he said finally. "But I can't let them know you're Galen Erso's daughter."

Jyn shook her head. "Why not?" she asked.

Saw knelt so his warm brown eyes were even with hers. "Jyn, I promise to tell you everything after supper. Xosad and the others are all leaving then. I'll tell you everything. But not in front of them."

"I won't say anything," Jyn said. "I just want to listen."

"He's your father, Jyn," Saw said. "Of course you'll say something. Stay here. I promise. Do you trust me?"

Jyn nodded reluctantly.

She could hear them on the other side of the door, laughing and talking, silverware clattering on the clay plates as they ate whatever it was Xosad had made for everyone. She tried to pick out each individual's voice, and then to discern their words, but it was all dulled by the heavy rock walls and steel door separating them.

She paced her room. Back and forth, back and forth. She wished she had the code replicator. She could distract herself with numbers.

She thought about that last day.

Jyn, whatever I do, I do it to protect you. Her father's voice had been almost calm, deep and solemn. He had spoken those words with such conviction and certainty, and he had looked straight into Jyn's eyes as he said them. When she closed her eyes, she could see his face. His hair was always unkempt; he never had time for a haircut. Mama had laughed at him about it all the time, saying she would have to tie him down just to trim his hair. And he had a little beard, something he hadn't bothered with on Coruscant. There were gray hairs in it, coarse and scraggly. They tickled Jyn's face whenever Papa hugged her.

She took a deep breath. He had been serious when he spoke to her then. His dark eyes unwavering. The lines on his face etched deep with worry.

Say you understand, he'd said. He had spoken those words like a promise. A covenant between them.

I understand, Jyn had replied in a clear, true voice. She felt so much younger then. But she had meant it. She understood what he was saying, and she believed it. She believed him.

Jyn sat down on her little bed on the floor and waited.

She heard the others say their good-byes. She heard the ships leaving. She heard Saw walk to her door, hesitate for several long moments.

And then he came inside.

"Jyn," he said, his voice heavy.

I do it to protect you.

"I want the truth," Jyn said.

Saw sat down on the floor in front of Jyn. He took a deep breath.

"Ever since I picked you up on Lah'mu, I've been looking for your father and trying to figure out what the Empire wanted with him," Saw said. "I know his research into crystals, I know the Empire must have a reason for it. He covered his tracks well. I've had some contacts of mine—not just Xosad and the others, different people—"

"Spies," Jyn supplied.

"You could call them that." Saw shrugged. "I've reached out. Tried to see if he needed help. Tried to tell him about you."

"Could you not find him?" Jyn asked.

Saw watched her without letting his face show emotion. "We found him," he said.

"Where is he? In prison somewhere?" Jyn's heart leapt to her throat. "Is he hurt?"

"No." Saw shook his head. "He's fine. He's on Coruscant."

The air left Jyn's body. "Coruscant. He could—I could go to him." It wouldn't be the same without Mama, but . . .

Saw was still shaking his head. "He could leave any time he wanted to," he said.

"Maybe he doesn't know where I am," Jyn said quickly. "You can take me to him, in your shuttle."

"Galen Erso is working alongside Orson Krennic." Saw spoke in clear tones, enunciating each word, as if he knew the truth would cut her and it would be cleaner if he used a sharp razor rather than a dull blade. "Your father is working—knowingly—with the Empire. He reports directly to Imperial forces. He has made it entirely clear to my sources that he has chosen a side, and that side is the Empire."

"No!" Jyn shouted, the word erupting from within her. "That's *not* true!"

"Just because you don't want to hear a truth doesn't make it less true," Saw said in that same calm voice.

"But you don't *know*," Jyn insisted, her voice turning into a plea. "It just *seems* like he's working for the Empire. Maybe he's being forced or . . ." Her voice trailed off at Saw's pitying look.

"Has he said it?" Jyn asked. "Has he said he chose the Empire?"

Saw shook his head.

It can't be true, Jyn thought. *Papa can't lie.* Everyone said so. Mama used to make fun of him for it. He was a terrible liar. Jyn wouldn't believe he left her for the Empire unless he *said* he did.

"Jyn . . ." Saw started, and the tone of his voice broke her heart and her resolve.

She shook her head frantically, the ends of her hair whipping her cheeks, her whole body screaming *no, no, no* over and over again.

"Galen Erso has chosen which side he wants to be on, and it's not ours."

Jyn stood up. "Mama *died*!" she screamed. "I *watched* her be killed by that man! And Papa works for him now?"

"By all appearances, they're friends," Saw said.

Jyn threw herself at Saw. She used everything she had learned in the weeks she'd been living with him, punching and kicking, slashing out at him. Anything to make him hurt the way she was hurting.

And Saw took it. He didn't raise a hand to defend himself. He let her slap him and slam her fist into his chest. He let her scream in his face without flinching. And when she started to tire, he wrapped his arms around her, pulling her close, and just held her.

"He's not coming for you," Saw said. "You can't trust him. The bastard's with the Empire now."

Jyn stared down at the floor, and Saw let the silence hang between them.

"I understand," Jyn said, the emotion drained from her voice. *My father is alive,* she thought. *My father is a coward.* She thought the word Saw had used. *My father is a bastard.*

CHAPTER SIX_

Time passed. Years. And Jyn's knowledge that Papa had left her for good, had chosen the Empire over her, was cemented by the proof of his continued absence.

But she didn't cry about it ever again.

Sometimes Saw left on "missions." Sometimes people came to Saw. Handfuls of men and women at a time, occasionally organized groups, more often a hodgepodge of discontented people who were looking for a fight. Jyn had thought the first night at Saw's outpost that he'd given her an old office as a sign of how unimportant she was, but she came to value her private room, especially when the bunkers filled up with more people than they could hold.

The better Jyn got at fighting, the more Saw let her participate when visitors came to the outpost. He instructed her very clearly: She was to listen. She was to judge. She was to decide whether or not the mission presented to Saw was worthwhile in the fight against the Empire. He always consulted Jyn. He didn't always take her advice, but he always listened, and that meant more to her than she could say.

Saw had gotten Jyn a code replicator of her own, something for her to tinker with to appear unobtrusive while he met with different people who were against the Empire. If she hid behind a screen, people forgot she was there, and she enjoyed the work.

Saw knocked on Jyn's door one evening after kinesthetic training. She'd been slicing holos, a practice Saw encouraged. Jyn would alter an image, and Saw would try to figure out what she had changed.

When Jyn opened the door, she was surprised to see another person standing next to Saw, a woman a head taller than him, with thick hair and skin darker than his.

"Jyn," Saw said, "do you remember Idryssa?"

Idryssa had come to Saw's base often when Jyn was younger but had not returned in a long time. Her skin sparkled with a slight greenish tint this time instead of blue, and Jyn realized that she wore some sort of makeup for the effect and had not been born with sparkling skin.

Jyn's gaze slid to Saw. "Are you going away on a mission?"

Idryssa smiled at her. "I'm just here to talk. Nice to see you again. It's been a long time. How old are you now?" Idryssa asked.

Jyn hated this question. It always came from people who thought she was too young, and if she told the truth—that she was fourteen—they would give her a pitying glance or *tsk* quietly. "Old enough," she said curtly.

Saw was relaxed around Idryssa, more so than he was when other partisans came to visit, even if Jyn didn't like the age question.

"I don't know what you expect of me," he told Idryssa in a good-natured tone. "I've got no info for you; I'm not the Ante."

Idryssa barked a laugh. "I couldn't afford you if you were."

"So do you have information for me?" Saw asked eagerly.

Idryssa shook her head. "A bunch of dead ends. The Empire is most definitely researching crystals, like you suggested, and the entire market for various minerals has been upended."

"I know all that," Saw said. "What I want to know is what the Empire plans to *do* with these resources."

Idryssa held her palms out and shrugged. She didn't know.

Jyn silently noted Idryssa's information, and she knew Saw had summoned her in part so she could hear. He hadn't given up trying to discover the Empire's purpose for Galen and his research, and Jyn hadn't forgotten, either.

Saw led them down the stone hallway to the long metal table in the common room. Idryssa sat across from him; Jyn sat at the end of the table, tinkering with a data chip she'd extracted from a holocube. She pretended to be uninterested as the adults started talking, but Saw had trained her well, and she analyzed their dialogue carefully. Jyn cut her eyes at Idryssa. She had an honest look about her, clear brown eyes that seemed guileless. She didn't look like the sort of person who would scrape together a fight against the Empire; she looked like the kind of woman who should be running a farm somewhere with lots of children. Jyn wondered if that was where Idryssa had been since the last time she'd seen her, so long before.

"We're starting small," Idryssa said, leaning toward Saw. "Organize a single base of operations, for starts."

"Bad idea," Saw said immediately.

Idryssa frowned.

"Look, I've been at this a long time," Saw said. "You have one base, when the Empire hits it, you lose everything."

"You have one base," she pointed out.

"No, I don't," Saw said.

Jyn's head shot up. Saw had more than this outpost? Was that where he went sometimes when he left her, to other homes, places where he didn't have to deal with her?

"There's been real interest from people high up," Idryssa continued.

Saw shot her a scathing look. "And you trust them?"

"They're the ones who got me the information you were asking about."

Saw waved his hand at her, prompting her to continue. "The Empire's supply runs have been fewer and more strategic." She propped her arms on the table, steepling her fingers. "Either they're done in secrecy and we don't know about them until too late, or they're done in public."

"Supply runs?" Jyn asked. Usually, Saw disapproved of her speaking during strategic conversations, but he had made a point to include her, and she sensed that he wanted her participation.

"For crystals," Idryssa said. "The Empire is particularly interested in kyber crystals, apparently."

"Oh!" Jyn feigned surprise.

"There was a small planet in the Sunshi system," Idryssa continued. "The Empire recently discovered kyber crystals there."

"What happened?" Jyn asked.

"They hollowed it out."

The words hung in the air between them, and Jyn tried to picture what it meant to mine a planet to death.

"The last shipment was a huge production," Idryssa

said, turning to Saw. "The Empire literally had a parade before the cargo left the planet."

"So?" Saw asked.

"That planet had been uninhabited. They brought civilian cruisers from the Core worlds and made a big show of the mining process," she said. "Alderaan and Chandrila were particularly invited, and the Emperor couldn't have made it more obvious that he wanted them to see the way the Empire has taken over the mining operations. But part of it, I think, was to ensure that we wouldn't attack and steal the shipment."

Saw's brow furrowed, creasing through the scars on his face. "I don't see why that would stop you."

Idryssa laughed bitterly. "I can see what the HoloNet would show on the feeds now. 'Anarchists Risk Lives of Senators,'" Idryssa said, spreading her hands as if reading a headline. "'Partisans Embrace Terrorism.'"

"You should," Saw said simply.

Idryssa blinked at him in obvious shock, then she grew very still. Jyn's attention shifted from her to him.

"I've heard the rumors," Idryssa said in a low voice. Jyn leaned forward. "But I didn't want to believe they were true."

"I do what needs to be done," Saw said. "And if you want your little 'coalition' to work, you'll do the same."

"Are you saying we should actually become a

terrorist organization? That we should slaughter anyone between us and the Empire?"

"Why not?" Saw asked. "That's how they'll spin it
anyway. Right, Jyn?"

Idryssa turned and looked at Jyn. Rather than
answering him, Jyn touched a button on the holocube. It sprang to life, shooting up the image of an
official Imperial media release. The symbol of the
Empire spun at the top, followed by a large headline
that read "Partisans Embrace Terrorism." The words
below were gibberish, but the signature at the bottom—
Lieutenant Colonel Senjax, military correspondent
for the Imperial Broadcast—looked real.

"Did you *just* do that?" Idryssa asked, impressed.

Jyn shrugged. "It wasn't that hard."

"Still, though."

Jyn pointed to the nonsense words under the headline. "Anyone could tell it wasn't real."

"Not if you filled that out." Idryssa stood up and
leaned closer. "You have every detail right—the insignia, the signature." She took the holocube from Jyn
and looked even closer. "You even have the serial
numbers correct, and the data chip identification code
is from an Imperial server file."

"No, it isn't," Jyn said. "I duped it."

Idryssa blinked. "Impressive." Across the table, Saw
beamed at Jyn.

Jyn was embarrassed to have so much attention on her. Without realizing what she was doing, she pulled her crystal necklace out from under her shirt and toyed with the stone. "My father taught me to pay attention to details," she said.

"Yes, I did," Saw said proudly.

Jyn sucked in a breath but didn't reply. Idryssa shot Jyn a curious look, but when Jyn wouldn't meet her eyes, she went back to her seat at the table. "Well, it's clear that anyone can say anything," she said, waving a hand toward the holocube. "But that doesn't mean we should attack civilians to inconvenience the Empire. I don't care what they say," she added. "I care what we *do*. And we do *not* kill innocent civilians just to disrupt the Empire's shipping lines."

"It's a price of war," Saw said simply.

"The Senate still hopes to avoid war."

Saw laughed bitterly. "The Senate?" Another laugh. "They don't realize we're still fighting the same war as before. We never quit fighting."

"We did," Idryssa said, her face melting in sympathy. "You're the only one still fighting that war."

Saw's face hardened. "So what if I am?" he roared at Idryssa. "War is war, and it *never* ends!"

Idryssa stood. She wasn't as broad as Saw, but she was tall and thin and her spine was strong as steel. "There is an end to war," she said. "I have to believe that. And so do the others I'm going to work with. We're going to make a difference, Saw, a change. There are senators interested in helping us. If we combine forces—"

Saw snorted. "Then we'll lose everything. Bureaucracy kills freedom."

Idryssa sank back into her seat. From Saw's face, it was clear that he thought he'd defeated Idryssa's ideology, but Jyn could tell that Idryssa felt only disappointment.

Saw got up and moved to the cabinet. "You remind me of Steela," he said, rooting around in the shelves. Jyn was surprised; he rarely brought up his sister. Jyn knew only that she had died fighting in the Clone Wars. Saw turned and met Idryssa's gaze. "That's not entirely a compliment," he added. He pulled out a bottle of lum and poured a glass for himself and one for Idryssa. The sharp, bitter alcoholic smell made Jyn scrunch her nose.

"I will never understand why the rebellion is so worried about labels," Saw continued as if he'd not just flared with rage. "Fear controls the masses. The Empire controls fear. If we tapped into that—if we used the same tactics the Empire does and brought about the same kind of fear, we'd control the people and give them the peace you are so anxious to have."

"That's not peace," Idryssa said simply.

It was clear that Saw didn't agree.

CHAPTER SEVEN_

Idryssa left early the next morning, and while she showed no signs of being hungover from the lum, Saw buried his head in his arms and dimmed the lights of the common room. Jyn ate her breakfast as quietly as she could and read her datapad.

It wasn't always easy to be in charge of her own education, and she had let most of the subjects her mother had taught her fall to the wayside as she focused on the things that interested her and that Saw clearly approved of, like seeing how much she could manipulate files and holos and data chips. But she did like to keep abreast of current events, even if she rarely spoke to Saw about them. After listening to Idryssa the night before, Jyn had stayed up late watching the last Senate meeting broadcasts. Despite the fact that Mon Mothma and Bail Organa had both spent so much time pleading with the Senate to recognize the state of the Empire, their speeches had been dismissed without further consideration. Jyn had zoomed in on the sharp angles of Senator Organa's face. He seemed like one of the best bets for the "Senate support" Idryssa had hinted at. He looked like the kind of man who'd declare war. But he wore the fine clothes of an Alderaanian, and Jyn doubted he'd have the strength to actually fight in one.

Saw would, though.

Saw already had. In the Clone Wars.

"You done?" Saw asked.

Jyn nodded, putting down her datapad and tossing her nutritive milk can in the trash. She followed Saw outside. He didn't flinch in the sunlight; he wasn't as affected by the lum as she'd thought.

That day was hand-to-hand combat practice, Jyn's favorite. Saw had tried her on various melee weapons, but her favorite was a pair of short truncheons. They felt like extensions of her arms, strong and empowering. Jyn glowered at Saw when he tried to pass her the bo staff and smiled brightly when he laughed in defeat and handed her the pair of short weighted batons. Saw took the bo staff for himself, then moved back, holding the weapon warily.

Jyn gripped the truncheons, watching his feet. Saw was quick with his hands, but she could tell when he was about to strike by how he positioned his feet.

He lunged, and she raised her truncheons defensively, knocking the staff aside.

"So," she grunted, stepping away after the initial attack, "Idryssa seemed nice."

"Too idealistic," Saw said. He feinted, and Jyn jumped, her arms raised, but he just laughed that she'd fallen for the trick.

"It makes sense, though," Jyn said, her eyes on Saw's staff. "You work with a lot of different partisan groups. If they all worked *together*, maybe . . ."

Saw struck quickly, jabbing Jyn in the side before she had a chance to defend herself. Jyn nodded, accepting the defeat, then raised her truncheons again.

"What would it take?" Jyn persisted when Saw didn't answer her.

"For what?"

She wasn't sure if Saw was genuinely confused or dodging her question. He often got so focused on the task at hand he forgot about everything else. Papa had been like that, too.

"For some sort of organized rebellion to form. Something that could take down the Empire."

Saw put his hands up, calling a pause in their sparring. He leaned against his staff. "It's not like that," he told Jyn. "It doesn't matter how many people stand up against the Empire. It doesn't matter how big a group it is."

"Then what matters?"

"The *kind* of people who fight." Saw watched her with his deep brown eyes. "If there's really going to be some anti-Imperial alliance, they need a . . ." He flicked his hand as he searched for the word.

"A leader?" Jyn supplied.

"Yes, but not just someone giving orders," Saw countered. "Someone the people believe in."

Jyn frowned at the truncheons in her hands. "I don't understand," she said.

"It's like I was telling you, with the droids and the clone armor," Saw said, indicating the mock battlefield he used for Jyn's training. "I tell you millions died in the Clone Wars, what do you feel?"

Jyn opened her mouth to speak, but Saw cut her off.

"You feel nothing, because you didn't know any of them, did you?"

Jyn shook her head.

"But I tell you that my sister died," Saw continued, "I tell you that Steela was the best part of me, and that she was going to change the world. Make it a better place. Hell, not just the world. The whole damn galaxy. She was stronger than any Jedi, stronger than the 'Force,' but that didn't matter." He sighed heavily, his eyes distant and sad. "I tell you that she died a hero. She saved a king and fought the enemy. But she was on the side of a cliff, and a gunship was shot down and crashed into it."

Jyn gasped, a tiny sound that Saw didn't hear.

"I tell you that I saw her, hanging on that rocky edge, her fingers gripping the stone. And there was a Jedi there. Oh, look at you. You got all hopeful at that. Didn't do a damn thing. The Jedi tried to save her, sure, but she didn't. Steela fell anyway. Fell to the bottom of the cliff, onto solid rock. Ever see what happens to a body that falls that far down onto stone? Bones don't just break, they *shatter*."

Saw looked at Jyn, but she didn't think he saw her.

"And I tell you that I was the one who shot down the ship that crashed into the cliff where she had been. I tell you that, and you feel something, yeah?"

Jyn couldn't move. Saw leaned over and rubbed the pad of his thumb across her cheek. It came away wet. She hadn't even known a tear had leaked out of her eye.

"And for what? They said her death was the price paid for the freedom of Onderon. Her body was barely cold before the Republic turned into the Empire. And it all started again. Another rebellion. More war. More death. I was smarter that time. I didn't make the same mistakes as I had when Steela was alive. Didn't matter. Didn't work. Onderon is under the Empire. And I'm here."

When Saw was speaking, for a moment Jyn saw him the way he used to be. A starry-eyed young man with a dream of justice and freedom. He must have been so brilliant then. But that young man died when Steela did, and in his place was this bitter, angry fighter.

"The resistance against the Empire needs Steela," Saw said. He searched Jyn's eyes, waiting to see if she understood.

"More fighters like her?" The idealistic, the heroes who stand up in the face of certain death.

"They need more fighters like her to die like she did," he growled. "The resistance needs a martyr. A tragedy. Something so horrific that people can't help but stand up and fight, too. You understand?"

"They need someone they can believe in," Jyn said, looking into Saw's eyes. He nodded like he was glad Jyn was understanding. "Like the Jedi, during the Clone Wars." It was impossible to study the galaxy without hearing something of the Jedi, and considering how much the Empire loathed even a mention of the religious cult, Jyn had assumed Saw would love and admire all Jedi.

Instead, he snarled.

"Don't give them another thought," Saw said, glaring. "Jedi think they can do anything, but where are they now? All dead. And before that? Sure, they helped. But not enough."

He stared down at his hand, and Jyn thought he was looking at the long jagged scar that cut through the thin skin between his thumb and first finger. But he made a fist.

"They talked about the Force, the Jedi did," he said in a lower voice. "Never understood what it was, but I saw it. It was like magic. They could move things with a wave of their hand." He swept his arm out.

Nothing in front of him moved.

"But they couldn't hold on," Saw continued. "For all their power, they couldn't hold on, not when it mattered."

Saw stood and started pacing down the gauntlet of droid bodies. He punched one, sending it swinging from its noose, the clanking of metal against metal reverberating across the island. "That's something neither side's figured out yet," he told the ground. "All you need is one good, solid tragedy, and the people will flock. Nothing unites people like that. If Idryssa wants to really rally people behind her, she needs to do it while standing on some graves."

There was a gleam in Saw's eyes, a spark that terrified Jyn.

And it *excited* her.

Saw turned to Jyn and swooped toward her in long strides. He wrapped his big hands around hers, pressing her fingers against the truncheons she still held. "That's what Steela taught me," he said. "One fighter with a sharp stick"—he held Jyn's hand up, brandishing a truncheon—"one fighter with a sharp stick and nothing left to lose can take the day. You just have to make sure that fighter *believes*."

CHAPTER EIGHT_

Seeing Idryssa must have spurred Saw into reuniting with some of his old compatriots. Xosad and his small crew came first, and then Reece arrived. This time, he wasn't alone; he had a group of three other humans and a Lasat who didn't talk much. They looked at Reece as if he was their leader, and Jyn had a hard time puzzling that out. He was not the kind of person she would have fought for.

The outpost was starting to feel more crowded than usual, and Jyn in particular felt outnumbered. Reece's men were young and immature, reckless and destructive. When Jyn was target practicing with her A180 modified blaster, Reece's crew picked up their own blasters and joined her. But they were not concerned with firing one shot and moving on to the next target; they massacred the dead droid bodies hung up on the rafters of the broken comm tower, laughing wildly as the metal burned.

"When are they leaving?" Jyn asked Saw in a low

voice on the third day after they'd invaded her home.

Saw laughed. "I know. They're insufferable. But they can be handy," he added in a louder voice.

"Really?" Jyn said, doubt dripping from the word.

"Really."

Jyn stared at Reece, evaluating him. He was about a decade older than her, but he lacked any discipline. He was broader, sure, with larger muscles, but she doubted he had ever formally trained.

"Like what you see?" Reece said, strutting over to Jyn.

"Not really," she said coolly.

"Keep a leash on your little girl," Reece told Saw. "She needs to have more respect."

Jyn's blood boiled, but Saw raised his hand. "Jyn's not a little girl, and if you have a problem with her, take it outside."

Reece laughed. "Yeah, okay," he said sarcastically at the same time Jyn snapped, "I'm fine with that."

Reece raised an eyebrow at her.

"Come on," she said, heading to the door.

Reece's men whooped at him so loudly that he had no choice but to follow. Saw lumbered behind them. Jyn went to the cleared area on the island where she and Saw practiced sparring daily and waited for Reece to face her.

"Cause no lasting damage and keep it clean," Saw said in a somewhat bored voice. "This is a spar; you're not fighting the Emperor here."

"I'll be gentle," Reece said, sneering at Jyn.

"I was talking to Jyn," Saw replied, stepping back.

Reece squared off in front of her. He had too much bravado; he was far too aware of the group of men circling them. Jyn kept her gaze on his face, knowing his tell would show there. She saw the instant his eyes changed from mocking to serious, and she had her arms raised in a block before he'd even finished making a fist. She knocked his arm aside with one of hers, driving a fist into his solar plexus with enough force to wind him.

Reece stumbled back, fury turning his pale face red as his men howled with laughter. Jyn kept light on her feet, careful.

She almost always sparred with Saw, and Saw kept his temper in check, especially with her. But Reece was not Saw. He boiled with anger at being mocked, and his next attack was as random and ferocious as an enraged animal. Jyn hadn't been ready for it, and she went down, slamming into the dirt.

She leapt up before Reece had a chance to turn around in triumph, scooting back and lowering her center as she watched him with narrowed eyes.

"You should have stayed down, little girl," Reece growled.

Jyn didn't bother answering. Words didn't hurt. Fists did. Tired of the defensive, Jyn struck first, feinting a punch, then leaning back into a kick that connected with Reece's shoulder. He took the force of it in stride, barely stumbling back, and Jyn kicked out again, aiming higher. He knocked aside her leg this time, throwing her off balance, and pushed against her, hard, so she thudded back to the ground. This time, he didn't assume she was out; he dropped his knees on her chest, painfully, smiling as the air whooshed out of her.

Her arms were still free, but Reece was positioned on top of her in such a way that she couldn't easily throw him off or gain any leverage. He smirked . . . and then his eyes narrowed. He leaned down so close to Jyn's face that for one horrifying moment she thought he was going to kiss her—but instead he yanked at the leather cord around her neck, pulling up her kyber crystal necklace.

"You've got us chasing the Empire halfway across the galaxy looking for these things," he yelled at Saw, "and your little girl has one around her neck? What are you playing at?" He flicked the kyber in Jyn's face and laughed when she flinched.

Jyn's lips moved. Reece was so focused on them that he didn't notice the way her fingers wrapped around a large stone on the ground.

"What was that, little girl?" Reece asked, leaning closer.

"I said," Jyn replied in a quiet voice, "that was my mother's." And with Reece's head so close to her own, she slammed the rock into the side of his skull. He fell off her, dazed, and Jyn stood, kicking him viciously in the stomach.

Reece rolled away, groaning, then stood.

Jyn let the rock fall from her hands, not breaking eye contact with him.

"That's—" Reece started.

"Cheating?" Jyn said. "I wasn't aware there were rules."

She headed back to the outpost as Reece's men swarmed him. When she passed Saw, he said in a low voice that only she could hear, "Nice pointed stick."

Jyn stayed in her room until Reece and his crew left that evening.

Saw knocked on her door to let her know he was gone. When Jyn let him inside, she noticed that he had a dark greenish-brown cloth in his hand.

"What's that for?" Jyn asked.

"You." Saw draped the cloth around Jyn's neck. "I want you to wear this from now on."

She tugged at the durable carbon-cotton scarf. "Why?"

Saw's gaze dropped. "I know you won't take off that necklace. I know what it means to you. But Jyn"—he finally met her gaze—"you can't let anyone else see it. Galen may have worked with kyber crystals, but they're rare. And the fact that you have one, and that I've made it known I'm asking about them . . ." He ran a hand over his smooth head. "It's not safe. We can't let others find out who you are. Who your father is."

"Reece works for you," Jyn said in a soft voice.

"Reece works for payment," Saw said. "And there are people who would pay him far more than I could if he knew you were Galen Erso's daughter."

Jyn tugged the scarf down, covering her neck and chest. She felt inexplicably exposed.

"He saw it," she said. "He knew it was a kyber." *I told him it was a gift from my mother,* she thought but didn't say. She didn't want Saw to know how foolish she'd been by just handing Reece another piece of the puzzle of who she was.

"And he knows that I've been very interested in Galen's work, and figuring out just what it is he's making for the Empire," Saw conceded. "But Reece is also thickheaded, and I doubt he's going to think about today beyond just how well you beat him. Still," he added, readjusting Jyn's new scarf, "just in case."

She pressed the cloth to her chest. "Just in case."

"Xosad and his men are still here. We're setting up our next mission." He spoke with an expectant tone that Jyn found curious. "Want to join in?" he asked, grinning.

Her eyes rounded. Saw had never, not once, allowed her to join him on a mission. He had ignored her pleading, eventually forbidding her from even asking anymore.

"If I had known you'd let me join you on missions as soon as I beat up a boy, I'd have done it a long time ago," she said.

"It wasn't that," Saw said. "I already knew you were strong enough."

He turned to her door. "Then what?" Jyn asked, bouncing on her heels. "What changed your mind?"

When he looked back at her, there was sadness in his eyes that belied his lingering smile. But he didn't answer her.

CHAPTER NINE_

Xosad and his crew were finishing dinner by the time Saw led Jyn into the room. She grabbed a plate for herself before everything was cleared away and ate quickly as the men started discussing the upcoming mission. The Togruta, Jari, slipped Jyn the last puff cake as Saw poured out the lum for the others.

"Did you hear about the T-7 ion disrupter rifles?" Xosad asked.

Saw shook his head. "Nasty business. Wish we could get our hands on some."

"The Empire's stockpiling. Have you heard from Idryssa?" Xosad meant to slip the last question in casually, but Jyn caught the sharp edge to it. The different people Saw worked with splintered off in ways she couldn't always trace.

"She's working with some other group," Saw said.

Xosad snorted disapprovingly, then got up and started clearing the dishes from the table.

"There's been a lot of movements around the mines. Mostly doonium and dolovite," Saw added.

Xosad's eyes shot to Jyn, then moved quickly away. "And kyber crystals." He had been there, along with his men, when Jyn had fought Reece.

Saw didn't miss the dig. "Leave my daughter alone," Saw said. There was a warning in his voice.

Xosad glanced back at Saw as he set the plates by the sink. Huge dark Saw who looked nothing like small pale Jyn. "No, she's not your daughter," he said genially. "And it seems strange you've got a girl here on Wrea with a kyber crystal. They're kind of rare, Saw," he added sarcastically.

Jyn adjusted her scarf.

"Xosad," Saw growled.

"I was there, too, Saw, at the Wanton Wellspring." Xosad narrowed his eyes at Jyn. "Has was my friend, too."

"Has talks too much."

"So are you who I think you are, little girl?" Xosad asked quietly, leaning so close that his lekku brushed Jyn's knees. She fought the urge to flinch away. "Because if you are, Saw's hidden a pile of credits on this miserable little planet."

"I told you," Saw said, right behind Xosad. "She. Is. My. *Daughter.*" He grabbed Xosad by the shoulder and yanked him around. His eyes were so narrowed that the scarred one had almost disappeared behind his squint. "Understand?" he growled.

Xosad threw up his slender arms. "Perfectly. You're a lovely family," he added.

"Yes, we are," Jyn said, kicking the back of Xosad's right knee and making him fall to the ground.

Saw barked a laugh, and despite being knocked down, even Xosad—and his crew—seemed amused by Jyn's little rebellion.

"You don't have to worry about him," Jari whispered to Jyn. He smiled at her pleasantly, but Jyn wasn't so sure of that.

"So what's the mission?" Jyn asked loudly, hoping to distract everyone from the tension surrounding her true identity.

Xosad got one of his other crew members, a Twi'lek named Bilder, to lay out the plans. "The Empire has sent a scouting mission to some remote planets in the Western Reaches. They're using a civilian ship," he said, and the holodisk showed a *CCR*-class pinnace. "The Empire has kept all of this *very* off the records, which of course means it's something they don't want us to notice."

"We did notice, though," Xosad said, grinning.

"It's a smaller ship, so the plan is simple enough. We intercept, board, and take the information they're hiding." Bilder pointed to the ship's connection point. "Our ship is compatible to dock with it, and we'll pose as an undercover Imperial ship delivering additional supplies."

"That's where you come in, Jyn," Saw said. "Think you can forge us what we'll need to convince them to let us dock?"

Jyn cocked her head. "Shouldn't be too hard," she said. "An Imperial manifest and clearance code, yeah?"

Bilder nodded. "With an official document of greeting, if we need it."

"I can do that." Jyn felt pride swell within her. She *could* do that, and easily. She used code replicators often, stockpiling credentials for Saw and his contacts. This would require a little more finesse, but she knew she could handle the challenge.

"Are we meeting up with anyone else?" Jyn asked.

Saw shook his head. "Small operation. If the Empire sees us coming, the ship'll ghost, or it'll get more reinforcements. Surprise is going to be our best asset. Xosad says there's no more than five people aboard the pinnace—two of whom are surveyors and scientists."

Jyn swallowed, hard. Surveyors and scientists. Just like her parents.

"Reece and his men are exploring a different lead, in the Outer Rim," Saw added. Jyn had to admit that even though Reece was a jerk, he was still useful. "There's a factory that seems to be receiving a lot of

Imperial shipments. There's a chance these two missions are connected. Hopefully, we can get some good information." He shot Xosad a look, and the Twi'lek nodded solemnly.

"Can we be ready in twenty?" Bilder asked. Jyn's stomach lurched; this was happening so quickly. But she didn't want to be the weak link on the crew.

As Xosad and his men went back to their ship to prepare, Jyn went to her room. She made sure the scarf Saw had given her covered her chest and the necklace, then she added a knife to her boot, strapped her old blaster to the holster around her right thigh, and secured the truncheons on her back. Her heart raced. She hadn't left Wrea since Saw had taken her there years before, and her excitement to be included was wrapped up in her readiness to go into space again.

Saw laughed when she walked out of her room. "You're forging codes, not going into battle."

Jyn's eager expression fell, and she turned back to her room. Saw dropped a heavy hand on her shoulder, stopping her. "Better to be prepared," he said in a low, serious voice.

"Let's go," Xosad called from the outpost door. They followed the Twi'lek out to his ship. Saw had Jyn stay in a jump seat in the back with the crew while he went into the cockpit with Xosad. Jyn didn't like the sensation of sitting in the back with no view outside, the safety harness of the jump seat cutting into her breastbone and shoulders as she lurched around. They couldn't make the jump into hyperspace without clearing Smuggler's Run, and Xosad wasn't a smooth pilot as he navigated the asteroid belt. The shields had to deflect more than one stray rock. Jyn wasn't ready for the jump when it finally came. Her stomach lurched and she cursed under her breath.

Jari shot her a sympathetic look.

"You can take that off now," Bilder said, indicating the safety harness. "Even Xosad can't mess up hyperspace travel."

"Don't jinx us," Jari grumbled.

Jyn undid the safety harness and slid out of the jump seat. Nothing about Xosad's ship seemed comfortable or friendly. Even the flooring, made of rough metal grating, bit into the soles of her boots.

Saw and Xosad emerged from the cockpit, and everyone moved to the table screwed into the floor in the common area. They each went immediately to a seat, giving Jyn the impression it was old habit. She lingered until everyone else was settled and then slid onto the edge of the bench beside Saw.

It took two more hyperspace jumps and a bit of flying to get to the system in the Western Reaches where they would intercept the Imperial pinnace. Jyn wondered which planet they were near. Saw hadn't been specific; he'd just said it was an ice world, which had reminded Jyn of a planet she'd been to as a kid with her mother. The memory was foggy; she mostly recalled playing in the crystal-like caves, sliding over the ice.

Saw didn't give her much time to linger in her daydreams. He had her working on the code replicator and the doc developer for most of the trip. When she finished, he carefully analyzed the results. "These'll do," he said in a tone that made Jyn feel as if she weren't good enough, but then he smiled at her, pride radiating from his eyes.

Xosad returned to the cockpit, scanning the system for the Imperial undercover ship. The ship lurched so violently that Jyn slid from the bench, her knee colliding painfully with the metal floor.

"I've made contact," he called back. "Give me those docs."

Saw stood up and strode toward the cockpit.

"Here's where it gets interesting," Jari mumbled, and his crewmates nodded grimly. Jyn felt a pressure on her lungs. What would happen if her codes didn't work? She suddenly felt small and unimportant, sure that she would be the reason the mission failed.

"We're in," Xosad called out, his voice echoing off the metal. "They took the bait."

CHAPTER TEN_

Xosad angled his ship next to the Imperial one. While launching from Wrea and maneuvering through Smuggler's Run had been a rocky ride, Xosad handled the close range of docking with the Imperial ship's port with a finesse that surprised Jyn.

"You stay back," Saw ordered Jyn. "Guard the port. Any of their men try to board our ship, shoot them."

Jyn glanced at the port that would open up to a transport tube connecting the two ships. She imagined a stormtrooper, white-and-black armor, running toward her through the tube. She nodded grimly.

Saw took position in front of the port. He was the face of the mission; Xosad's crew of Twi'leks and a Togruta would be suspicious. As soon as the transport tube extended between the ships and the port area was repressurized, the doors opened. Through a short tunnel and from behind the others, Jyn could see the interior of a small ship, sleek white plastoid and chrome glistening in contrast to the rough and dull metal of Xosad's ship.

Two stormtroopers stood at the entrance of the transport tube, blocking the way onto their ship. "This is somewhat unexpected," said a man wearing Imperial gray, striding forward. "We weren't supposed to get resupplied for another standard month."

"Then you're going to be really surprised by this," Saw said, whipping out his blaster and shooting both stormtroopers before they had a chance to retaliate. The Imperial officer ran, and Saw gave chase.

Xosad and his men surged forward after Saw, leaving Jyn behind. It had all happened so suddenly that she was breathless. There had been so much waiting—traveling through space to get there, arranging the hookup, waiting for the tube to extend. And now the others were already on the Imperial ship and Jyn was alone in front of the transport tube with two stormtroopers motionless on the other side.

Through the transport tube, she could hear the sounds of blaster fire. The dull thuds of bodies. Shouting.

Jyn pulled out her blaster and held it tightly in her hands. She wished she was beside Saw, even if he was in the thick of the battle. She didn't like being alone. Her imagination filled with terrors.

Footsteps. Coming closer. Fast. Someone was running toward her.

She saw him before he saw her. A man, his dark

skin vivid against the gray suit he wore, stained with bright red blood on one sleeve. He stopped at the stormtroopers after stumbling over their bodies, an expression of utter terror—or maybe disgust—evident on his face.

Then he looked up and saw Jyn.

He stepped over the first stormtrooper.

"You're a little young thing. And they left you on guard duty, huh?" he asked. His voice was calm, like he was talking to a frightened animal. Jyn squeezed her blaster tighter.

"Don't come forward," she said, raising it.

"You didn't do this." The scientist looked down as he stepped over the second stormtrooper's body. He was in the tunnel now. "You didn't kill them."

"I said," Jyn warned, "don't come any closer." Her voice shook, but the blaster was steady in her hand.

The scientist had one hand in the large pocket of his coat. There was something there, hidden behind the cloth. Something hard and metallic. A blaster?

"Stop!" Jyn shouted.

He took another step closer.

"If you were going to shoot me, you would have by now," he said. Another step. He was halfway across the transport tube now. "You look like a good girl," he said.

"I'm not," Jyn whispered, her finger on the trigger.

He didn't hear her. "You're not a terrorist like those

men. I don't know how they roped you into this, but if you let me, I can help you." Two more steps. He was closer to Jyn now than to the stormtroopers' bodies.

"Not another step," Jyn said, aiming the blaster.

The scientist raised one hand as if surrendering, but there was an easy smile on his face, and he kept his other hand in his coat pocket, holding . . . holding whatever was there. Jyn's eyes flicked from the hard outline to the man's kind eyes. She couldn't imagine someone who looked like this scientist hiding a blaster in his coat, but . . .

"I'm going to board your ship," the scientist said with certainty. "I'm going to break the transport tube connection and use your comm to contact my superiors. You're going to let me. Because you're a good girl."

"I'm not," Jyn said, louder this time, her finger twitching but still not pulling the trigger.

He took another step.

A blaster shot erupted, and the scientist dropped. Jyn was so surprised that she screamed, a short burst of pure emotion, and dropped her own, unfired blaster. Jari stood at the other end of the transport tunnel, his blaster drawn.

"What were you doing?" he asked, concern rippling his forehead. "Why didn't you fire?"

"I—I . . ." Jyn's voice trailed off, her eyes drinking in the way the scientist didn't move.

"Time to go." Saw's voice cut through the air, and for the first time, Jyn realized that there was no more blaster fire, no more thuds and shouting.

It was already over.

Saw, Xosad, and the others stomped across the transport tube, ignoring the body of the scientist. Jyn stumbled back, holstering her blaster. Saw slammed the port door shut, spinning the locks into place, and joined Xosad in the cockpit.

Jyn ran to the door, looking out the small viewport as the transport tube disconnected. Explosive decompression forced the stormtroopers and the scientist to shoot across the short distance, their bodies slamming into the side of the ship before bouncing off amid the rest of the debris from the open Imperial pinnace. Jyn jumped away from the window, covering her mouth in disgust, bile rising in her throat. Xosad's ship took off, heading to a place it could safely jump to lightspeed.

Jyn watched as the Imperial ship and its scattered contents floated through the emptiness of space.

Once in hyperspace, Saw and Xosad joined the others in the common room of the ship to discuss what they'd uncovered.

"Those were the same scientists who were part of

the Ilum mission the Empire sent out three months ago," Saw said.

Xosad nodded. "Whatever the Empire is doing, these events definitely seem linked."

Bilder piled up a stack of datapads he'd taken from the Imperial ship. "This will take a while to analyze," he said.

"Jyn can help." Saw glanced at her. He had yet to notice that she had not spoken at all since the ship headed back toward home. "Jyn?" he said quietly.

"I can help," she repeated automatically.

The others continued talking, discussing what they'd found in the lab and what the implications of it all might be. Jyn slipped quietly off the bench seat. The room felt tiny now, claustrophobic, and Jyn wanted nothing more than to get off the ship, but there was nothing outside, just hyperspace and death, death like the scientist floating in the black.

She found her way to a little hallway that, she suspected, led to bunks for Xosad and his men. She didn't want to violate their privacy, so she just sank to the floor, her knees to her chin, her back against the metal wall.

She didn't look up when she heard familiar footsteps making their way toward her. She would know Saw anywhere.

"Hey," he said, crouching so his face was even with hers.

"I've seen death before," Jyn said hollowly. "Worse than that. But . . ."

"It's always rough when it's your first kill." Saw's voice was sympathetic, but Jyn didn't have the courage to tell him that she had not shot the scientist; Jari had.

"I remember a mission not that long ago," Saw continued, shifting so he was sitting beside Jyn. "It was one of those 'we're so outnumbered and may not make it out alive' missions that I always seem to find myself in. The Empire . . ." Saw shook his head. "They *take*. They take and they take and they take. They're like a child, and we have to be the ones to say 'no more.'"

Jyn nodded, not really listening. *My mother didn't hesitate when she fired her blaster,* she thought.

"We wanted to protect some planets that the Empire wanted to destroy. Not outright, not even the Empire's that evil. But they were mining, and they didn't care about the people or the environment. They were going to suck those planets dry. And we weren't going to let them."

I wonder if she killed anyone. It was Jyn's mother who had told her always to set the blaster to stun. But Jyn hadn't done that since the blaster became hers. And her mother had shot to kill back on Lah'mu. She'd missed Krennic's heart, but that was where she'd aimed.

"Do you hear me, Jyn? We weren't going to let the Empire win."

Jyn turned to Saw, her eyes focusing on his lips as if she could see the words coming from his mouth.

"And our plan was, if we couldn't stop the Empire, we'd at least make sure they didn't get what they wanted. How did that Hiitian put it? 'What we fail to protect, we will leave in ruins.'"

Saw reached up, wrapping Jyn's cold fingers in his palm. "I don't think I understood what he meant until today," he told her.

"We weren't trying to protect any planets today," Jyn said.

"I'm not talking about any planets."

He reached up and tucked a strand of Jyn's brown hair behind her ear.

"You can't protect me," Jyn said.

"At least I taught you how to protect yourself." And there was pride there, true pride for what Saw assumed Jyn had done that day.

She ducked her head, unable to look at him.

LOCATION: Wobani

PRISONER: Liana Hallik, #6295A

CRIMES: Forgery of Imperial Documents, Resisting Arrest, Possession of an Unsanctioned Weapon

MONTH 02_

Jyn had no sense of time at the prison camp on Wobani. There were no windows in her cell, the only light coming from the hallway in the center. It was so humid during the day that even the stones sweated and so cold at night that they sometimes frosted over. It reminded her of the cave where she had hidden on Lah'mu. She thought of that cave more and more. Sometimes when she woke in the middle of the night, she had to remind herself that she wasn't eight years old, hiding from stormtroopers.

And that Saw wasn't coming to save her.

Her cell was tiny, even more so since they had paired her with a new cellmate, a Lunnix named Zorahda. Zorahda was older than most of the other prisoners, with white fur covering her body and fading yellow eyes, but she never cowered in front of the stormtroopers and did her best to show no weakness. It wasn't hard; a flash of her smooth black teeth behind the fine white whiskers on her lips was enough to keep most at bay.

The cells were narrow, with mattresses crammed onto slabs built into the walls. The beds were cramped for Jyn's short frame; for Zorahda's two-meter-tall lanky body, they were almost impossible. On her first night at LEG-817, she had stretched out on the floor of the narrow space between the cubbies. A stormtrooper on patrol had paused by their cell door.

"All prisoners in their beds during night shift," he ordered.

Zorahda had flicked him a rude gesture with her long fingers.

The stormtrooper called for backup and stun prods. Zorahda scrambled to get up and curl into the little cubby, but it was too late. The warden watched, smiling, as four stormtroopers first stunned Zorahda with high-voltage shocks and then beat her until reddish-brown blood matted her snowy fur.

Jyn had wanted to offer some sort of comfort, but she knew it would be worse if a stormtrooper saw her showing sympathy or compassion. It hadn't taken long to learn that lesson.

Every morning, an alarm pulsed through the prison to mark the start of a new workday. Food—a single ration cube—appeared in the small compartment by each prisoner's bed. Jyn stuffed hers in her mouth, ignoring the saltiness, and chewed as she quickly got ready for the day. The stormtroopers selected farm detail laborers first. This was the best and easiest job, the one everyone wanted. After the first selection, everyone was forced into the halls and assigned other work details.

Zorahda finished her ablutions and stood beside Jyn as soon as she was ready. They could hear the tedious process of prisoner relocation starting far down the hall. The stormtroopers made their first choices; neither Jyn nor Zorahda would get to work on the farms that day. Jyn watched the lucky prisoners with envy as they filed down the hall.

"I hate it here," Zorahda said in a low voice full of bitterness.

Jyn nodded but didn't answer. There wasn't much to add to that.

A stormtrooper unlocked their door and cuffed them. The heavy binders were huge on Jyn's wrists, weighing down her arms. On Zorahda, they pinched painfully. Neither complained.

Once the day's work detail was lined up, they were forced into a frustrating quick step that was between walking and jogging. The prisoners with longer legs, like the Gigorans or the lone Wookiee on Jyn's level, awkwardly shortened their gaits while the ones with shorter legs, most noticeably a family of Ociocks, flat-out ran to avoid being trampled. At the end of the aisle, their scandocs were flashed and they were pointed to various turbo tank transport units to complete the day's labor in the factories.

The prison towered over the factories spread around its base like supplicants. Nearest to the prison were factories developing small parts—screws and bolts used in ship manufacturing mostly. Rumor was that stormtrooper armor had originally been manu-factured on Wobani, but Jyn saw no evidence of that. Just countless screws and bolts, enough to make more Star Destroyers than could possibly be needed in the galaxy. Other factories on the planet developed ship panels used in floors and walls that were then sent off-world for construction. It was hard, brutal work with liquid-hot metals, and Jyn hated being assigned details in those factories. She spared another bitter longing for the missed farm detail, which at least was outside in the fresh air.

Not that Jyn had a choice. Every day, the prisoners worked in different groups, at different tasks. It was a way to prevent alliances from forming. It didn't mat-ter what their bodies were like, what skills they had.

The physically weak worked along with the strong, and if they were lucky, their fellow prisoners helped them complete the labor. Jyn had made the mistake of mentioning that she had tech skills and could be assigned to the engineering department. She had been beaten for her trouble and had never once been allowed near tech because of it.

Her prison badge beeped. "Panels," the stormtrooper who'd scanned her said, jerking his thumb toward a turbo tank.

Jyn trudged to the tank, where she was scanned again and given a partitioned seat made of hard metal. Stormtroopers patrolled the center aisle, but no one was talking or even looking at each other. They knew they had a hard day of labor in front of them. Working droid harvestors and irrigation units in the fields or aligning screws and inspecting bolts on the main production line wasn't that difficult, just tedious. Smelting panels meant singed hair and burned skin, aching muscles and bleary eyes and dry throats and lungs full of ash.

The turbo tank rumbled to life as soon as it was full, clattering over the rough ground of Wobani as it made its way to the panels factory. The work detail filed out after the short trip and droids instructed them on their tasks for the day.

That was part of the indignity of it all; this was work

droids could do more easily and more efficiently. In fact, droids did most of the work in the factories during the night shifts while the prisoners slept. But the Empire was willing to sacrifice some of that efficiency to make the prisoners fulfill a negligible quota.

Jyn's job that day was to notch the bottom of a series of wall panels in two-meter-by-half-meter sections. She stood in front of a production line with her accelerated particle cutter, slicing down twice and across once, letting the metal bits fall from the notches with bone-clattering thunks. The hair on her arms had long been burned away by the work, and although the tempered helmet she was given fit poorly, at least it protected her head from the full brunt of the heat.

Jyn lifted, sliced, and moved the metal panels down the line. A small part of her wondered just what the Empire wanted with this many notched wall panels. She hadn't been the first to wonder at their production line. Common assumption was that the Empire was building a larger fleet, but the sheer quantity of pieces the prisoners had worked on over the years, since long before Jyn arrived, sparked a rumor that the Empire was simply remelting the finished metal pieces and forcing the prisoners to do the same work on the same metal over and over and over again.

Jyn had long before quit bothering to figure out why the Empire did what it did.

Why did the Empire bother killing her mother and taking her father? If they were doing anything with his research, she had yet to see it. Saw had driven himself half-mad, spending most of Jyn's childhood chasing down ghosts of her father in an attempt to figure out the Empire's plans. In the end, he had found nothing.

Inexplicably, Saw's words filtered through Jyn's tired mind. *One fighter with a sharp stick and nothing left to lose can take the day.* Her finger twitched over the accelerated particle cutter. Even if she could rip it from its mounting, there was no way she could take out more than a single stormtrooper before she was cut down. The prisoners were given tools that could easily destroy their captors, but there was no escape.

The metal piece she'd notched from the main panel she was working on dropped to the ground. Rather than thunking, it shattered, metal shards splintering around her.

"Halt production!" a stormtrooper called. Red lights flared and the bone-jarring grinding of metal echoed throughout the factory. All the prisoners dropped to their knees, hands up, as they had been trained. Jyn wanted to brush away the metal shavings digging into her legs, but she knew better than to move out of position.

Stormtroopers and a few Imperial engineers

swarmed to Jyn's section of the line. Jyn kept her head down.

"Something wrong with this duralium-enforced steel," one of the engineers said. "This panel is far too brittle."

"Look at the striation lines," another engineer said, kneeling. An RA-7 inventory droid picked up one of the larger pieces of the shattered metal so the others could more easily examine it.

"Initial scan indicates an improper combination of alloys," the droid said. "This was from batch three two-four-three; four hundred other units were poured from that batch."

The head Imperial officer cursed and turned to a datapad, punching up information. Jyn's arms ached from being raised for so long, but she didn't move as the officers, stormtroopers, and droids stood around, talking about the tensile strength of the metal alloy and ignoring her completely, as if she were nothing but another bit of scrap metal.

"We'll have to halt production and pull every panel made from that batch," the head officer finally said, turning on his heel and marching back toward his office. "And it will be tedious to find them; they're scattered throughout the factories."

"Looks like your lucky day," a stormtrooper near Jyn

said as the crowd around her dispersed. In a moment, an announcement blared through the factory, calling Jyn's work unit back to the prison transport for an early shift dismissal.

Jyn finally dropped her arms, letting them sag by her body as the blood tingled back to her fingers. She pushed her hands into the floor to stand, wincing as a sharp piece of shattered metal pressed against her palm. Jyn shifted her hand.

The metal shard was roughly twelve centimeters long, one end squared and the other sharp as a blade. It could not have looked more like a knife if it had been purposefully made to be one. Jyn stared at it for a long moment.

One fighter with a sharp stick . . .

It was impossible. It was stupid. But it was there.

A chance.

Without letting herself think any further, Jyn palmed the sharpened piece of metal. Just wrapping her fingers around the square base made her feel stronger, more powerful than she had since she'd come to Wobani. Since before then. Hope surged through her, straightening her spine, clearing her eyes.

"You, there," came a voice through a stormtrooper helmet.

Jyn's fingers turned to ice, and the metal shard dropped, clattering so loudly against the cement floor of the factory that it seemed as if every single person and droid in the building heard it.

"Unsanctioned weapon found on a prisoner," the stormtrooper said. Another stormtrooper rushed Jyn, slamming her against the wall.

"It wasn't—it was just—" Jyn started, but a magnetic charge collar was snapped around her neck, and it became difficult to swallow, let alone talk. In moments, her hands were cuffed and two stormtroopers with stun prods stood in front of her.

The first stormtrooper bent down, picking up the happenstance knife. He held it loosely in his palm, testing the weight, and then he turned to Jyn.

"You were going to use this as a weapon," he accused.

Jyn shook her head frantically.

"Call the warden," the stormtrooper said.

It was three hours into the night shift when the stormtroopers dumped Jyn's battered body onto the floor of her prison cell. Zorahda started awake, staring as Jyn struggled to stand and make it to her bed. She did not move to help Jyn. She didn't show sympathy or compassion. It hadn't taken long to learn that lesson.

CHAPTER ELEVEN_

Jyn was never sure when it happened that Wrea became less her and Saw's home and more of a headquarters for Saw's cadre of partisans. Xosad left, but Jari and the others stayed. Some of Reece's people came back, saying they'd rather take orders from someone with actual experience. Idryssa sent some new recruits. Saw took them all—if they proved themselves worthwhile. It was typical for there to be at least a half dozen or more people staying at the outpost. Some came and left quickly, and Jyn never saw them again. Others stayed.

Jyn struggled to maintain her daily regime of training as Wrea grew crowded. When Saw was home, there was always a handful of people who joined her for sparring matches and target practice. She was distinctly aware of the way they tried to show off for Saw, of the way they wanted to catch his eye.

"They never bother when you're gone," she grumbled to him in a rare moment of privacy as she shaved his head for him, a task she'd taken over when she proved far more adept at it than he.

Saw laughed. "Are you saying you want me gone?"

Jyn punched him in the arm. "They're trying to impress you," she said, exasperated.

Saw had laughed again, but Jyn didn't think he really noticed the effect he had on others. He assumed the new recruits were hanging around Wrea because they believed in his cause; he didn't fully understand that they just believed in him.

On the bright side, there was a lot to learn from the newcomers. She was not too proud to admit that Codo was a better fighter; whenever she could, she'd request him as a sparring partner and try to learn his moves. Maia was slender and quiet, but no one had better aim. Staven knew ballistics. Jyn followed them around, learning as she could.

Because a small part of her—a part that she wanted to keep hidden even from herself—wanted to impress Saw, too. As more and more people came to Wrea, vied for his attention, forced him into the role of both leader and mentor, Jyn longed for the days when it had been just the two of them.

Saw was changing, too, seemingly before her eyes. He left on more and more missions, and Jyn had nothing to do but stand by the comm, waiting to hear word from him, hoping the worst hadn't happened yet. It took everything in her not to comm him when all she got was silence, but she knew her role. She kept her vigil.

He had been gone for a week when he came back from a mission with fresh wounds on his face and a badly broken leg. Jyn tried to ask him what happened, but he just grunted that the mission was a success and dismissed her worry. His leg bothered him, though, and as he was stuck at the outpost while it healed, he snapped at everyone. Including Jyn. She was actually glad when he finally left for another mission, and that feeling hollowed her out.

"What's wrong, little one?" asked Maia, who'd been at the outpost for over four months by then.

Jyn hung her legs over the edge of the island, staring down at the little grotto where some of the boys were swimming. The sun was starting to set.

"Everything's changing," she said sullenly.

"Everything usually does," Maia said.

"I don't like it," Jyn said.

Maia flexed her hands, and Jyn couldn't help noticing the synthskin gloves she had taken to wearing. She'd won them in a bet against Codo, and she enjoyed showing them off whenever there was a chance he might notice. Sure enough, Codo tried to splash them with water from his position in the sea. It didn't reach them, but Maia laughed at the shouted curses that followed.

"Saw means something special to you, doesn't he?" Maia asked Jyn after Codo and the other boys had swum off.

Jyn shrugged. She couldn't deny it, but she didn't want to say it out loud, either.

"Saw means something to a lot of people," Maia said when Jyn didn't answer her. "I heard about him as a hero of Onderon, from my godfather, Lux. Staven's family was saved when Saw organized a supply run past Imperial blockades to feed them. Saw fought in the Clone Wars; he's fought in battles since then. He's half legend."

Jyn sniffed.

"But," Maia added, "while Saw means something to all of us, *you* mean something to him."

Jyn's head whipped around, but she didn't know what to say. Maia nodded knowingly.

"Don't doubt that, little one," she said. "Sometimes I think you're the only one he really cares about."

"Oy!" someone called from the ladder that descended to the sea. The boys were climbing back up from the grotto. Staven made his way over to Maia and Jyn, his blue hair dripping wet. "We're taking a break, you want in?"

Jyn frowned and stared back out over the sea. "Taking a break" was code among the regulars on Wrea for "getting drunk while Saw is gone," and she was never, ever invited.

"Sure." Maia stood up, brushing the sand off her bottom. She and Staven headed back to the outpost.

Staven paused. "You want in?" he repeated.

"Me?" Jyn's voice was higher, more childish than she would have liked.

"Yeah," Staven said with a laugh. "You. Coming?"

Jyn jumped up and followed him and the others back to the outpost. Someone produced a jug of pale blue liquid, but it smelled sour, strong enough to burn the hairs in Jyn's nose. When Staven poured her a cup of the fermented bantha milk, it was half as full as anyone else's, but she didn't complain.

They swapped war stories and dirty jokes, and Jyn sipped the foul liquid, her insides growing warmer and her laugh growing louder. Codo clapped her on the back, shouting, "She's one of ours!" as Jyn chugged the dregs of alcohol from her glass. "To Jyn!" he cheered, grabbing the jug and refilling his cup. He blinked at her. "Jyn. Um. I forgot your last name."

A little bell rang in Jyn's mind, a warning. She and Saw had always been careful, *always*, never to mention her last name. She was just Jyn.

"To Jyn Gerrera!" Maia cried, tipping her cup back. The rest of the table followed suit.

As she stumbled off to bed that night, Jyn thought, *Maybe this isn't so bad after all.*

CHAPTER TWELVE_

When Saw returned from his mission, he still had a bit of a limp, but his leg was mostly healed. He took Maia and Codo into one of the private rooms branching off the hallway, and before Jyn had a chance to realize what was happening, Maia and Codo were gone, off on a mission of their own.

"You said I would be going on more missions," Jyn told him. She couldn't help noticing how different Wrea felt with Maia and Codo gone, with Saw back. She didn't want to think about which scenario she preferred.

Saw tilted his head back. "How old are you again?" he asked.

Jyn wanted to lie, to pretend she was older than she was, but she answered truthfully. "Fourteen. Almost fifteen."

Saw looked up, scanning the group of soldiers scattered around Wrea. "Staven!" he barked.

Staven ran up, his hand twitching as if he wanted

to salute Saw but just barely kept himself in check. "Yes, sir?" he said.

"Get me a detonator kit."

Staven nodded and ran to one of the rooms in the armory. He returned minutes later with a small box. He held it out to Saw, but Saw jerked his head to Jyn. Staven turned, holding the box out for Jyn to take. She picked it up, surprised by the weight. She glanced at Saw, then turned her attention to the box, opening it slowly.

Inside were all the pieces needed for a standard detonator. Two halves of a palm-sized disc, the detonite, the wiring compartment and timer, the remote override.

Saw glanced at the time on his comlink. "You have three minutes," he said.

Jyn's heart leapt in her chest. *This is a test,* she realized, slowly, even as her fingers were extracting the items from the box, putting them together with speed she hadn't known she had. The rough construction of the detonator was easy enough, but the remote override and the wiring was always tricky. She felt the seconds tick by. She allowed herself one moment to look up. Everyone on the island was silent, watching. Staven stood over her shoulder, watching her work, his eyes narrowed as he examined every move her fingers made. He was the expert in explosives, and she was very aware that he was judging her just as harshly as Saw was.

Once the remote override was done, Jyn focused on the wiring compartment. This was the trickiest part of piecing together a detonator, and she hated it. She always got the wires mixed up. Her fingers shook. She was very, very conscious of everyone watching. Of the time ticking by.

"One minute," Saw said.

That's not helping, she wanted to snap, but she kept her mouth shut and her mind focused. She slid the wires into place, snapped the cover over the detonator, and looked up, pride making her chin tilt in triumph.

And then she saw Staven's face.

He shook his head sadly.

"Show her what she did," Saw said, disappointment dripping from his voice.

Staven opened the detonator, peeling back the overlay and displaying the wiring compartment for Jyn. Her eyes danced over the myriad wires, seeking her mistake . . . *there.* A blue wire where a green wire should have been. The timer would be messed up, measuring in hours instead of minutes.

"If you'd given me some warning, I would have been prepared," Jyn said. "It's not fair to just throw this at me last minute."

Saw raised an eyebrow.

Too late, Jyn realized her mistake. In a mission, she would have no time to prepare. In a mission, she would be operating under more stressful conditions than Saw's timer and Staven's watchful eye.

"Your mistake could have cost the lives of everyone else on your mission," Staven said.

Saw said nothing. The disappointment was evident on his face. Jyn blinked away tears as he turned silently and walked away.

⬧

Someone knocked on Jyn's bedroom door.

She wasn't going to open it. Jyn knew it wasn't Saw; she could hear him talking and laughing down the hall. But the knock came again and then a third time, more insistent, so she got up and opened the door.

"Can I come in?" Staven asked.

Jyn shrugged and turned away, flopping back down on her bed. Staven stepped tentatively inside the room—a rarity. The outpost was full of open doors, the bunkers always overflowing with people, the great room a mass of bodies—but Jyn's room was *hers*, and no one but her or Saw was allowed inside.

"I thought you might want some supper." Staven placed a bowl on the crate Jyn used as a bedside table. She didn't look at it.

"He hates me," she muttered to the floor.

"He doesn't." Staven said it simply, as if there was no question of it. But he hadn't seen the disdain on Saw's face.

"I could have done it right," Jyn said, anger and defeat mixing in her voice. "It wasn't fair."

She looked up when Staven didn't reply. He held her gaze a few moments, then said, "It doesn't matter if it was fair or not. It only matters that you messed up, and doing something like that could hurt or kill a teammate.

"This life," Staven continued, glancing toward the open door, where the sound of the others' voices leaked through, "it's dark. You know what I mean?"

Jyn shrugged.

"You can't let the darkness overtake you."

When Jyn shut her eyes, she saw the hatch, the one she had hidden in after her mother was killed, her father taken. She thought about the way day had faded into night, the way she had been alone for the first time in her life, the realization that the people who loved her best were gone and no one else knew she was there.

There had been a lantern. A little lantern, so dim that it almost didn't matter. That little lantern had been her companion against the dark.

And then Saw had come.

He had come for her. No one else had. And he

hadn't left her. Staven knelt, trying to get down to Jyn's level. "When I was learning explosives," he said, "I miswired a detonator, too." He paused as if carefully choosing his words. "But no one caught my mistake. Until it blew up. I hurt someone, someone on my own team. He lost his hand. And it was my fault."

Jyn flexed her own fingers, wondering what it would feel like if they were gone.

"He's never going to trust me on a mission now," Jyn muttered, looking away.

"I don't think he wants to send you on a mission."

"I've been on missions before; I'm good enough!" Jyn jumped up, her hands curling into fists. "I am! So what if I made a mistake today, I know I'm good enough for another mission!" This wasn't ego talking; Jyn knew she outmatched most of the regulars in the bunkers, and her mistake that day notwithstanding, she was more than qualified for her own operation.

Staven nodded slowly. "You are," he said. "But I don't think Saw wants to admit that."

CHAPTER THIRTEEN_

Saw sent Jyn on her first solo mission not long after that. She suspected this was mostly thanks to Staven's influence, but perhaps it was Saw's way of honoring her for her fifteenth birthday, an occasion that otherwise went unnoticed.

"We're dropping you on Horuz," he said. "That's one of the dark planets we've been watching."

Dark planets—Jyn knew what that meant. Sixteen planets on Saw's list, each with communication blackouts and much higher protocols than the Empire usually placed on planets that didn't seem that significant. Several of Saw's missions had been revolving around the so-called dark planets, and Saw was convinced that it had something to do with Jyn's father and whatever it was he'd been researching, but he rarely talked to Jyn about that those days, and he never mentioned his motivations to any of the others.

Saw held out an imagecaster, and a young man with two long dark braids revolved in the light. "This is Dorin Bell," Saw said. "We think he was recruited by the Empire about a year ago."

Jyn looked around the empty room. *Who is this "we"?* she thought.

"He's been working with kybers," Saw continued in a softer voice, and Jyn knew that she was hearing that only because she was close to Saw. He wouldn't get so personal with others in his cadre.

When he continued, his voice was back to being full of authority and cold detachment. "I've gotten word that he's going to be scouting the southern hemisphere of Horuz with only a small protection detail."

"What's my mission?" Jyn asked, staring at the holo of the man.

Saw shot her a look. He reached back and pulled out a modified long-range blaster rifle fitted with a sniper scope and an additional power cell that would overcharge the plasma.

Jyn stared at it.

"Maia said you would be good for this," Saw said, doubt creeping into his voice.

Jyn thought of the target practice she'd done with Maia, the careful aim from across the island. She glanced at the image of Dorin Bell.

"What did he do?" Jyn asked. She meant, *Why does he deserve to die?*

Saw didn't answer immediately, and when Jyn

looked into his eyes, she was a little terrified of what she saw there. "Does it matter?" he asked in his soldier voice.

Yes, Jyn thought.

"No," Jyn said.

Saw nodded, happy with her answer. "Staven will take you to the drop point," he said, and with that, Jyn was dismissed.

◈

Jyn stopped by her room, preparing carefully, checking her weapons, packing a small satchel of essentials. She turned to face the door and caught her reflection in the smooth metal.

She was surprised at the woman she saw there.

Saw didn't like mirrors, and the sea outside was always too rocky to be reflective. And Jyn rarely cared about her appearance. But she paused now, staring at herself.

First she saw her eyes. Her father used to say that she had stardust in her eyes, that's what made them such an unusual color. She could still hear his voice, his whiskers scratching her chin as he hugged her and whispered, *I love you, Stardust.*

Jyn shook herself, dispelling the memory. She set her jaw, steeling her spine, letting her sorrow give her strength.

And then she saw her mother in her reflection.

Jyn reached out, touching the smooth surface of the door, her fingertips pressing against the cold metal. That was the way her mother had stood. Tall. Proud.

Determined.

Jyn spent so much of her life hoping she could be different from her father, sometimes she forgot how much she wished she could be half as brave as her mother. She squared her shoulders.

She would prove that she was.

On the ship ride to Horuz, Staven went over additional details with Jyn. He described the landscape, the timing, the drop point and rendezvous point. "We've set some other traps for him and the work detail," he added. "But Saw likes having insurance."

Jyn's fingers ran over the barrel of the long-range blaster. It did not escape her notice when they pulled out of hyperspace that Staven was using forged ship clearance codes that Jyn had made for Saw in her spare time.

Staven dropped Jyn off near a little canyon. "If they follow our intel," he said, "they'll be walking on a trail down there." He pointed over the edge of the cliff, at the dusty canyon floor. "But if not, the other access point is that way." He pointed south, at another trail cut into the small forest. From Jyn's vantage point, she had cover and a clear view of both trails. "Either way," Staven concluded, "they'll likely end up there." He indicated a point about a kilometer away from Jyn. She viewed it through her sniper scope. That was her target.

Staven left, and she was alone.

Saw had arranged for Jyn to arrive on Horuz early, so she had hours to wait. Hours to wait, with a blaster in her hand.

I can do this, she thought, and knew it to be true.

She didn't let herself think of whether or not she wanted to.

When the Imperial scouts finally came, long after the time she'd been expecting them, Jyn was nearly asleep. She scrambled to attention. They came from the second trail, through the trees. Jyn was glad of her position, of the way she was mostly hidden on the canyon ridge.

She drew in a breath. The blaster was set up with a small tripod. She'd calculated the distance, the angles. She watched the dust cloud rise as the small transport unit pulled to a stop just outside of the area Staven had said they would be.

Jyn took a deep breath.

The first time she was supposed to pull the trigger, it had been a scientist. One that reminded her of her father. And he'd been right in front of her. She could hear him, smell him.

This was better. This was farther away. Impersonal.

Jyn squared Dorin Bell in her sights. He was younger than Jyn had expected. He was smiling. Jyn moved the scope down, to Dorin's chest, where she didn't have to see the easy curve of his lips, the light in his eyes. Jyn focused on the gray of the Imperial uniform, the little black shield badge over Dorin's heart.

She looked over the scope. From that distance, they hardly looked like people at all.

Jyn angled her head down, pressing her eye into the scope. She charged the modified blaster, and the additional power cell hummed.

Her finger felt the curve of the trigger.

It's just like target practice, she told herself, but her mind was screaming at her, over and over: *It's not, it's not, it's not.*

She thought of Saw. Of the disappointment on his face when she'd failed the detonator test.

She squeezed the trigger.

The blaster jumped in her hand, the overclocked power cell so hot that it left a scalding blister on her palm. She didn't notice that though; she was distracted by the billow of smoke and dust that rose up from the area where, moments before, the Imperials had been standing. A booming echo rang across the land.

"The traps," she muttered. Staven had told her that

she was insurance, that there were traps laid where the Imperials were expected to be. Something must have triggered them; she assumed they were land mines, based on the explosion. Jyn forced herself to watch the cloud dissipate, to look for survivors. To prepare.

When the dust and smoke cleared, she used her sniper scope to examine the carnage. She saw Dorin Bell's body, broken, bleeding, and she squinted at his wounds, inspecting them. She was equally ashamed and relieved that it had been the land mines, not her blast that had killed him.

CHAPTER FOURTEEN_

After that mission, Jyn never knew when she woke up if Saw would send her outside to train or if he'd tell her to load up and meet him on the ship. She liked the unexpectedness of her life and the fact that she was a partner, not a student. Most of their missions were to worlds in the Outer Rim, typically along trade routes. Saw was preoccupied with the Empire's increased focus on cargo, certain that it was gearing up for a major weapons development. Ore from Siriamp, Jelucan, and Centori; the occupied mines on Ilum . . . Saw went over galactic maps nightly, trying to connect the pieces of the Empire's plans. While he did that, Jyn scoured all the records she could, gathering information on how to falsify clearance codes and develop scandocs so that Saw could continue his missions. The Empire was showing more and more interest in the planets on the edges of civilization, and the previously neglected reaches of the Outer Rim were starting to feel very crowded indeed.

So she was a little surprised when Saw told her their next mission would be to Inusagi, a wealthy planet in the Mid Rim.

"What's the mission?" Jyn asked, confused.

Saw frowned. "Not our normal fare, but it pays well," he confessed.

"Normal fare" meant getting closer to Jyn's father. Jyn felt the obsession Saw did just as acutely, although for a different reason. She didn't care what her father was making for the Empire; she just wanted to face him one last time. She wasn't sure if she'd use the chance to punch him or ask him why he had abandoned her, but she hoped that, one day, she'd get the opportunity to do at least one of those things.

"If this isn't linked to the Empire, what is it?" Jyn asked.

"It's still linked to the Empire, just not the big mission," Saw said. He tossed her a holocube, and when Jyn activated it, she found herself staring into the face of a Zabrak woman. It was hard to tell on the cheap holocube, but Jyn guessed she had yellowish skin, with green-black horns like a crown around her head. She wore a heavy faceplate that covered her forehead and shot between her eyes, down to her nose. It curled over the top of her head, adding metal spikes between her natural horns.

"Arane Oreida," Saw said. "Hates most humans, by the way. Good thing I'm so handsome." He crinkled his scarred face in a ferocious grin.

Jyn frowned. "If she hates humans, then why—"

"Arane is notoriously suspicious," Saw said. "We're given pieces, not the whole. She's paying for my services."

"And those services are . . . ?" Jyn asked.

"She needs two fighters," Saw said. "Me and Maia, I think. Maybe Codo."

Jyn's heart sank. She was still, after everything, not good enough.

"You're in this, too, kid," Saw said, ruffling Jyn's hair. "There are a lot of players on this one. We each have a specific role."

"So what are we doing?"

Saw nodded to the holocube, and Jyn activated it. "The operatives in Group C, under Stoneface's command," Arane started in an imperious voice.

"My code name," Saw said. He tilted his face to the light, setting his jaw in a hard line. Jyn giggled.

"Obtain clearance codes for ships landing on Inusagi. Arrange for access for operatives in Alpha Group to the main floor of the palace during the dedication ceremony. Guests have been sent a special imagecaster branded for the occasion and with an XLD security chip."

Jyn shrugged. "That's not very secure."

Saw spoke over Arane's holographic image. "It's a party, not a top-secret military function. So you think you can handle something like that?"

"Sure," Jyn said. "The clearance codes—no problem. The invites may be more difficult. If I had one to copy . . . ?"

Arane had sent one legitimate imagecaster invitation and provided Saw with a dozen blanks. "We absolutely need ten," Saw said. "So there's a little room for error. But if you can make all twelve work, that's better."

Jyn inspected the official imagecaster. "Shouldn't be a problem," she said. "I'll need some things."

Saw took careful notes of everything Jyn suggested he get so she could replicate the invitations, then immediately sent one of his underlings to the nearest world with a tradepost. They had less than a standard month to complete the task, but Jyn was fairly certain she would need only half that time.

The outside of the imagecaster was painted in swirling designs of red and gold, the display base made of what looked like actual golden honeycomb. A scandoc had cleverly been inserted into the bottom of the imagecaster, and when Jyn twirled the three legs at the perimeter, the holo started automatically.

A young woman who looked a few years older than

Jyn, in her early twenties, was illuminated in the holographic light. Rather than show just her face, the small image showed the girl's whole body. The imagecaster was an expensive model, and the girl was illuminated in vivid detail, her clothes seemingly woven from light. Her rich brown skin seemed to glow even more against the bright red embroidered cloth that she wore tightly wound around her body. A cascade of silky black hair extended almost to her knees, curling slightly at the ends.

"As the chieftess of Inusagi," the woman said, her voice tinkling through the small speakers of the imagecaster, "I welcome you to our planet's annual sakoola blossom festival. This imagecaster will also allow you entry to the special dedication ceremony in honor of our first Imperial governor. Please present it to the royal guard upon your arrival, but until then, I encourage you to learn more about Inusagi and our royal heritage." The girl threw her arms up at the end of her speech, as if celebrating a great win.

Before the holo cut off, the woman lowered her arms, her shoulders sinking, and there was a flash of emotion on her tiny, illuminated face, one that spoke of defeat.

Jyn scanned the contents of the imagecaster. The information on Inusagi was cursory at best, highlighting its contributions to the Empire and glossing over the years of "negotiations"—many of which grew violent—before the planet's fall into the Empire's hands. Inusagi had remained chiefly unimportant for centuries, benefiting from its position near wealthier planets but without key exports itself. It had mostly been successful in its attempts to remain neutral throughout the years, but clearly that neutrality was over. A planet was either for the Empire, or it was crushed under the Empire's heels.

The final holo held a message from the Empire. "Inusagi is a planet rich in culture and arts," Lieutenant Colonel Senjax, official military correspondent for the Imperial Broadcast, said. Unlike the chieftess's opening speech, the lieutenant colonel's holo showed him from the chest up, as if he were speaking directly to Jyn. "The Empire is pleased to bring this diverse planet under its wing. Inusagi's strong alliance with the Empire will prove that new beginnings under our beloved Emperor can lead to prosperity and happiness for all the galaxy's citizens. We look forward to greeting you at the sakoola blossom festival."

"Oh, I bet you can't wait to see us," Jyn told the flickering image just before she turned off the device.

CHAPTER FIFTEEN_

"Nice work," Saw said when Jyn finished duplicating the last invitation. "I honestly can't tell which is the original."

Jyn beamed at him. It had taken a lot of work to replicate both the outer appearance of the imagecasters and the internal information. Copying the holos over had been simple enough, but duping the scandocs had required much more time and patience. She had spent so much of the past few years developing the physical side of her training that she'd almost forgotten how wonderful it was to focus on something that was entirely a mental activity.

Saw glanced up at Jyn. "You constantly amaze me," he said. "Not many people could have done this, but I knew you could."

"I enjoyed figuring it out," she said, shrugging despite her pride at his words. "It was like solving a puzzle."

"Must run in your blood," Saw said.

Jyn's head whipped up. "No, it doesn't." Her eyes

flashed. Saw rarely spoke that directly about her father.

Saw nodded—his way of admitting he shouldn't have reminded Jyn of her past. "Ready to go?" he asked.

Jyn nodded eagerly. She hadn't been sure she'd be invited to join Saw on the mission. This partisan group led by the Zabrak . . . Jyn had never worked with them before, although she suspected Saw had, during one of the missions when he'd left her behind.

Saw tossed the imagecasters into a large canvas bag that was already full of something soft, then shrugged the bag onto his shoulder. He led the way to his ship. Maia was already there, smiling at Jyn.

Saw climbed into the pilot's seat, and they headed off.

"Excited?" Maia asked Jyn. They both swayed as Saw maneuvered the ship through the asteroid belt.

Jyn nodded. "But it's a bit odd, isn't it? I don't even know what you and Saw are doing on Inusagi, other than that you're meeting others. Why didn't that woman—"

"Arane," Maia supplied.

Jyn nodded. "Why didn't she just hire Saw to do it all? Instead of passing these imagecasters off to strangers, we could have worked as a team."

Maia nodded darkly. "I don't think Saw likes it, either," she said in a low voice. "But the anti-Imperial groups are too spread out. We have to work together when we can. This could be a good thing, a sign of a forthcoming alliance."

Jyn frowned, remembering what Saw had said about Arane not liking humans. Even though Saw worked with Jari and Xosad and others who weren't human, the majority of his cadre was. She somehow doubted that Arane wanted anything to do with Saw other than paying him to do whatever dirty work she didn't want the nonhumans doing.

The ship jumped to hyperspace, and Jyn heard the familiar thump of Saw's boots on the metal flooring. "This is the way Arane works," he said, shooting Jyn and Maia a look that told them he'd heard their conversation. "Keeps things secure."

"But we usually don't work like this," Jyn said.

Saw frowned. "Maybe we should."

"Or maybe," Maia interrupted, "we should work closer together. Idryssa—"

Saw growled, and Maia clamped her lips shut.

He jerked his head toward the back of the ship. "Go change," he said, tossing Jyn the large satchel he'd carried aboard.

Jyn opened it to reveal a set of Inusagian robes in petal green, with gold embroidery on the hem that matched the sparkling sakoola blossoms Jyn had seen in the imagecaster's holo.

"We need to blend in," Saw said, grimacing.

"It'll do you good to clean up," Maia said, pulling out her own bag from the storage unit.

"Go on," Saw growled.

Jyn headed to a more private corner and stripped her clothes. She thought of the beautiful, young, and obviously naïve chieftess of Inusagi as she took off her usual pants and shirt and replaced them with the finely embroidered cloth. She carefully tucked her kyber crystal necklace under the robe and smoothed the material over her body. She was usually proud of the way she didn't look like a girl—she would much rather show off her biceps than her breasts—but that day she relished her curves, winding the cloth tightly around her torso and admiring the way it swished around her legs and hips when she moved. She pulled her hair out of its usual messy bun, arranging it as best she could so it curled down her back. Saw didn't exactly keep cosmetics around, but Jyn dusted her face with the talc she found in the bag and bit her lips to make them pinker.

"Nice," Maia said. She wore a similar set of robes, but there was extra padding around her body, making her look fatter than she was. Maia had also stripped the synthskin gloves from her hands. She kept twisting her fingers, as if unused to feeling the world with her actual skin.

"You clean up well," Jyn said, looking past Maia at Saw.

The suit was a bit tight around his broad chest, but the colors brought out the deep brown tones of his skin. The fine material made him look almost regal. Jyn felt as though she was wearing a costume, but Saw looked like a king.

"This is yours," he said, tossing her a green purse that was embroidered to match her robes. Inside, the dozen imagecaster invitations were nestled in small pockets in the liner.

"The other members of the group will recognize you by your robes." Saw indicated the elaborate, distinctive embroidery all along the hem. "The code word is *cloud*. Get the others inside."

Jyn nodded her understanding. The ship lurched out of hyperspace, but her stomach had been left somewhere behind her in space. The mission felt . . . off. She didn't like working with Arane, with her obvious disdain for humans. She didn't like how fractured the mission was.

Saw gave his clearance codes, and Jyn smiled with satisfaction as they were approved to dock in the spaceport without question. He maneuvered the ship down, and Jyn eagerly leaned over, looking out at Inusagi's beautiful landscape. An azure river cut through the lush green hills and valleys near the capital city, a ribbon of blue that spun off into curlicues and large pools. She knew from her research that Inusagi's landscape had been cultivated over centuries, and each pool represented a different community led by a noble house. The largest pool spilled over the cliff, forming a waterfall into the ocean. The chieftess's palace was built on the cliff, a long rectangle of milky brown stone, one side facing the calm pools overlooking each of the lesser noble houses, one side facing the waterfall and the tumultuous sea at its base.

Saw swooped the shuttle down into the spaceport, built a little distance from the river. As soon as they were docked, apprehension started curling in Jyn's stomach.

"Once you pass out all the invites, come back here," Saw said, standing. "Wait for me."

"You said you only needed ten invites," Jyn said. There were a dozen in her bag. She withdrew two and handed them to Maia and Saw.

"Come back here," Saw repeated, his voice sterner, a clear warning that she was not to use one of the imagecasters for herself. "We each have a part to play."

He moved stiffly out of the cockpit, and although his suit was fitted to his body, she knew it was hiding weapons. Maia nudged her forward, and Jyn glanced at the padding beneath her friend's robes, wondering which blasters were wrapped under the silk.

CHAPTER SIXTEEN_

Zip ports carried groups of people from the docking area to the palace. The large glass bubbles resembled eggs on their sides, and they were put on a magnetic track that took a scenic route around the decorative pool and up to the center courtyard of the palace. Saw positioned Jyn near the glass so she could see, but as their zip port moved them closer to the chieftess's home, Saw subtly pushed his way deeper into the center of the glass egg, distancing himself from Jyn. Maia had hung back with the ship, taking the next zip port.

Colorful tents had been erected around the chieftess's large pool, and it was clear the sakoola festival was in full swing for the locals. The delicious scent of some sort of sweet fried dough permeated the zip port, and Jyn could hear hawkers enticing people to buy souvenir nets with which to catch the sakoola petals. Mostly children ran around waving the nets, which had been decorated with colorful ribbons, but more than a few adults carried them as an accessory to their festive clothes.

When the zip port stopped between the courtyard and the east end of the pool, everyone filed out. Saw let the crowd separate him from Jyn. She watched as he went straight to the palace, holding out the image-caster. A flash of apprehension shot through her, but the guards in front of the palace didn't question Saw's invitation in the slightest. He strode through the doors and was gone.

While the west end of the pool overflowed with street vendors and children, the east end, closer to the palace, was more reserved. The colors were muted, and rather than tents, discreet benches had been placed along the water's edge and interspersed among the trees.

The sakoola trees had long slender branches that drifted easily in the near-constant breezes of Inusagi. The yellow petals that floated throughout the area were as soft as silk, with a hint of gold along the edges that didn't seem natural but was beautiful nonetheless. People strolled through the trees in small groups or alone, talking in reserved voices.

Jyn chose a bench by the pool where there were fewer trees and she was more visible. As she sat, she caught the tail end of a conversation between a couple watching the palace steps and the stormtroopers who lined them.

"It's not democracy if our chieftess is forced to sign

a treaty with the Empire," the woman hissed. She wore robes similar to Jyn's—a long stretch of embroidered cloth wound tightly around her upper body and trailed down her legs.

Jyn had thought her companion was a man, by the clothes, but when the person spoke, Jyn realized it was another woman. "The Empire is here whether we like it or not," she said. "At least they're peaceful."

"Peaceful," the first woman snorted. "Silence isn't the same as peace."

Nevertheless, when they rounded the path and saw Jyn listening to them, they both went quiet.

Another man meandered down the path, nodding at the two women before he sat beside Jyn. "Lots of people talk the big talk," he said in a strange accent.

Jyn nodded, her eyes scanning the sakoola trees, waiting for her first contact.

"But in the end, they're about as threatening as a cloud," the man added.

Jyn froze. The code word. She glanced over at the man, and his eyes narrowed. Jyn casually slid her hand in the purse, palmed an imagecaster, and slipped it into the man's hand. He nodded, his beard moving over his chest, and strolled away casually. A few moments later, he headed to the stairs and entered the palace.

While the sakoola festival was a large tourist event, Jyn saw only a handful of attendees who weren't human, and most of them kept close together, soon heading toward the more open festival on the other side of the pool. Everyone who approached Jyn and said the code word was human—many young men, a few women, and one old crone who looked as if she had a hunchback, although Jyn wondered if it was a disguise to hide weapons. Jyn was down to just a handful of image-caster invitations—one to give the last member of the mission and the spares she had made.

A wave of melancholy washed over Jyn, unexpected and unbidden. But she couldn't help thinking how much her mother would have loved this experience. Lyra had always been seeking out the ways in which worlds were unique; she valued the differences in the galaxy. She would have loved Inusagi.

More people crowded near where Jyn sat, as if expecting something. They faced the pool, and Jyn turned to see what they were watching. Soon the still, glassy surface of the water broke, and diamond-shaped creatures as tall as Jyn swooped out of the water, gliding across the surface. They were pale and hairless, very thin with almost invisible facial features. Their movements were part flying, part swimming as they glided over the surface of the water. A thin membrane connected their heads to the tips of their fingers, and from there down to their ankles.

"What are they?" Jyn asked a woman nearby.

"Rayeths," the woman answered. She sounded sad, which made no sense; the Rayeths' water dance was breathtakingly gorgeous, almost magical in the way they soared across the pool.

Soon a group of six Rayeths glided up to the edge of the pool, close to Jyn. They were so thin it seemed as if they would float away like the sakoola blossoms, but as soon as they stood, the Rayeths wrapped their membraned arms around their bodies, forming a narrow, almost cocoon-like shell around their torsos that gave way to looser folds flapping near their ankles.

The six Rayeths made something of a small parade as they left the pool and marched toward the grand staircase of the palace. Tension crackled through the crowd that had grown, and no one spoke as the Rayeths walked through the floating sakoola blossoms and up the first few stairs. Jyn watched as more stormtroopers, as well as some local guards, formed a barrier on the staircase, barring the Rayeths' entrance.

The Rayeth in the front said something, but Jyn was too far away to hear it. She worried at first that the delicate white creatures would be struck down, but after a few moments, the Rayeths turned, beginning the long walk back the way they had gone. No one in the crowd gathered around the pool said a thing as the Rayeths hung their heads, denied entrance to the palace and shamed in front of everyone. They slid into the water silently, spreading out their arms and quickly disappearing under the surface.

"Such a shame," someone near Jyn murmured. "A tradition broken."

"Stupid animals," someone else muttered. "At least the Empire knows they're not important. They shouldn't be allowed on the surface."

They're people, Jyn thought viciously. *Not animals.*

But she didn't say a word aloud.

CHAPTER SEVENTEEN_

The last contact walked straight up to Jyn. "Cloud," he grunted in a low voice. She handed him the image-caster and watched him enter the palace. She was half surprised it worked for him; he was the least subtle of all her contacts.

Saw had told her to go straight back to the ship after she passed out the invitations, but she still had extra imagecasters, and she could use one for herself. And after seeing the Rayeths denied entry into the palace, Jyn was more than a little curious about just what lay beyond those forbidden doors.

Besides, all the other missions she'd done with Saw hadn't ended in a party in a palace. The most glamorous thing she'd done lately was release mynock repellent around the asteroids closest to Wrea.

"Just a peek," she told herself, wrapping her fingers around an imagecaster. She mounted the steps of the palace slowly, her eyes on the stormtroopers. They looked bored, waving her inside with one hand after she scanned her imagecaster on the ident lock.

Fallen sakoola petals formed a path down the hallway, but even without them, Jyn could have followed the sounds of the crowd to the large ballroom that was sunken into the heart of the palace. Pillars wrapped in ivy supported a glass ceiling over the ballroom, and several dozen steps led down to the main floor. Jyn's Inusagian robes whispered against the stone as she descended into the ballroom. Her eyes darted around, looking for Saw or the other contacts in the partisan group, but she didn't see anyone else.

They must have used the invites for entry into the building, she thought. The palace was huge, with high domed ceilings; they could be anywhere by then, uncovering the secrets of the Empire that had been hidden in its base there in the chieftess's palace.

Just a few minutes, Jyn told herself. The ballroom was packed with people, most lingering around the buffet table, on which sat an array of Inusagian delicacies, fruits and honeys, breads and cheeses. Different wines were being passed around by server droids, a selection from Inusagi but also a few finer bottles from Core worlds, including a blue one featuring Alderaanian wine that was being served only to the more elite guests, who stood on a platform near the art sculpture that occupied the center of the ballroom.

The sculpture was made of flowers. Jyn had never seen something so beautiful—and so pointless. The flowers would surely die after a few standard weeks, and the entire thing would wilt. For now, though, it was breathtaking, a show of extravagance. The base of the sculpture was made with greenery, thick waxy leaves woven together with ivy, and that gave way to fiery red blossoms with orange centers, crowned with bright golden-yellow sakoola blossoms. The image the flowers created was a bird on fire.

"It's lovely, isn't is?" a man near Jyn said when he saw her leaning back to see the full sculpture.

She had to admit it was. "What kind of bird is it?" she asked. She only then realized she hadn't seen any birds in the garden by the pool; the closest thing to flight that she'd seen was the Rayeths gliding over water.

"It's a starbird," the man said. "Your mother didn't tell you the legend?"

He thinks I'm Inusagian, Jyn thought, remembering her robes. "My mother died," she said, looking down demurely.

A flash of pity crossed the man's face. "It's an old tale anyway," he said. "People forget the old tales. But the starbird lives inside the heart of every star in the galaxy. When a star goes out, the bird dies a fiery death, its wings spanning millions of kilometers, stretching out over the dark abyss of space. The starbird turns to stardust."

Jyn stiffened.

"All that's left is the heart. And the dust spreads out over the galaxy, then forms again. The man cupped his hands, as if he could hold the stardust. "And the starbird is reborn." He opened his palms, and Jyn half expected a mythical bird to soar into the air.

But there was nothing.

"Disrespectful is what it is," said an older woman who had been listening to them, frowning.

"Disrespectful?" the man asked, but there was an icy edge to his voice.

The woman sniffed at him, turning away. She moved over to a group of Imperial officers gathered near a platform.

"Thanks for the story," Jyn said, moving away from the man. She didn't want anyone to really notice her, and if the man wasn't liked, it wouldn't help her to stick near him.

"Friends, members of the Inusagian court," a voice echoed, amplified by the speaker droids that had buzzed above the crowd, hovering over everyone's heads. All eyes turned to the dais installed under the flowery sculpture.

The chieftess looked much smaller than she had in the holo. Her eyes were sunken and her skin ashen. Her hair hung limply down her back. The only thing that looked regal about her was the silvery-white robes she wore, the bands of cloth wrapped around her torso in a way that reminded Jyn of the Rayeths wrapping their arms around themselves as they approached the palace.

"We welcome you all as we celebrate the beautiful festival of sakoola blossoms," the chieftess said. She glanced behind her at the statue made of flowers.

"Yes, thank you," someone said before the chieftess could continue. An Imperial officer stepped forward, and the microphone shifted toward him. "We are pleased to share this festive day with an event equally joyous: the installation of Inusagi's first Imperial governor!" He waited for polite applause and kept waiting until there were enough cheers to satisfy him. "Thank you, thank you," he continued as the welcome abated. "Governor Cor Tophervin is a personal friend of our great Emperor Palpatine, and it is an honor to dedicate his service to the Empire and the planet of Inusagi today. Cor, please step forward," the officer said, sweeping his arm out.

Jyn made her way to the back of the crowd. It was clear what this little party was really about—a show of power and prestige from the Empire. It seemed almost like a mockery to turn a festival in honor of the planet's beauty into an excuse to showcase an Imperial governor.

Most of the crowd edged closer to the stage, but Jyn unobtrusively stepped farther back. It was time to go.

A handful of stormtroopers lined the bottom of the stairs in the sunken ballroom. Before they could stop her, Jyn made a motion to show that she was feeling sick, and one stepped back so she could dart up the stairs and toward the hallway that led out of the palace. She paused before leaving, her robes brushing through the trail of sakoola petals, the pillars surrounding the ballroom casting long, reaching shadows.

There was movement there.

Jyn squinted into the darkness.

Ten people moved forward, silently. Among them were a bald man with a bushy beard, an old woman no longer hunchbacked, a blunt man with big, angry eyes. Maia. And Saw.

Each held a dual canister FC-1 flechette launcher. Jyn had studied weapons with Saw long enough to know exactly what such a weapon would do. Her eyes widened as her mind ran over the statistics she knew by heart. Each flechette launcher would hold six antipersonnel canisters. Each canister held hundreds of tiny, razor-sharp flechettes made of durasteel that, when fired, would slice through the crowd, penetrating up to ten centimeters, regardless of whether they hit a stormtrooper's armor or a soft Inusagian gown.

Flechettes were deck sweepers, capable of decimating a crowd in minutes.

Jyn couldn't move as she watched the partisans take their positions around the pillars. Ten people. Sixty shots. Thousands of tiny razors flying through the air.

Her eyes flew to the chieftess as she stepped forward and the newly installed Imperial governor finished his speech.

"Welcome to Inusagi, Governor Tophervin," the chieftess said in a defeated voice. She held something in her hand—a remote—and when she activated it, millions of golden sakoola petals floated from the sky, drifting like snow over the crowd. Cries of wonder and delight filled the ballroom.

Jyn almost didn't hear the first launcher fire.

The flechettes were silver, cutting through the golden petals. People dropped, soaked in blood, before anyone thought to scream. The new governor's body fell off the stage. The chieftess crumpled at the feet of the flowery starbird, her silvery-white gown stained red.

In mere minutes, the floor was covered in blood and bodies.

CHAPTER EIGHTEEN_

Jyn waited in the shuttle for Saw. She sat in the cockpit, staring out the viewport as Saw dropped his FC-1 on the deck and booted the launch sequence. But she knew—because of the way he didn't talk to her, didn't look at her—that he had noticed her in the palace. He knew that she knew.

Maia didn't return.

Jyn had seen that, too. As soon as the alarm went up, the chaos and panic had served the partisans. Jyn had a head start; she was already at the zip ports when the alarm started. Through the glass, she had watched as people ran from the palace. Her eyes darted from person to person, looking for Saw. She'd seen Maia. A stormtrooper had tried to stop her—her robes were ripped, exposing the padding and the hidden armory under the silk.

The zip port had started to move away, zooming Jyn back to the ship, but she saw Maia fight with the stormtrooper, the blaster he raised, Maia's limp body crumpling to the ground.

Jyn said nothing as Saw boarded the ship and they raced away. There was a little trouble at the exit, but so many people were trying to escape the planet by the time they reached the sky that the Empire had no chance of stopping everyone. Even so, Jyn checked the scanner codes she'd forged for Saw's ship and knew that any record of them on Inusagi showed only a small transport-class vessel with full clearance.

They did not speak as they hit hyperspace. Jyn watched the blue-gray trail of stars, letting her eyes blur. Saw got up and went to the back of the ship. She didn't know what he was doing, but she heard the metallic sound of the flechette launcher being picked up, and then, farther off, the sound of it being locked away.

When they reached Smuggler's Run, Saw stopped the ship, overlooking the asteroid belt.

"Inusagi is near Naboo, the Emperor's home planet," Saw said, turning to Jyn. "An attack of this measure, this close to home, will send a message that needs to be sent. The new governor was a close ally to the Emperor, and the chieftess a key player. Not that the chieftess had much choice," he conceded.

"This was a murder mission, Saw," Jyn told the dead rocks floating in space. "We weren't fighting for good or supporting the resistance or taking down the Empire. That was a massacre."

"Oh, Jyn," Saw said, his voice cracking, "what do you think war is?"

A flicker of movement darted between the asteroids. No matter how much repellant she used, the mynocks always came back.

"Let's go home," she whispered. She slid out of her seat, moving as far away from Saw as she could go.

She found Maia's synthskin gloves. She held them close to her face, but all she could smell was the carbon scoring.

❖

Sometimes at night, when the broken communications tower creaked in the wind, Jyn still heard the thousands of flechettes flying through the air, slicing the drifting sakoola blossoms apart. On those nights, the damp stone of the outpost walls smelled of blood, and Jyn would pull the quilt over her head, forming a tent, and spend all night looking up old holos of her father.

❖

"There's a leak," Saw announced to the group at large a few days after Inusagi and Maia's death.

"A . . . leak?" Staven asked. He had been the most bereft without Maia.

Saw nodded grimly. "I'll find it," he promised, and a chill descended over the room. Jyn's eyes darted from person to person. These were no longer her friends, her compatriots. She wondered which one had betrayed Saw.

"Is that why Maia died?" Codo asked.

"Maybe," Saw growled.

Saw began taking a larger role in the training of the cadre as a whole. He stood on top of the broken comm tower, screaming orders down at his soldiers as they ran through drill after drill. "Not like that!" he bellowed as Jyn crouched with Jari and Codo in a mock battle. "You cluster together like that, you all die!"

Codo scooted off for a different vantage point, but Jari hung back. "He's paranoid," he whispered, glaring at Saw.

"He's *right*," Jyn said, pushing Jari away as Staven, sparring for the other side, descended on them.

The new recruits to Saw's cadre of partisans were given even harsher training. Many quit within days, but the few that remained—including, Jyn was sad to see, the human Reece Tallent—became the most fervent supporters of Saw's methods.

"Why did you have to come back?" Jyn said as Reece took a seat beside her after a long day of target practice.

"I lost most of my original crew to Saw," Reece said. Jyn was a little surprised to remember that was true; she no longer thought of the men who'd defected from

Reece and joined Saw as Reece's. "Figured I should get some training myself."

Jyn evaluated him. Over the past year, Reece had lost some of his cockiness. Maybe Saw would do him good.

Still, she was surprised when Saw selected Reece for his next mission. "You too," he said, pointing at Jari. The Togruta looked surprised. "And Jyn."

"What's the mission?" Jyn asked as they boarded the little shuttle. This was one of the newer ships, purchased with money from the mission on Inusagi.

"You're to help with the clearance codes," Saw said, and Jyn got to work with her code replicator. She stayed focused on the task at hand, and it wasn't until she was finished that she realized an uneasy silence had fallen on the small crew.

Saw grunted his approval at the clearance codes she'd forged. Soon after, he pulled the ship out of hyperspace. Jyn didn't recognize the planet. No Imperial checkpoint scanned her new codes, but there was an Imperial outpost and barracks not far away. As soon as the ship landed, Saw led the small crew to a safe house.

"I told you there was a leak in our unit," he said. "Probably someone who wants to defect."

Jari, Jyn, and Reece gave each other worried looks.

"Did you discover who it was?" Jari asked.

Saw stared at the Togruta. "Yes," he replied shortly.

He spread out a map of the planet, and they all crowded around the holocube to see. "Imperial barracks here," he said, pointing to a location about four klicks east of the safe house. "They've been receiving transmissions from our base."

"From *our* base?" Jyn gasped.

Saw nodded grimly.

"The traitor has told them of a few of our missions, and they've gone sour. We've lost a ship. Some men."

"Men like Bilder," Jari said in a low voice.

Saw nodded. Jyn lowered her eyes. She hadn't even realized the Twi'lek was gone; she just thought he'd been on a long mission. How many of the people who'd left the outpost and never returned had died? Why didn't Saw mourn them, let the others mourn them?

If Jyn hadn't witnessed Maia's death, would she have spent the rest of her life thinking Maia was off on some mission or had left the group?

"And the Gamorreans," Saw added.

Jyn frowned. The giant Gamorrean brothers hadn't been a part of Saw's cadre for long, but they had looked invincible.

"How did you track down the traitor?" Jari asked.

Saw stared at him a long time. "I have my means," he said finally.

"Is the traitor at the Imperial compound?" Reece asked.

"No," Saw said, still staring at Jari.

Jyn's eyes flicked between Saw and the Togruta. She noticed the way Saw kept his hand hidden in his coat.

No, she thought, and she wasn't sure if she had said it out loud.

Saw revealed his blaster. "Tie him up," he said.

Reece was the first to jump into action; Jyn was still too shocked. Jari tried to jerk away, but Saw fired a blast into his shoulder. Moaning, Jari couldn't protest as Saw held the blaster to his head and Reece bound him with plastoid ties.

"Blindfold him." Saw tossed a scrap of cloth at Jyn.

Her hands shook as she wound the cloth over the Togruta's eyes and his montrals. "Jyn," Jari said in a low voice. "It wasn't me, it wasn't. Bilder was my friend. I would never betray—"

"And gag him," Saw ordered. Reece stuffed another cloth in Jari's mouth.

"Saw," Jyn said in a small voice, a pleading voice.

Saw's eyes softened—just for a moment—when he looked at her. He motioned for her to come closer. "He knows," he whispered in her ear, but she didn't understand what he was saying.

Saw holstered his blaster and grabbed Jari by the plastoid ties, dragging him to the airspeeder parked in front of the safe house. Jyn followed on his heels, but Saw needed no help, punching the open wound on Jari's shoulder when the Togruta made one last desperate attempt to escape.

Jyn and Reece ran to the roof of the safe house, both of them watching as Saw sped across the open field toward the Imperial barracks. Saw pushed the airspeeder faster and faster.

"Here." Reece had a pair of quadnocs. Jyn didn't question where he got them; she just accepted them and watched as Saw zoomed toward the Imperial barracks. She could see white-and-black stormtroopers pointing at the blur that was Saw and Jari.

Saw drew the airspeeder up short just in front of the barracks. The stormtroopers were shouting something, but Saw didn't say anything back. He just kicked Jari off the airspeeder and started back toward the safe house.

"We have to go," Jyn said. She threw the quadnocs at Reece, and together they ran toward the spaceport. Saw had been so enraged by Jari's betrayal that he hadn't stopped to consider how quickly they'd need to leave after that little stunt.

Jyn and Reece were racing up the boarding ramp into the ship when Saw brought the airspeeder up short. He threw himself on board, initiated the launch sequence, and burst out of the spaceport. Reece examined the scanner. "At least three on our tail," he said.

"We can make it," Saw growled, leaning into the throttle.

Jyn's heart was racing, beating out a staccato rhythm that felt impossibly fast. As Saw burst past the Imperial ships, through the planet's atmosphere, and into hyperspace, all she could think about was the way Jari had whispered that he was innocent, that Saw was paranoid, that Bilder had been his friend.

CHAPTER NINETEEN_

Saw stomped off the ship as soon as it landed on their island on Wrea. Reece looked over at Jyn.

"That was . . . illuminating," he said.

"Really?" Jyn shot back.

Reece nodded. He moved to sit beside Jyn, and she was surprised at the way she didn't move away from him. "Saw is a difficult man, and one not to betray. I think he wanted us both to learn that lesson as much as Jari."

"I would never betray Saw," Jyn said.

"Perhaps it was more for your benefit in terms of assurance," Reece said. When Jyn shot him a confused look, he continued, "He was proving how far he'd go to protect you."

Jyn's eyes unfocused. Was that what it had been? But . . . Jari hadn't been a threat. At least, not that she had known.

She didn't like these doubts. This fear.

What had Saw meant when he said, *He knows?*

"How well do you know Saw?" Reece asked.

The question surprised Jyn. "Very well," she said. "He's like a father."

"And you trust him?"

"Absolutely."

Reece gave her a doubtful look.

"He saved me," Jyn said simply. She wasn't sure why she was telling Reece, whom she'd never really liked, but the darkness helped her speak. "I was in a bunker. A hatch. I was just a little girl. And I thought I was going to die. But . . . Saw saved me." Reece didn't speak, so Jyn continued. "I still think of that cave. It was so dark. I waited for so long. When I'm scared, it sometimes feels like I'm back there."

"Trapped inside a cave inside your mind," Reece said softly.

Jyn nodded in the dark. "But Saw always comes," she said.

Saw turned the great room from a lounge and eating area into a command center. He always had at least three missions in the air, planning a half dozen more. The area was littered with holocubes showing planets and Imperial posts, and the comm never stopped buzzing with new intel.

"So close," he'd tell Jyn, grinning.

But he didn't send her on any more missions.

Sometimes, when the missions landed at night, Saw would leave his impromptu command center. Jyn could always identify him by the way he stomped down the hall. On those nights, he boarded the ships that arrived.

He never spoke of what he did. But Jyn could guess. She could hear the screams.

She cornered him once. He was wiping blood from his hands, a distant look in his eyes.

"Saw," she said.

He stopped short.

"Did you see—" he started.

She shook her head. "No." She hadn't seen. But she had heard. She suspected everyone on the island had heard.

"Why?" she asked. Why the secrecy, the lies. The torture.

Saw followed Jyn into her room. "They know," he said.

It was an echo of what he'd said about Jari. "Know what?" Jyn demanded.

Saw leaned in close. He jabbed a finger at her chest, but rather than pressing into her flesh, his finger hit the kyber crystal necklace she kept hidden under her shirt. "They. Know," he said slowly, watching the realization dawn in Jyn's eyes.

Someone knew who her father was.

Who *she* was.

Idryssa Barruck seemed surprised at how crowded Saw's outpost was when her Z-95 landed.

"Nice ship," Jyn said as she disembarked.

"Who are all these people?" Idryssa asked.

"You're not the only one with 'alliances,'" Saw said, calling out to Idryssa as he crossed the island.

"Saw," Idryssa said, smiling at him in a way no one had smiled at Saw recently.

Saw's face crinkled up. "Id." There was warmth in his voice, and respect. But then the look melted into sourness. "I don't need another lecture." He motioned for Jyn and Idryssa to follow him into the outpost. He cleared the command center with a wave of his hand, only Reece pausing to nod at Idryssa as he left. Reece and Idryssa had been a part of the old crowd. Saw trusted them in ways he didn't the newcomers.

But Jari was one of Xosad's crew, a part of the old crowd, too, Jyn thought. *And that didn't save him.*

"Why are you here?" Saw asked Idryssa.

Idryssa still seemed a little shocked by Saw's outpost. "This isn't what I expected," she said.

"I've been busy."

"I can tell." Idryssa's face darkened. "And Inusagi . . ."

Jyn wanted to cover her ears. The attack—particularly the slaughter of the chieftess and the newly appointed governor—had been widely publicized. There was talk of banning flechette launchers from civilian use, and new measures were being taken to ensure safety from the "terrorists" and "anarchists" who'd gunned down the innocents. Jyn didn't want to think about Inusagi again.

Neither, it seemed, did Saw. "Drop it," he growled.

"That was . . . bad." Idryssa didn't take her eyes off Saw's. "Saw, that is not what we stood for."

"There is no 'we.' "

"There could be, you know," Idryssa said. She stared at a holocube. Saw reached around her and turned it off. "We've offered. You could command your own unit."

"I don't want to take orders, and I don't want to give them." Saw heaved himself into a chair.

"Isn't that what you did when you worked for Arane's partisans?" Idryssa asked. "She gave the orders. You pulled the trigger."

"That's different."

Idryssa didn't respond as she looked over at Jyn.

"Are you bringing us a mission?" Jyn asked.

"Not exactly," Idryssa said. Her eyes questioned Saw—could she talk in front of Jyn? Saw nodded curtly.

"This isn't something my people have the means or"—her gaze flicked to Saw again—"the incentive to pursue."

Saw straightened, and Jyn leaned forward. Her thoughts went immediately to her father. As much as she wanted to dismiss him, she couldn't help hoping, somehow, that Idryssa had found him, that he really was a prisoner somewhere and that she and Saw could save him.

"This have to do with kyber crystals?" Saw asked.

Idryssa shook her head, and Jyn's heart sank. "You sent me coordinates of mines for ore as well. Remember?"

"Doonium and dolovite," Saw said. "Key components of Star Destroyers."

"But there hasn't been a marked increase of production for Star Destroyers," Jyn added. "At least not that we have found."

"Nor us," Idryssa conceded. "But we *have* traced a large percentage of the ore being shipped to factories on the planet Tamsye Prime, near the Tion Hegemony. One in particular is being operated under extremely oppressive terms."

Saw glowered. "The usual debt system?"

Idryssa nodded grimly.

"Debt system?" Jyn asked.

Idryssa turned her attention to Jyn. "Tamsye Prime has the manufacturing factories and laborers; the Empire wants them. The Empire offers to 'loan' equipment, resources, and so on. Seems like a great deal, but the credits add up, until everyone's basically an indentured servant, working off the debt the Empire pressed upon them."

"Slavery, more like," Saw growled. Jyn could tell this system struck close to home for him, and she wondered what mission he'd had in the past that made Imperial indentured servitude such a sore point. "So what are we doing?" he asked Idryssa. "Blowing up the factory?"

Idryssa shook her head. "The Empire would just bill the planet for new and more expensive materials, adding to their debt." She paused. "Besides, we both know that no deck sweep will ever clear out the Empire. Or," she added, "at least I hope we both know that now."

"Id." Saw's voice held a warning. "I have never done anything that the Empire didn't do first."

"That's not a very high standard, Saw."

"So then, how do we help the people of Tamsye Prime?" Jyn asked, interrupting what threatened to be the start of another fight.

Idryssa looked down at the table.

"We don't," Saw said. Jyn looked startled, but he shook his head, silencing her. "You said your people don't have the means to fight this. That just means you want *us* to do the work, but you're not going to pay us."

"Saw—" Idryssa started, but he cut her off.

"You may not like Arane, but she pays well. And I can't fight if I can't get supplies, can't feed my daughter." He gestured to Jyn.

And you can't outfit any of the other partisans, Jyn thought, thinking of all the soldiers that had been displaced to give them privacy in the command center. She imagined Codo and Staven and Reece and the others standing idly outside, tapping their feet impatiently.

"Saw, have you ever thought that we could do more if we worked together?" Idryssa said. Jyn narrowed her eyes, noting the smooth way Idryssa had shifted the conversation.

"You recruiting for that squadron of yours?" Saw sneered.

"It's not that different from your outposts," Idryssa insisted. "If you joined up with us . . ."

"I'll think about it," he said in a tone that Jyn knew meant he didn't want to discuss it further. But she also could tell he was intrigued.

"I know you like to be in charge," Idryssa pressed. "But something like this . . . it would be for the greater good."

"Greater good?" Saw asked, his voice rising. "I've heard that excuse before. But it's not for the greater good that you're here today, is it?"

Idryssa cut her eyes away. "It's not like that."

"What do you mean?" Jyn asked.

Saw didn't look away from Idryssa. "It's those higher-ups you were talking about, isn't it?"

"What is?" Jyn asked again.

"Idryssa's squadron." Saw smirked. "You went to them first, didn't you? But they didn't want to get their hands dirty on this." Saw kept talking, even though Idryssa opened her mouth to protest. "You told me once you wanted to help. 'A free galaxy,' isn't that what you said? You had such ideals. How's that working now, when you see people who need help but the best thing you can do is just hope someone like me will pick up the slack."

"It's not like that!" Idryssa said, more powerfully this time. "I tried, Saw, is that what you want to hear? I pitched this plan to the generals. But there are other battles we have to fight first."

"Tell that to the people on Tamsye Prime, the ones who aren't worth it." Saw smirked, but there was no triumph in his voice, just disappointment.

"We cannot fight every battle." Idryssa glared defiantly back at Saw. "But if you can get me intelligence about what it's like on the ground at Tamsye Prime, I can get them to consider a raid. I'm not asking much, Saw. Just a scouting mission, that's all."

Saw stared at her, then looked away. "Get out," he finally said, his voice softer than his words. "I've got a mission to plan."

CHAPTER TWENTY_

Saw stared at the holocube of Tamsye Prime Idryssa had left behind. With an Imperial blockade around the planet and an Imperial presence at the factory, a scouting mission would be no easy task.

"Get Reece," Saw growled.

Jyn jumped up, but before she left the room, Saw called her back. "And Codo."

Jyn dashed out of the outpost. Idryssa's starfighter was already a blur in the sky, and everyone else who'd been ousted from the command center stood in a huddle, talking in low voices. They quieted when Jyn approached. They stood straighter; they looked at her with expectant eyes.

Jyn's steps slowed; her spine stiffened. She was speaking for Saw, and they knew it, and they respected her for it.

"Reece," she said, "and Codo."

The two men broke off from the group. Reece walked with a triumphant bounce in his step. Codo looked nervous, and Jyn realized that he hadn't been sent on many missions lately.

Saw laid out the mission for the men after Jyn led them to the command center.

"I've been tracing that ore for years," Saw said in a musing tone, mostly to himself. "The Empire has kept even its shipping logs on lockdown. I'll find a mine, track where the doonium or dolovite is being carted. Split up to refineries. Shipped to worlds for holding. Sent one way, backtracked another. If Id is right and this is where the ore is being shaped into whatever it is the Empire is building, it's worth checking out."

They stared at the holo of Tamsye Prime. A Star Destroyer orbited the planet, and beyond that, Jyn could see notes of Imperial outposts surrounding the perimeter of a landmass in the southern hemisphere. A series of manufacturing plants had been developed on the continent, originally by a large family who'd turned the colony into an economically viable endeavor. The family had been bought out by the Empire and lived in luxury on Bespin. The people who'd spent generations working to turn Tamsye Prime into a home for their families toiled under the Empire's harsher rule. There was only one spaceport, and the only other way off the land mass required sneaking past Imperial troops and then swimming a vast ocean.

"One main access point," Saw said, pointing to the

spaceport. He reached for the holo, blowing up the area so they could see it in greater detail. He scanned the text descriptions attached to the landmarks. "This planet was a player in the Clone Wars," he growled. "They developed shell munitions for the Republic."

"Shell munitions?" Jyn asked, surprised. She knew the history of weapons but had never actually fired something that used bullets instead of plasma. Even the flechette launcher used a plasma-based firing mechanism, not something as crude as gunpowder.

Saw grunted. "It wasn't common but was especially effective for large landmasses. I've seen shell ammunition take down a mountainside." His eyes grew distant, and Jyn knew, at least for a moment, Saw was back in the Clone Wars. "That's what I can't get Idryssa to understand," he said finally.

"What?" Codo asked. He sounded nervous.

"She's following a cause. She believes in this squadron, the idea of joining forces against the Empire. But people don't follow an idea."

"But she's still fighting the Empire," Codo protested. "Isn't that enough to get more people to rise up?"

Jyn shook her head. She thought of the way the others listened to her because she was speaking for Saw. People didn't follow an idea, not even something as big as fighting the Empire. They followed a person. Someone like Saw.

"So what's the target objective?" Reece asked, all business.

"Strictly scouting," Saw said as if the idea was distasteful.

"If her group won't do this and we're not getting paid, why bother?" Codo asked.

"Why bother?" Reece snapped back. "Why are you even here?"

Jyn caught Saw's eyes. She saw the gleam in them, the anticipation. Tamsye Prime held a munitions factory, and the blockade and blacked-out comms were too similar to the other planets Saw had been watching, the ones he suspected were linked to whatever it was her father was working on for the Empire. This mission was just close enough to Saw's obsession to be too enticing to pass up.

Reece and Codo were still bickering, but they fell silent as Saw spoke. "We need an in," he said. "If we can get our boots on the ground, we can find a way to get Idryssa the information for her group to launch a larger-scale attack against the Empire." Jyn could tell he didn't like working through red tape, but he also didn't have the manpower to fight a Star Destroyer.

"I could forge us credentials," Jyn offered. "Go in under the guise of inspecting the plants."

Saw shook his head. He pointed to the Star Destroyer. "An operation this big? Everything's documented. We can't just show up. Even if your forgery was perfect—which I'm sure it would be—there would be no record of an inspection, and that would raise too many red flags."

"We could pose as workers?" Codo suggested.

Saw was still looking at the holo, still shaking his head. "The workers on Tamsye Prime were born on Tamsye Prime. The Empire's done that before. Take over a whole planet's labor force, recruiting only from within. Keeps it secure. And ensures they don't rebel."

Jyn looked at him curiously, unsure of his meaning.

"If you're alone, you don't care as much." Saw's eyes were watery and seemed tired as he shifted his attention to Jyn. "If you've got no one left, it doesn't matter as much what happens to you. There's a sort of fearlessness in being alone. But when you start to love someone else . . . It's ironic."

"What is?" Jyn asked softly.

"You find out that you have so much more to fight for, but it becomes that much more dangerous to fight at all." Saw took a deep, shaking breath. "Anyway, the Empire knows this. They employ not just the man, but his wife, his children. So if the man thinks of rebelling, the people he loves pay the price. Ensures no one protests."

Jyn shifted her gaze to the holo, blinking away unexpected tears. Saw's words reminded her of Galen

Erso. Jyn didn't let herself think the word *Papa* anymore. Galen was her father, but not Papa.

Jyn used to wake up in a cold sweat, reliving the day her mother was killed and her father was taken. Her father's fate was more terrifying to her than her mother's. Death's pain was finite. The Empire's was not. In Jyn's worst nightmares, the Empire came for her, too, kidnapping her from her old home.

But no one ever came. And Jyn knew it was because no one needed her. Not her father, who had never tried to find her, but also not the Empire. There was no point in taking her to use against her father if he worked for the Empire willingly. The families on Tamsye Prime were all leveraged against each other, but Jyn couldn't be leverage if no one cared about her.

"I have an idea," Reece said, his voice cutting through Jyn's dark thoughts.

"What is it?" Saw asked.

Reece stood up and started pacing. "The timing may not work out, but . . ."

"Out with it!" Saw demanded.

"I've got a few contacts on Coruscant, from my old group," Reece said. Saw nodded in acknowledgement. Reece rarely spoke about how his former team had splintered and broken apart around him, how many of the men who used to call him boss deferred to Saw. "One of them works with the propaganda department.

I remember hearing something. . . . Tamsye Prime sounds familiar. . . ."

He dashed to the comm unit and punched in some codes. Saw bristled; he didn't like communications happening without his approval, but Reece whooped in triumph a moment later. "Yes!" he said. "They're shooting a propaganda documentary, and Tamsye Prime is on the list. If you can get us scandocs, we can be assigned as tertiary units to help with the recording."

"I can do scandocs," Jyn said immediately.

Saw nodded his approval. "Yes," he said, thinking. "That could work. Shoot for the Empire but send the info to Idryssa's group instead." He turned to Reece. "Set that up," he ordered.

Reece pulled up a chair at the comm unit and got to work. Saw sent Codo to acquire cam droids, and Reece gave Jyn the specs she'd need to start on the forged scandocs.

This is the way it should be, Jyn thought as she applied herself to developing new scandocs. Idryssa may have joined some sort of bigger movement working with other partisans, but they were too big to actually *do* anything. This—this immediate action—was the way to fight the Empire.

CHAPTER TWENTY-ONE_

Reece set everything up with his contact on Coruscant. Their cover was a replacement crew for a propaganda holo the Empire was developing. They had to move fast, but the contact was confident that their cover would hold.

Jyn showed Reece the forged scandocs and badges for his approval. "These are good," he said. "They're expecting us—my contact already filed our names for the work detail—so they're not going to look too closely, but even if they did, these would still pass inspection."

Despite herself, Jyn felt pride swelling in her chest at his compliment.

Codo returned the next day with a bevy of camera droids, each set to upload directly to Idryssa's camp rather than to an Imperial server. They ran over the plan again and again, from cover story to two different emergency escape possibilities.

"The one area we want to avoid on Tamsye Prime," Saw told them, using the holo of the planet to showcase

the landscape, "is here." He indicated a munitions testing ground. "Particularly this area, where they were
experimenting with shelled artillery. We don't know
what's there, but let's not find out."

Jyn nodded, memorizing the roads. The spaceport
wasn't that far from the munitions testing ground; if
they got cornered there, it would be easier to make a
run for their ship than veer into that area.

"We ready?" Saw asked, looking from Jyn to Reece
to Codo.

They nodded. They were as prepared as they
could be.

"Let's go," he said grimly.

Jyn had Imperial clearance codes ready by the time
they broke out of hyperspace near Tamsye Prime and
the Star Destroyer orbiting it. They were cleared to
land in moments, and Reece took his small cruiser
down into the spaceport.

Jyn's stomach was twisted in knots, though she
didn't know why. This was by far an easier mission
than any of the others she'd been on. And it filled her
with more hope than she cared to admit. She understood why Idryssa wanted to be a part of a larger group
fighting the Empire. Sometimes with Saw's missions,

it didn't feel like fighting the Empire; it just felt like fighting. But with this, there was a chance they could make a real, true difference, not just for the people of Tamsye Prime but also for the galaxy as a whole.

Reece stood as soon as he docked the ship, moving straight to the gangway. Saw and Jyn hung back, booting up the camera droids and directing them off the ship. Reece was playing the part of overseer; Jyn and Saw were his subordinates. Codo was their pilot; he was staying with the ship.

A pair of stormtroopers were waiting for them as they left the ship.

"Identification," the first said in an authoritative voice.

"Of course, of course," Reece said. He presented all the official documentation Jyn had forged for them. She breathed deeply, willing her heart not to leap from her chest. The stormtrooper handed back their scandocs when he was done. Jyn smiled down at the fake name she'd given herself, Kestrel Dawn.

"We've been expecting you," the stormtrooper said. "This way." The two stormtroopers turned on their heels and led the three of them and their droids through the spaceport and toward the exit.

Jyn took stock of the ships that were docked as they walked past. Three were obviously Imperial; the largest cruiser was probably the one used by Lieutenant Colonel Senjax, and the two others may have been transports for more stormtroopers or something else. There was a small fleet of branded ships with the Tamsye Prime factory logo emblazoned on them and a few smaller ships, perhaps privately owned, although Jyn doubted it.

Once outside, Jyn could see why Tamsye Prime was used only for manufacturing. The planet appeared good for little else. The surface of Tamsye Prime was unforgiving, the wind whistling through the hard shiny rock. It reminded Jyn of a darker version of the planet Alpinn, which she'd visited as a child. Alpinn was littered with shining white crystals that formed eerie formations and caves. Tamsye Prime's rocky surface was a mixture of soft brown rocks that crumbled to fine dust and hard, shiny black igneous rocks that spired up like frozen water spouts or curled down like waves. Jyn couldn't imagine what kind of drills must have been needed to break into the black rocky surface to build the spaceport and factories.

Lieutenant Colonel Senjax waited for them outside the main facility. "Ah, we can begin," he said, a pleasant smile plastered on his face. Jyn blinked in surprise. She'd seen his image before, on the HoloNet, presenting to the public the new ways the Empire worked for the people of the galaxy and promoted peace among the planets. But there was something surprising about seeing him in person, tall and blonde and pale, with ice-blue eyes and a perfectly chiseled face and immaculate white teeth lined up in neat little rows as he bestowed them all with his smile. He was perfect, so perfect that Jyn felt like a grub worm next to him.

But he was also much more human than she'd expected. He was the face of the Empire, and his was a face she felt inexplicably drawn to, as if she could trust him. When Jyn thought of the Empire, it was a monster wearing a black helmet and killing her mother. Lieutenant Colonel Senjax wasn't a monster.

She was very glad she was supposed to play the part of nothing but an underling to Reece; she wasn't really sure she trusted herself to speak in that moment.

Lieutenant Colonel Senjax took the time to introduce himself to everyone in the small press group, from the paid actors who must surely have already known him down to Jyn and Saw. He stopped short of greeting the camera droids and laughingly turned to Jyn. "It feels rude not to speak to protocol droids or ones that look human and can talk back. I suppose the camera droids don't really care."

"N-no, sir," Jyn stuttered.

"Well, let's get to work!" the lieutenant colonel said cheerfully, turning to the factory. "Let's show the people of the galaxy just how wonderful the Empire can be!"

It struck Jyn as she followed the group into the huge factory that Lieutenant Colonel Senjax hadn't said the Empire was already wonderful, just that it had the potential to be.

CHAPTER TWENTY-TWO_

Reece stayed near the front with the main camera droid as Lieutenant Colonel Senjax provided a constant chatter. "It's best to treat these things as naturally as possible," he told one of the reporters, smiling. "This isn't an interview or even a true report. This is a conversation with the galaxy."

Saw rolled his eyes, and Jyn hit him.

Reece dropped back. "Everything going well?" he asked in a low voice.

"Our end is good," Saw said. "You?"

"We're getting everything." Reece tapped his nose, then jogged to catch up with the front of the group.

Saw frowned after him, then looked up at the camera droids buzzing overhead. Jyn knew what he was thinking. Saw didn't like scouting missions. They were too passive. He'd be happier if they could blow the factory sky-high and transport every person on the planet to a safer home.

Except the stormtroopers. Saw was much more at home bashing helmets together than trotting behind them, pretending to work for the Empire.

The factory was oddly quiet. Jyn looked around at the rows of workers piecing together stormtrooper blasters. Everyone was silent, attentive to their work, and focused. They didn't even look up as the holo crew passed. They'd been prepped and warned not to make a disturbance.

Jyn and the others left the main assembly line and veered into another branch of the factory. A plasma lathe dominated the floor. Giant cranes lined the ceiling, and when she squinted, Jyn could see that the roof itself was hinged. They could work on satellites taller than the building with a plasma lathe that large.

"I know," Saw said in a low voice as they followed the PR group.

"These tools . . ." Jyn frowned.

"Yeah," Saw said. "Id's info was good. This place definitely is building . . . something." There was frustration in his voice. Just being in the factory, they felt they were close to uncovering something big, but the information was still tantalizingly out of reach.

"Like that." Jyn jerked her head to a crystalline spectrometer built into the wall. "Pa—my father used one of those. A smaller one, but that's a tool for kyber crystals."

Saw whipped his head around and stared at the giant piece of equipment and the array of lasers extending from it. Reece, noticing the way they lingered, motioned for them to catch up. Then his gaze fell on what Saw was staring at, and he narrowed his eyes, looking back at Jyn.

A chill danced up her spine. There was something . . . hungry about the way Reece looked at her. She was certain he knew what the crystalline spectrometer was and that he remembered the kyber crystal she kept hidden under her shirt. She readjusted the carbon-cotton scarf covering her neck.

In the heart of the factory, Lieutenant Colonel Senjax paused. "Why don't you set up here," he told the reporters. Members of his crew jumped to life, arranging chairs, adjusting lighting, directing the camera droids to find the best angles. He turned to Saw and Jyn, who were pretending to work on the camera droids.

"You two, come with me," he said, motioning toward them.

Saw frowned but couldn't reasonably deny the request. He and Jyn followed Lieutenant Colonel Senjax down the hall and into a small empty room.

"Is something wrong?" Saw asked. Jyn could feel the tension radiating from him.

"People forget—because I'm something of a celebrity, a public face—people forget that I'm still an

Imperial officer," Lieutenant Colonel Senjax said. He looked past Saw. "Ah, yes, come in, come in."

A pair of stormtroopers entered the room, followed by Reece.

"What is this?" Saw growled. Jyn's hands balled into fists.

"These are the anarchists you alerted my department of?" Lieutenant Colonel Senjax asked Reece.

He nodded. "Saw Gerrera," Reece said.

Lieutenant Colonel Senjax's eyes were alight. "This is excellent," he said. "That name has been on our lists for quite some time."

"This was a setup?" Saw said, disbelief in his voice—not disbelief that Reece would betray them but that he hadn't caught on earlier. "Did Id—was she in on it?"

"Idryssa was a fool who took my suggestions easily." Reece laughed. "But she was just a fool. By the way"—he turned back to the lieutenant colonel—"check where the signal of the camera droids is transmitting; it should lead you to a larger cell."

"Traitor," Saw growled at Reece.

"You betrayed me first," Reece said in a bored tone. "You took my men. So I'm taking yours."

The comms Reece had sent from Saw's base, the "contact" he obviously never had. He'd been signaling the Empire directly. Jyn prayed that everyone back at the outpost had the sense to evacuate, knew the procedures and remembered the plans Saw had drilled into them.

And then Jyn thought of Jari. Had he been a traitor, too, or was he framed by Reece? Or—a dark thought flashed through her mind—had Saw just been so paranoid he saw a traitor where none had been?

"This is revenge from all those years ago?" Saw laughed. "You were a little boy then, and you're a little boy now."

The insult struck home; Reece's face reddened with anger, and Jyn thought of how he'd looked when she'd beaten him in the sparring match.

His eyes landed on her. "And that one," Reece said, pointing to Jyn. "You may be interested in her as well—and I'll obviously be expecting higher payment if you are. Saw's tried to keep her identity undercover, but I suspect she may be—"

He never finished the sentence. Saw moved with lightning speed, ripping the blaster from the stormtrooper positioned behind him and firing at Reece. Reece dropped like a stone, but Jyn was surprised to see that he was still breathing, still alive. The stormtrooper's blaster had been set to stun.

Saw turned it toward the lieutenant colonel, but the other stormtrooper knocked his arm, sending the shot wild. Lieutenant Colonel Senjax commed for backup, and Jyn threw herself at the stormtrooper, fighting him back. She wasn't armed well—Reece had told them specifically that they'd be scanned before working next to the lieutenant colonel and any blasters would be confiscated—but she had a knife in her boot. She withdrew it as fast as she could, slamming it into the stormtrooper's elbow.

"We have to go!" Saw shouted at her. The outer room was large, but there was only one exit and entry, and already more stormtroopers were charging inside.

Saw wheeled around, pressing the barrel of the blaster against Lieutenant Colonel Senjax's skull. "Jyn," he said, "get Reece."

Jyn didn't question him; she grabbed Reece's limp arms and dragged him behind her. Using the lieutenant colonel as cover, Saw and Jyn exited the room.

The rest of the crew stood, shocked. The stormtroopers were listening to orders in their helmets. Jyn sent an emergency comm to Codo in the ship. For a moment, they all stared at each other.

And then the entire building shook.

"An aerial attack?" Jyn gasped, catching a glimpse of black TIE fighters through the high windows.

Lieutenant Colonel Senjax laughed mirthlessly. "This factory is on its way out," he said. "The Empire is finished with it. It's worthless. If you think they'll let the building stand when they could destroy you . . ."

But the people, Jyn thought as an alarm blared through the building and all the workers tried to evacuate.

Lieutenant Colonel Senjax used the chaos to wrench free, jerking from Saw's grasp and knocking the blaster aside. Jyn picked it up from the ground, letting Reece's limp body drop, and fired at the retreating officer. Saw pulled her behind the edge of the plasma lathe, giving her cover.

The lieutenant colonel raced out of view, but the wall behind him erupted in flames. Debris rained down on them, rock and metal, flames and timbers. The crystalline spectrometer shook free from the wall, the laser array spinning.

Saw leapt toward Jyn, grabbing her by the arm and yanking her behind him. "We have to go!" he screamed.

Panic flooded Jyn's senses. Everywhere was chaos and burning. Through the exposed roof, Jyn could see more TIE fighters screaming through the air. Everyone scattered, racing down the hall to the exit. Rumbling filled the room.

Someone was shouting her name, pulling on her.

Saw.

"Come on!" he shouted in her face.

Just past him, Jyn noted the giant power cells lining the wall. She blinked, shock overwhelming her system. She watched as if frozen as a green beam of plasma from a TIE fighter's cannon whizzed through the air, striking the power cells.

The world exploded.

Saw threw himself at Jyn, covering her body with his. They landed on the floor with a skull-cracking crash, and Jyn was knocked out of her dazed shock. Fire and metal rained down on them.

Saw bucked in pain, screaming in agony, a sound Jyn would never forget. She scrambled out from under him.

Blood blossomed all over his body.

CHAPTER TWENTY-THREE_

Jyn analyzed the wounds as quickly as she could. A mixture of sharp metal debris and something else— a chemical of some kind, she wasn't sure—had fallen over them. The chemical burns were deep, but they were mostly seared shut. The same could not be said of the wounds caused by the metal debris. Dozens of deep, long cuts littered Saw's body, but the worst was where a long, flat triangular-shaped piece of metal that had pierced Saw's shoulder, clean through to his chest. Jyn knew not to remove the metal; she just hoped it hadn't sliced any arteries. Saw still bled, but he might not bleed to death, and not dying was about the only thing Jyn hoped for at that point.

Reece groaned. Somehow, despite being unconscious and unprotected, he'd escaped the main blast mostly unscathed. His face was covered in blood-streaked soot, but the superficial head wound was nothing.

Jyn kicked him. "Get up!" she screamed. "Help me!"

He groaned again, rolling over, then his eyes

widened, taking in the horror of everything around him.

"Help me!" Jyn shouted again, struggling with Saw's body. He had passed out from the pain. Or at least Jyn hoped it was the pain. His shirt was so soaked that it dripped blood, but he still had a pulse, breath. It wasn't over yet.

Reece, still stunned and possibly in shock, lifted one of Saw's arms around his shoulders, and Jyn supported the other side, holding him so as not to disturb the metal in his shoulder. She kept the blaster she'd stolen from the stormtrooper in her other hand in case they met resistance. They hobble-ran through the raining debris.

"They're toying with us," Reece said, choking on smoke. "We'll never escape."

Jyn thought about the crystalline spectrometer, the hinged roof that was even now falling aside, flattening everything in its wake. They stumbled to the door.

"Jyn," Saw groaned.

They cleared the building. The spaceport was a kilometer away, and it was, miraculously, not destroyed. Reece picked up his pace, but Saw, becoming more conscious of what was happening and his injuries, pulled away. He made a noise, deep and guttural, animal-like, a bellow of rage and regret. Reece yanked him forward, but Saw struggled against him, stumbling and pushing Reece away.

"Traitor," Saw growled. He slipped from Jyn's tenuous grasp, falling to the ground, hissing in pain as the metal shard in his shoulder shifted.

In her desperate attempt to flee, Jyn had almost let herself forget that Reece had been the cause of all this. She raised her blaster, pointing at him, and he froze.

Saw had not forgotten. He was bleeding, broken, maybe even dying, but he looked more dangerous than Jyn had ever seen him.

"Saw!" Codo—stupid, simple Codo—stood in the path leading to the spaceport. He started running as a TIE fighter zoomed overhead.

Jyn kept her eyes and her blaster on Reece. Saw muttered something, spluttering through the blood in his mouth.

"What?" Jyn asked, not taking her eyes from Reece.

"Go." He struggled to sit up, and when he coughed, blood leaked over his dry, cracked lips. He jerked his head to the left, toward the munitions testing ground. "Hide." He coughed again.

"I'm coming with you." Jyn was surprised at the steel in her voice.

"Give me a day," Saw said. "He—" He coughed again. "He knows."

"We will take care of Reece," Jyn said, looking the traitor right in the eyes. She was satisfied to see the terror in them.

"No!" Saw roared. Jyn flicked her gaze back to him. "*I* will take care of Reece."

Codo finally reached them, and Jyn tossed him her blaster. He was confused, but he knew enough to keep it trained on Reece.

Jyn dropped to her knees by Saw's side. "Wait in a shell turret," he said. He pressed a small blaster into her hand; she had no idea where he'd gotten it. "Until daylight." He withdrew a pair of knives from a hidden sheath inside his pants. He pressed one into Jyn's hand but kept the other one.

"You're not leaving me behind, are you?" Jyn asked urgently.

Saw's big eyes stared into hers, and she could see all the love in them. "He knows who you really are," he said. "A secret like that, once exposed, can never be hidden again."

"You're coming back for me, right?" All she could think about was Saw's growing paranoia, the way he had treated Jari and some of the others. "Promise?" she said in a small voice.

Another explosion rattled the ground.

Saw struggled up, sucked in a deep breath, and

shouted, "Go!" Blood from his mouth sprayed across her face.

The noise startled Codo so much that he lowered the blaster he held on Reece. Reece moved like lightning, jerking the weapon from Codo's grip and whirling around, aiming wildly. Jyn wasn't sure if he intended to shoot her or Saw, but he never got the chance. Saw lunged up, driving the blade of his knife into Reece's leg and jerking down with all his weight, the blade dragging a jagged slice through his flesh. Reece screamed in agony but didn't drop the blaster. He smashed the grip against Saw's skull, beating him repeatedly when he didn't release his hold.

"Run!" Saw shouted again.

Jyn ran.

She blew past Codo, who was sputtering out questions, and ran to the munitions testing ground, breaking through the weak gate and ignoring the warning signs. The area had been used during the Clone Wars and then boarded up.

She had seen the reports of buried mines, of unexploded torpedoes embedded in the black rock, but she didn't think about that now. The ground was still pockmarked and scarred from blasts, but near the fence was a series of small rectangular buildings that faced the testing ground.

Jyn ran for the closest shell turret, a bunker just

big enough to hold one or two people if they crouched. It was made of black igneous rock and gritty mortar that blended into the background of the landscape. Jyn dove for the tiny hut. There was a single entrance— more like a tunnel—and two slits for windows.

The bunker was dark inside, with just slits of light carving into the shadows. Jyn pressed her face against the narrow window, looking out.

She could see Saw and Reece, still fighting in the road, oblivious to the TIE fighters and the screaming survivors, to Codo and the chance to escape. Despite his injuries and the metal shard sticking out of his shoulder, Saw had managed to throw himself over Reece, using his body weight to keep him down. They were both smeared with his blood.

"Help me, boy!" Saw roared at Codo. Codo dropped to the ground, pressing his hands against Reece's wrists.

Saw's bloody-toothed grin was so malicious that Jyn could see it from her hiding place. He said something— Jyn couldn't hear it—but despite the fact that Tamsye Prime was still under attack, Saw wasn't going to delay his revenge one moment longer. He slid the blade of his knife down the side of Reece's face, as if he was going to peel the skin from his head. Jyn gripped the twin of that blade in her own hand so hard that she started shaking.

Reece screamed, high-pitched and desperate, and

squirmed, trying to get out from under Saw. Codo was pure white, fear blanching his face as he watched Saw dig the knife into Reece's shoulder, twisting the blade, creating a mirror of the injury Saw himself bore.

Something crashed. Something loud. Tinkling sounds of rock and debris scattered across the shell turret's roof, and on the road, Codo ducked for cover.

"We have to go!" Codo shouted.

He stood, heaving Saw up and helping him stand. Reece lay on the ground, whimpering, one arm splayed out. Saw looked around, his eyes scanning the munitions testing ground. He couldn't see Jyn; it was impossible, but for a moment, she pretended that he could. Through the slit in the shell turret, she stared at him, memorizing him in that moment, blood-soaked and wild.

He turned away. Saw said something to Codo, and Codo grabbed Reece by the ankle, dragging him as he supported Saw and they made their slow way back to the spaceport.

Through the noise of her entire world crashing around her, Jyn heard an engine roaring to life. She scooted out of the tunnel just in time to see a ship—a small Imperial shuttle—streak across the sky. Smart of Saw to steal an Imperial ship. None of the men knew how to use Jyn's code replicator, but an Imperial ship could make its way through the attack anyway, with a little luck. It dodged the TIE fighters, taking out one with a plasma cannon before breaking atmosphere and disappearing from sight.

Jyn was alone.

LOCATION: Wobani

PRISONER: Liana Hallik, #6295A

CRIMES: Forgery of Imperial Documents, Resisting Arrest, Possession of an Unsanctioned Weapon, Aggravated Assault

MONTH 03_

Eat a ration cube.

    Collapse into bed.

    Wake to the alarm.

    Eat a ration cube.

    Rush to dress and stand by the door.

    Accept the heavy cuffs.

    Trudge to work assignments.

    Board a turbo tank.

    Rattle over the planet's rocky landscape to the work assignment.

    Work.

    Work.

    Work.

    Work.

Eat a ration cube.

Work.

Rattle back over the planet's rocky landscape to the prison cells.

Eat a ration cube.

Collapse into bed.

❖

The days drifted one into another, the only difference being what the day's labor assignment was and, occasionally, new faces in the crowds. Some she recognized. Working with Saw meant that she had been exposed to various partisan groups throughout the galaxy, and it wasn't that surprising that anyone with rebellious intentions wound up there.

Jyn never tried to reach out to any of the people she recognized. There was little point. She saw them in passing, maybe shared a day's labor with them. But the Empire's system of varying whom people worked with ensured that no attachments could be made or exploited. Jyn spent whole days without saying a single word. Zorahda had begun withdrawing into herself and didn't respond on the few days when Jyn tried to make conversation.

"Another day," she said as she and her cellmate stood by their prison door, waiting for cuffs.

Zorahda grunted at her.

At work assignment, Zorahda was sent to the farms and Jyn was sent to transport loading. It was monotonous, but it was by far not the worst possible position at the camp. Droids oversaw the main shipping placement, and Jyn and the others in her group operated the repulsorlifts that shifted the crates of ore into position. The Empire could have had droids do the entire operation, which just added to the insult of making prisoners complete the tasks.

A door opened near the hangar as Jyn moved the latest crate from the mines into position on the loading line. She caught a glimpse of the warden and looked quickly away. Her eyes met another prisoner's, and she shared a momentary look of worry with the Rodian. Wherever the warden was, nothing good could happen.

"As you can see," the warden said, his voice carrying across the floor, "we have an excellent production cycle."

Jyn dared a glance up as she lifted her crate. A man in an Imperial admiral's uniform surveyed the transport loading line, looking down his long nose. He had dark skin, shaved hair, and eyes that were more black than brown. He was clearly an Imperial soldier down to his bones, but he wasn't the man who had killed her mother, so Jyn ignored him.

The warden and his Imperial guest walked along the perimeter of the catwalk, then down the stairs and onto the floor. The admiral didn't seem to be very keen on being among the prisoners and dust, but the warden was overwhelmed with pride. He prattled about production rates and the low cost of the labor. *He's nervous,* Jyn realized. This Imperial officer made the warden nervous.

"It is not as efficient as it could be," the admiral said, cutting through the warden's ceaseless talk.

The warden's river of words dried up. "We have, of course, experimented with longer work hours. We've found that fifteen standard hours of labor a day gives the ideal combination of efficient, mistake-free labor and little chance for any seditiousness to grow."

The admiral put up a hand. "Droids can work longer than fifteen hours a day. And they need less . . . maintenance." The admiral's eyes drifted to a man who was missing an arm, struggling to operate both the directional and repulsor controls at the same time.

"Any worker who falls behind production for more than three marks is sent to top level," the warden said immediately.

The admiral made a sound of mild approval, and the warden's shoulders relaxed a bit. Jyn kept her head down. The top level was whispered about throughout the cells. A few weeks before, Jyn had witnessed the youngest member of the Ociock family a few cells down from hers being taken away. She hadn't known what the top level was, but when the stormtroopers reached for the little girl, who was sobbing so hard that her tears and snot smeared on the downy feathers of her face, the other Ociocks on her level had screeched a blood-curdling cry of sorrow and alarm, their beaks open wide and pointing straight up. They flew at the stormtroopers, clawing at their armor uselessly with long taloned fingers. Jyn had been pushed into the fray in the chaotic hallway, and she tried to help, tried to give the little girl one last hug from her mother.

She'd been given an extra charge of aggravated assault and a mark for top level for her trouble. She'd gotten another mark for her improvised knife, but the stormtroopers hadn't bothered informing her of it as they'd beaten her.

Jyn never saw the Ociock girl again. Her family's talons had been clipped off, cut to the quick, and then they had been sent back to work in the mines.

"And yet," the admiral said, strolling past Jyn's line, "I feel like more could be done within those fifteen hours of labor."

Jyn kept her head down. Punch the red button, lift the handle, shift the crate. Punch the red button, lift the handle, shift the crate. Head down. She knew this Imperial officer's tone. She knew what it meant. Head down. Punch the red button. Lift the handle. Shift the—

"You, there." The admiral's voice cut through the sound of the repulsorlifts.

"M-me?"

Jyn glanced up. She knew this man. Knew him from the outside. She'd met him first on Inusagi, although she hadn't known his name. And again, later, on Skuhl, when she'd punched him in the face.

Berk.

Jyn hadn't known the man had been arrested and sentenced to Wobani. He carried himself like one of the old ones, the prisoners who'd been there for a while. He had scars she didn't recognize and a grim set to his mouth that made him look ancient.

"You." The admiral smiled, and a chill ran down Jyn's spine.

Berk's shoulders were broad, his biceps like knotted ropes. But he looked like a child next to the much shorter officer, cowed and afraid.

"Do you think your fellow criminals could be enticed to work harder?" the admiral asked in dulcet tones.

"I—" Berk glanced from the warden to the admiral. If he said no, the warden would be proven right. If he said yes, the admiral would be. "Yes," he said.

"And *how* do you think we could entice these low-lives to contribute more precious labor to the glorious Empire?" the admiral asked.

There was no answer Berk could give. If he asked for more food or more breaks, then he risked what little they did have being taken away in a cruel mockery of justice. "I . . . I don't . . ."

"You don't know," the admiral sneered.

Berk shook his head, his eyes wide.

"Fortunately, I do." The admiral looked away from Berk and toward the other workers in the transport room. Without even trying, he'd commanded the attention of every person on the floor. The crates had stopped. Everyone was watching. Waiting.

"If I offer you some sort of *reward* for working harder," the admiral continued, addressing the room at large, "then that's not really fair, is it? This is a punishment. You are criminals against the Empire. You deserve no reward.

"Besides," he continued, "people don't work harder for rewards. That's a child's way of thinking. What really makes people work harder is fear."

In one fluid motion, the admiral pulled out his blaster and shot Berk in the head. Before his body hit the floor, every single worker had turned back to the task.

Jyn had never worked harder in her life than she did that day.

CHAPTER TWENTY-FOUR_

Jyn examined her situation in a cold, analytical way. She had gotten at least that much from her father—the ability to detach and look at the world as a scientist, not a human.

First, she was alone. Saw was gone. Codo was gone. Outside the bunker, there were Imperials and the people of Tamsye Prime. She could rely on none of them. With the entire world crumbling to the ground, burning and destroyed, no one would show kindness to a stranger.

Second, Jyn had two weapons: Saw's knife and the blaster. She didn't have any of her own weapons; her cover had not allowed for them. These weren't the worst weapons she could have at the moment, but they were nothing compared with the Star Destroyer and TIE fighters and countless stormtroopers.

Third, she was safe for now but couldn't stay where she was. The bunker was oppressively small. She couldn't stand up straight; at best she could hunch over, her spine pressed against the roof. She wondered what the shell turret had been made for. Droids that easily slid into position? Clone troopers who didn't mind their conditions?

It didn't matter. When she added up all the facts of her situation, Jyn was left with a simple truth: she couldn't stay there, but she had no way to leave.

Saw had told her to wait until the next day.

She curled up on the ground of the bunker and closed her eyes, waiting for the nightmare to be over. She had hidden in a hatch before, had waited a day, and Saw had come for her.

He would come again.

◈

The attack ended sometime before dusk. The ground was still bright from fires. Stormtroopers rolled out, ordering everyone to return to their homes or, if their homes were burning, to at least clear the streets. Jyn watched through the slits in the turret.

She tried to peer through the tiny openings and see the stars above, but smoke shrouded the area in darkness.

◈

Daylight crept through the tiny openings in the turret. Jyn watched it slink across the dirt floor, drawing closer and closer to her hand, the hand that gripped the knife.

She was eight years old again, hiding in the cave, staring up at the hatch. She didn't know if anyone would come, but Saw did.

Saw did.

Outside was silent.

And Jyn knew.

He wasn't coming back for her. Not this time.

An announcement blared throughout the settlement, followed by a low pulsing alarm. Jyn looked through the slits in the shell turret and watched in surprise as Imperial transport ships landed and the stormtroopers still on the ground boarded them. People from Tamsye Prime stood in the wreckage of their town, watching as the soldiers flew off.

Some of them cheered. Their oppressors were leaving.

Jyn's heart sank. She scrabbled out of the shell turret, her eyes to the skies. The Star Destroyer was still up there, high above. Preparing.

She remembered what Lieutenant Colonel Senjax had said: *The Empire has no further use for Tamsye Prime.*

The TIE fighters had decimated the factories, destroying any evidence of what the Empire had been making in its facilities. But the people still knew.

They had worked on whatever it was. They knew.

Jyn was hardly surprised when the first plasma beam shot from the Star Destroyer. She watched almost impassively as it cut through the air, sending down flames and destruction.

Escaping from the factory had not given her much time to look around; running from Reece had narrowed her focus to a pinpoint. But now, with the Star Destroyer low in the sky, fading into the billows of smoke rising from the ground, Jyn saw just how great and terrible the destruction was. And just how much worse it was going to be.

She had to go. *Now.*

As Jyn raced toward the spaceport, another blast from the Star Destroyer shook the ground. Closer this time. And not too far away, a secondary explosion. She didn't look back, but she was keenly aware that she was on a munitions testing ground that was being fired upon. Any leftover torpedos or mines or whatever other monstrosities that remained from the Clone Wars munitions manufacturing days would be set off inadvertently by the Empire's plasma blasts.

The stones of the shell turret rattled as the ground shook from explosive shock. Jyn scrabbled over the sharp, rocky ground, ignoring the cuts that sprang up on her fingers and sliced her pants.

Nothing but smoke and ash was behind her.

Distantly, an alarm cut through the sounds of scream-ing, a steady, high-pitched pulse that seemed oddly rhythmic amid the staccato bursts of random explo-sions and blaster fire. People covered in soot and streaked with blood stood out in the streets, staring up at the Star Destroyer in horror.

I have to go. The words echoed in Jyn's mind, the only truth she knew. She had to leave this planet. She had to escape.

Jyn turned her back on the rubble and faced the spaceport. *Ships.* Reece's ship was still there.

Not that she knew how to fly it.

But it was a start. She had only luck left, and she could only hope it hadn't run out entirely.

Jyn darted out of the munitions testing ground toward the spaceport. As soon as the shock of the attack wore off, this was going to be the most popular place on the entire planet, but none of the natives on Tamsye Prime had yet thought of escape. When something bad happened, people's natural instinct was to go home. It had not yet occurred to the people of Tamsye Prime that there was anywhere else to go.

She went straight to Reece's ship, thankfully still open. She raced first to her own locker, withdrawing the small satchel of her belongings that she'd brought with her on the trip. A change of clothes, her trun-cheons, and the code replicator.

Then she went into the cockpit.

She'd seen Saw fly their shuttle a hundred times over the years. She'd watched as Reece piloted this ship. But the array of buttons and gauges, dials and levers was completely alien to her. She had no idea how to even begin launch sequence, let alone fly past a Star Destroyer.

Another rumble, closer this time. The Empire had been toying with them; now Jyn wasn't sure if there would be any survivors at all. She dashed back out of Reece's ship, wildly looking around as if some sort of escape would just appear. Maybe she could take one of the other ships, the smaller planet hopper. . . . She scanned the spaceport and saw a young man beating on the outside of one of the few remaining Imperial shuttles.

"Hey!" she shouted. When he looked up, she called, "Can you fly this thing?" She jerked her thumb toward Reece's ship.

"I work transport; I can fly anything," he called back. "But it won't do any good. They'll blow anything that's not Imperial out of the sky!"

Jyn thought fast. "I've got Imperial clearance codes," she shouted. "And those things are locked up tight."

The man hesitated, weighing his odds. Finally, he nodded, making up his mind, and ran over to Jyn. She was already turning around and started pulling up the metal ramp as soon as he boarded.

The man knew his way around a ship. He went straight to the cockpit and threw himself into the pilot's chair. Jyn sat down in the copilot's seat, her code replicator in her hand and hooked up to the ship's mainframe.

"We should get others," the man said, hesitating. "There are survivors. . . . We could help them. . . ."

Jyn paused. She *wanted* to help others, but when she pushed past her emotions, she knew there was no way they could organize an evacuation. So she focused on the code replicator. If Saw and Reece escaped on an Imperial ship, the Star Destroyer would be even more hesitant to let another ship slide through its grasp. This had to be perfect.

"It wouldn't take long," the man said, turning around as if there were a group of survivors waiting behind him for permission to board.

"There's no time!" Jyn screamed at him when he still didn't launch the ship. "Go!"

He slammed his hand down on the console and initiated launch sequence. The engine roared to life, and they shot into the sky.

Jyn tapped on the code replicator furiously. She used an Imperial code she'd been working on in her spare time, one with high levels of complex security. She didn't know if it would work, and if she used it now, she knew it would never work again; as soon as the Empire saw her trick, they'd crack down on the codes. But if she was ever going to use it, now was the time. She uploaded the code into the ship's system, masking the ship's identification and labeling it as a medical emergency with high-level clearance for evacuation. She used all her best work on this one shot.

Their ship burst from the planet's atmosphere, burning off oxygen as it entered the vacuum of space. "They're scanning us," the pilot said tightly, his eyes on the screens spread before him. The Star Destroyer hung ominously in the black.

"Don't hesitate," Jyn said. "Keep going; keep going."

Another ship broke atmosphere behind them, the little planet hopper Jyn had seen in the corner of the spaceport. Apparently, more survivors were trying to escape. The scan for that ship was much quicker; in moments, it was shot from the sky, reduced to nothing but debris.

Her code replicator beeped, the sound blending into the alert on the pilot's main console. "We've passed clearance," the pilot said, his voice filled with wonder.

"Go!" Jyn shouted. Their saving grace had been the emergence of the other ship, distracting the Imperials from a close scan. As Jyn watched, TIE fighters

deployed; their visual on the ship would doom Jyn and the pilot.

The pilot punched it, heading straight for the hyperspace route, programming the coordinates with a flurry of fingers. Jyn's hands curled over the sides of her seat, her eyes darting between the pilot and the approaching TIE fighters.

The stars blended together, light and fog forming around them as they flew through hyperspace and away from the carnage of Tamsye Prime.

CHAPTER TWENTY-FIVE_

Jyn sagged in her seat, relief washing over her. She'd escaped.

She turned to the pilot. She wanted to ask his name, thank him for flying, but he stared straight ahead, his spine stiff, tear tracks tracing through the grime and soot on his face.

They had escaped, but he had lost his home, his family, everything he loved.

There was nothing she could say to that.

Jyn curled her legs up, drawing her knees to her chin as she mimicked the pilot and stared out at the blue-gray of hyperspace, nothing but silence between them as they traveled through the stars.

They emerged from hyperspace sooner than Jyn would have expected. A small planet with a lone, barren moon hung before them.

"Where are we?" Jyn asked.

"I don't ever want to do that again," the pilot said in a soft voice.

"Do what?"

"Abandon everyone else just so I can live. We could have saved more," the pilot said, still staring straight ahead. "We could have saved someone other than ourselves."

Guilt enshrouded the pilot. It sank into his skin, it pulled at his bones.

Jyn could feel the same sorrow reaching for her. It filled her lungs like smoke; it made her blood heavy and slow. She closed her eyes, pushing the smell of fire and the sounds of desperate screaming away from her thoughts. If there was one thing she'd learned in her sixteen years of life, it was that she couldn't afford to think in regrets. "The Empire will know by now that my codes were forged," she said in a calm, matter-of-fact voice. "They will likely try to locate this ship. We need to land, and we need to leave it behind."

"I know some junkers," the pilot said.

Jyn raised her eyebrows in surprise.

"I'd been planning to escape," he added. "I'd already set up a whole network of contacts so I could disappear. I just never . . ." He blew out his breath. "I never thought it'd be like this."

Jyn nodded in agreement. It was a good plan—land

the ship and let it be dismantled for parts, impossible to trace. The pilot used the ship's comm system to set it up, then veered out of orbit and toward a landing station.

It all happened surprisingly quickly; the pilot landed the ship, the junkers offered him credits for it. There were no negotiations. The pilot handed Jyn half the credits as her share, and then the junkers offered them a ride on their cargo transport into the main town.

And that was it. When the cargo transport stopped in the center of the dusty little town, the pilot said good-bye and walked off. Jyn got out with her bag of gear, and the transport zoomed away.

She didn't even know the name of the planet she was on.

The town was small, without much in the way of homes. A cantina, a few buildings, a tiny spaceport. The landscape was flat, with little more than scrub brush, and although the big yellow sun beat down on her, the air was chilly. Inside the cantina, Jyn knew she could purchase time on a comm. She could reach out to Saw. Maybe he was looking for her. . . .

She shook her head. No. Either he hadn't survived his wounds—a distinct possibility—or he had never intended to come back for her. There was no middle ground. There never was with Saw.

Jyn rubbed her arms and made her way to the spaceport.

"What you want?" a Lannik said, looking up at Jyn as she approached.

She looked behind him. Three ships were docked—a freighter, a cargo-class transport system, and a personal cruiser that had seen better days.

"Anyone looking for passengers?" Jyn asked.

"No one needs a mutt hanging around," the Lannik growled. He scratched one of his impossibly large, long ears, and the metal hoops piercing the cartilage jingled.

"I can pay!" Jyn protested.

"*Pay*," he sneered.

Behind him, a woman was using mag-lifts to load crates into the freighter.

"Hey!" Jyn called, ignoring the protests of the Lannik. "You need any help?"

The woman leaned back, pressing a hand into her lumbar. She looked Jyn up and down, but she kept her face impassive. She was human, with dark brown skin and black hair and eyes that Jyn hoped were kind.

"You looking for a job?" the woman called back.

The Lannik spit his disgust at Jyn and walked away, mumbling about vagabonds and thieves.

"Yeah," Jyn said, jogging up to the woman. "Got a job for me?"

"I'm not sticking around," she said.

"Suits me."

"Aren't you a little young to be flying?" she said, frowning.

"Old enough," Jyn shot back.

"You don't mind leaving the planet?"

Jyn laughed mirthlessly. "Why would I stay?"

"You don't even care where you're going?"

"Nope." Jyn stuck her hands in her pockets.

The woman leaned back on her heels. "Can you fix a broken droid?" she asked.

"Absolutely," Jyn lied.

The woman stuck her hand out. "Name's Akshaya Ponta," she said.

"Jyn." Jyn said immediately. She was tired; she knew better than to give her real name. "Jyn Dawn."

Akshaya gestured to the SC3000 freighter behind her. Someone had handpainted the ship's call sign on the hull: *Ponta One*. "Welcome aboard," she said.

⬥

Jyn helped Akshaya finish loading up the ship. She was surprised to see that the crates were filled with ore; this hadn't looked like a mining planet.

"I ship for the little guys," Akshaya said. "Small operations, usually family-owned, not the corporate or government stuff."

Akshaya took Jyn to a common area in the heart of the freighter. A small table was bolted to the floor, and there was a bowl of meiloorun fruit in the center. Jyn stared at it, hunger and exhaustion sweeping over her. She let her pack drop to the floor.

"What's that?" Akshaya asked.

Jyn looked down to where she was pointing. Her pack had opened slightly, and the blaster Saw had given her on Tamsye Prime peeked through the top of the bag.

"That can't be on this ship," Akshaya said firmly.

"You won't see it again," Jyn promised, picking the pack back up and closing the top.

Akshaya shook her head. "No, give it to me. I'll get rid of it."

Jyn stared at her with wide eyes. "Look, I appreciate the ride off this rock," she said. "But a blaster is a tool, and I intend to use it in the future. You can't just get rid of it."

Anger flashed in Akshaya's eyes, but it melted away quickly. "I don't really know who you are or where you've come from," she said in a gentle voice. "But I don't live like that, with the need to be armed just to feel safe."

"It's not—" Jyn started.

Akshaya was already shaking her head. "No weapons," she said again. "I'm a peaceful operation. I don't get involved with violence. Skuhl—the planet where I'm based—is neutral. You want to join my operation, you follow my rules."

She crossed her arms and waited for Jyn's reply.

"You need to make a choice," Akshaya said, her tone growing louder. "Choose a peaceful life with my unit, or go back to a life where you need a blaster."

Jyn weighed her options quickly. Finally, with a sigh, she handed over the blaster. She had enough credits, she knew, to purchase another one. A better one. It was more important that she get off-world than that she keep her blaster.

"Thank you," Akshaya said, taking it. "There's a spare bunk down there," she added, pointing. "Help yourself to some grub and rest up. The droid can wait. When you're ready, the pieces are there." She pointed to a small door off the hallway. "I'm going to take care of this," she said, hefting the blaster in her hand and walking off the ship.

Jyn gratefully sank into a seat by the table as Akshaya left. *No need to tell her about the knife in my boot,* she thought as she sucked the pulp from the skins of the fruit. She'd eaten three before Akshaya came back.

After the jump to hyperspace, Jyn made her way to the bunk Akshaya had offered and sank onto the bare mattress with such bone-weary relief that she fell asleep immediately.

❖

Bang! Jyn startled awake, scrambling up. Her stomach churned with fear and disorientation before she was able to remind herself where she was and how she'd gotten there.

Saw had left her.

The planet had burned.

She was on a ship.

Another bang rattled through the metal of the SC3000, and Jyn forced her aching body up. She stumbled blearily through the hall and saw Akshaya signing off on a second load of cargo. Jyn had slept the entire time they were in hyperspace, through the landing, and even through the new cargo being loaded into the main bay.

"Sorry," she said sheepishly.

"Don't apologize," Akshaya said with a friendly smile. "You clearly needed a rest. That it?" she asked the droid with the cargo. It beeped its assent and left the ship.

"I mostly do little hops from system to system," Akshaya said, heading back to the cockpit. Jyn followed her. "I like it, getting to see the different worlds, meeting the people. Always a friend on each world."

"Sounds nice," Jyn said absently.

"Keeps me up to date with the news, too," Akshaya said. She settled into the pilot's seat and waited for Jyn to strap into the copilot chair. She launched the ship, and Jyn got a glimpse of the planet—green and lush, with an exposed quarry off to the side—before they broke atmosphere. "For example," Akshaya continued, "today I dropped in the diner before picking up my cargo, and I heard about a planet that had experienced some trouble."

Ice water washed down Jyn's spine. She didn't say anything.

"Little rock of a world, mostly used for factories. Named Tamsye Prime. Looks like some sort of tragedy happened. Factories are all gone. Not much left there at all," Akshaya said, keeping her eyes straight ahead.

She glanced at Jyn, worry evident on her face. Jyn had been right about Akshaya's kind eyes.

"Seems to me," Akshaya said, "someone from a planet like that may not know where to go or what to do."

Akshaya punched in the next coordinates, and the ship jumped to lightspeed.

Jyn released the safety harness of her chair and stood. "I guess I should get to work on that broken droid," she said, avoiding Akshaya's eyes. She didn't know what to do with her pity or concern. Akshaya didn't follow her as she went back down the hall.

Jyn opened the door to the little closet where Akshaya had said the droid was. It was a small astro-mech unit, an older class, more outdated than some of the junk Jyn used to spar with on Saw's outpost. She pulled the motivator out, then found a bag of bits and pieces that had broken off it and spread them out on the table.

I have no idea what I'm doing, she thought, staring down at the parts. She could tinker with her code replicator all day, finding the patterns and pulling at the algorithms, but with something mechanical like this . . . she was utterly lost.

Still, she gave it a go. She knew enough about how to destroy a droid to guess at how one should look when it wasn't broken, but the internal mechanisms were far more complicated than she'd thought.

She'd been working for about an hour when they emerged from hyperspace. Jyn made her way back up front to the cockpit.

"An Imperial checkpoint," Akshaya said, sighing heavily. "More and more of them these days."

"Are your docs in order?" Jyn asked urgently.

Akshaya hesitated. "I may be behind on my cargo license," she said. "Which means an inspection and a fine." She sounded defeated.

Jyn ran back to her bunk, grabbed the code replicator out of her bag, and ran back to the ship's main console. She plopped on the floor, quickly working as an alarm started ringing throughout the ship. A warning blared over the main screen.

IMPERIAL TRANSPORT CODE: VIOLATION

Jyn had done this sort of thing for Saw enough to know she had only moments to spare. The Empire would run an initial scan at a checkpoint, and those usually triggered alarms. They'd run a deeper scan in a few minutes. If Jyn could forge proper codes between then and now, the Imperial officers would likely not bother to physically check the ship.

She tapped on the datapad hooked into the ship's core as quickly as possible, uploading the authenticator code generator into the processor. She marked the permissions for the cargo as home crafts. There was a market in the Core worlds for "genuine" crafts from smaller, Outer Rim planets, and that would both explain the ship's log visiting a half dozen different planets and make the cargo completely uninteresting to any Imperial inspectors.

The alarm cut off abruptly, and a new code flashed through the ship's receptors.

IMPERIAL TRANSPORT CODE: APPROVED

Akshaya, startled, quickly resumed her seat in the pilot's chair and set the ship on course toward the planet. She kept shooting Jyn curious looks. When they landed, rather than get to work, Akshaya put her hand over Jyn's, keeping her in the chair.

"How did you learn to do that?" she asked.

Jyn shrugged.

"No," Akshaya said, her voice firm. "You're on my ship, I expect honesty. Did you come from Tamsye Prime?"

Jyn swallowed. "Yes," she said.

"Were you born there?"

"No," Jyn said. "I . . . I was raised on another planet."

"By your parents?"

"No," Jyn said in a soft voice.

"You're a bit of a wanderer, aren't you?" Akshaya said. Her eyes crinkled at the corners, and she reached over to smooth down Jyn's hair. It was such a motherly action that Jyn couldn't help leaning into the touch.

"It's not safe for you," Akshaya chided. "Just bouncing around from planet to planet. When we get back to Skuhl, you can stay with me for a bit, okay? Get back on your feet properly."

Akshaya stood, clapping her hands, ready to get back to work.

"Um," Jyn said.

"Yes?"

"If we're being honest, then I'd better add that I have no idea how to fix your droid."

Akshaya laughed. "Don't worry," she said. "With that little trick, you've already paid for your passage."

Jyn allowed herself a tiny smile of relief, then followed Akshaya off the ship.

CHAPTER TWENTY-SIX_

Skuhl was not what Jyn had expected. Akshaya docked her ship in a private hangar outside of town, and Jyn grabbed her lone bag. She hated not knowing what to expect next. When she stepped outside, Jyn was blasted with cool air, so refreshing that she just stood there, sucking it in the same way she'd gulped down the meiloorun fruit. The planet was gorgeously serene. Flat in every direction, with fields of blue-green grass that moved like ocean waves in the breeze. The sky was a rich blue, and a single sun peeked through fluffy white clouds.

It reminded her of Lah'mu but flatter and grassier and bluer.

Behind the hangar was something of a town—a warehouse where Akshaya's cargo was being sent, some sort of factory, a few shops, a diner, and a cluster of homes. The main street cutting through the town was decorated with baskets of flowers hanging from poles lined with bells that tinkled in a beautiful melody. The people walking down the street greeted each other in a friendly way, as if they all knew each other. Even from there, Jyn could hear cheerful music and smell the roasting meat from the inviting diner. At the opposite end of the town, Jyn could just make out a small space-port, not good for much beyond shuttles and planet hoppers.

Akshaya's house stood just a little downhill from the hangar. It was a small clapboard building, painted bright blue, a color that blended in perfectly with the clear sky and the blue-green grasslands that stretched into the distance. The door was red, and yellow designs had been painted around each window. It was the strangest house Jyn had ever seen, but it seemed to fit well there.

When Akshaya pushed open the front door, some-one called out.

"Mum?"

"Hadder," Akshaya said, "come and greet our guest."

A boy about Jyn's age peered around the corner. He had the same dark brown skin with red undertones that Akshaya had, and the same black hair, though his was cropped to chin length. His eyes widened when he saw Jyn standing behind his mother.

"Hey," he said.

"Hello." Jyn stuck out her hand.

"Where'd Mum find you?" His tone was friendly but curious.

"Near old Hamma's place," Akshaya said, shoving her son goodnaturedly into the room and leading Jyn inside before closing the door.

"My name is Jyn," Jyn said.

"Where is she staying?" Hadder asked his mother.

Jyn had been staring at the beautiful mandalas painted on every possible surface in the room—walls, floors, ceiling. But the question made her focus on Akshaya.

"Where do you *want* to stay, Jyn?" Akshaya asked politely.

Jyn shrugged with one shoulder. "It doesn't matter," she said. "I could . . . stay on the ship?"

Hadder started to speak, but his mother cut him off. "You could. Do you want to? You could stay here if you like."

Jyn's eyes darted around the warm house. "Here?"

Akshaya seemed to be asking her son a question with her eyes. "You know I don't care," Hadder said. Akshaya nodded as if she'd made a decision.

"You can have Tanith's room," she said.

Akshaya's house was small, and the bedroom Akshaya showed Jyn was a lot like a ship's bunk. She suspected that the room was originally part of a larger one and that the whitewashed wall had been added more recently. The small bedroom had just enough space for a pallet on the floor, a small shelf that contained a wooden box, a vase with dried flowers, and little else. It seemed stark and empty compared with the beautiful bright mandalas and designs decorating the rest of the house.

"You're welcome to stay here as long as you like," Akshaya said graciously.

Jyn nodded, although she wasn't sure how much of that she believed. But she didn't want to go back to hiding and being alone.

"I'm just on the other side," Hadder added, pointing to the whitewashed wall.

Jyn dropped her bag on the floor.

"That's settled then," Akshaya said. She turned to her son. "Is dinner ready? I'm starving."

"I mean, I made bunn," Hadder said, although Jyn wasn't sure what bunn was, "but we have a new housemate! We should celebrate!"

Hadder hustled Akshaya and Jyn back to the door. Akshaya laughed. "Any excuse to eat out, huh?" she said.

Jyn glanced behind her as they headed into town, noting that Akshaya hadn't locked the door to the house. Come to think of it, she hadn't locked up her ship, either. Even when they were the only ones on Wrea, she and Saw had kept everything secure.

As dusk dipped into night, fewer people were on the main street, but it was still well lit. Those who lived directly in town lingered on their stoops, chatting with neighbors. A few waved in greeting to Akshaya or Hadder, making the trip down the road take twice as long as they stopped to give updates. Most looked at Jyn curiously, but Akshaya ignored the pointed looks and discreet questions.

"You're the most interesting thing to happen here in ages," Hadder said in an undertone as he pushed open the door to the diner.

Jyn was a little surprised at how big the diner actually was, and how crowded.

"There's a refinery on the other end," Akshaya supplied, guessing what Jyn's expression meant.

Jyn recalled the building that had looked like a factory. It made sense. Akshaya carted ore from small mining facilities to the refinery and then took the refined stock to manufacturing planets to sell it. This section of the Outer Rim was rather close to some rising Mid Rim worlds, and trade was growing.

"I'm surprised there are so many different kinds of people here," Jyn commented as she sat down with Hadder at a table near the bar.

Jyn looked around. A Drabatan was laughing loudly with a Cyran. Over in the corner sat a group of Winrocs, talking darkly among themselves. The owner of the diner was a Chagrian, his mottled blue skin the same color as the sky outside. He caught Jyn staring at his lethorns and flicked a forked black tongue at her, winking when she smiled at him.

Akshaya ordered plates of food, which were served family style for their table. A steamed, sticky grain made up the base of all their choices, but there were hot dumplings in pale brown broth and thick gummy noodles that had been sautéed in oil with long strips of green vegetables. Jyn slurped noisily, and Hadder copied her, laughing.

It was such a warm, comforting experience that Jyn allowed herself to believe the moment would last.

Over the bar, an old-fashioned viewscreen showed the news. Jyn was fake-fighting with Hadder over who got the fourth and last sugared dumpling when someone across the room shouted, "Hey, everyone, look!"

Nearly everyone turned to the news, and the owner adjusted the volume.

"We turn now to our ongoing coverage of the disaster on an Outer Rim world, Tamsye Prime, a small manufacturing planet." The reporter was a female human, and she spoke with sincerity that sounded real.

Jyn felt Akshaya stiffen beside her. Hadder's eyes darted from his mother to Jyn, then back to the screen.

"For the first time since the attack, Lieutenant Colonel Senjax is with us today," the reporter continued. The camera droids shifted, showing the Imperial officer.

Jyn sucked in a breath. If Lieutenant Colonel Senjax had been the Empire's pretty boy before the attack, now he was the dignified hero with battle scars to prove it. He'd lost an eye, and it had been replaced with an artful mechanical optic implant that glittered with decorative sweeps of gold. A scar had been etched down the left side of his face, disappearing under his crisp uniform. His hair was shorter now, giving him the appearance of having aged significantly in just a few days.

"Thank you," Lieutenant Colonel Senjax told the reporter. His voice held none of the lighthearted, easygoing joy that it had when Jyn had met him. "The terrorists who attacked Tamsye Prime had a single goal," he continued, looking straight out. It felt as if he was staring directly at Jyn. "The factories on that planet were key in manufacturing items the Empire uses for the defense of its citizens. This was a focused, pointed attack, and the anarchists who implemented it did not care that they destroyed not just the plant, which can be replaced, but also the lives of more than a thousand beloved citizens."

Jyn's heart twisted in rage. How could this man lie so easily? He knew as well as Jyn that it had been the Empire he loved that had both betrayed and hurt him. She wondered just what they had given him or threatened him with to make him speak on their behalf so soon after the attack.

"I was on the ground at the time," Lieutenant Colonel Senjax continued, "and I regret to inform the galaxy that the terrorist's goals of annihilation made them far deadlier than typical separatist groups. However, the group has been utterly crushed, every single member who implemented the attack has been caught and punished."

"Saw," Jyn whispered, water springing to her eyes. She'd assumed Saw had escaped. Had he and Codo been caught? But . . . the rest of the report was a lie. Maybe this was, too.

"The Empire sent aid to Tamsye Prime immediately. In the medical bay, I was beside many citizens." Lieutenant Colonel Senjax ducked his head. "I'm sad to say, there were few survivors."

At this, a hush followed by frantic whispers swept the crowd in the diner. Tamsye Prime wasn't that far away from Skuhl. Some muttered individual names, people they had known who had likely been killed in the attack.

"Remember," Lieutenant Colonel Senjax continued, "the actions of a few anarchist terrorists cause much harm, destroying lives throughout the galaxy. But the Empire is working to protect you. With the new defense budget approved by the Senate this morning, I have no doubt our Empire will be even stronger than before. These small groups are no true threat to the Empire. Rest assured, you are safe."

"That didn't happen." Jyn looked to Akshaya and Hadder. "None of that—it wasn't like that! I was *there*! It wasn't terrorists . . . it was—"

"Shhh," Akshaya demanded. Hadder's eyes filled with worry. "We're going," Akshaya said, dropping some credits on the table and bustling Jyn and Hadder out. They didn't stop on the street to talk to anyone else; Akshaya was practically running by the time they reached the end of town, and she didn't let them speak until they were back in the privacy of the little blue house.

"The *Empire* did that!" Jyn said. "I was *there*!"

"You were on Tamsye Prime?" Hadder asked.

Jyn nodded furiously. "And I saw the Star Destroyer. I saw the turbolaser fire. I saw the—" She stopped, unable to continue. She could still smell the sharp stench of burning.

"It's over," Akshaya said firmly. "Whatever happened there, best to not bring it up again."

"But if the Empire . . ." Hadder started, but Akshaya slashed her hand in the air, silencing him.

"We are several systems away from Tamsye Prime," she said. "The Empire doesn't reach this far."

"The Empire reaches everywhere," Jyn whispered. "And we're not that far away."

Akshaya threw an arm around her and pulled her into a hug that Jyn didn't return. "It's over," she repeated. "You're safe here. I promise."

Jyn closed her eyes and tried to believe it.

CHAPTER TWENTY-SEVEN_

Jyn woke early the next morning. She crept down the hall to the kitchen, hoping she could find some caf and a brew pot. She was surprised to see Hadder already up.

"Bunn doesn't cook itself," he said, lifting the top of a big pressurized steamer. Jyn recognized the same long, sticky grains that had been the base of much of the food at the diner; bunn must be locally grown and very popular. Hadder had refilled the steamer the previous evening and let grains cook all night. From the large quantity of bunn in the basin, Jyn figured it was going to feature in every meal she had on Skuhl.

"Want breakfast?" Hadder asked pleasantly.

Jyn nodded.

Hadder moved around the kitchen efficiently, frying up two eggs, setting caf to brew, flipping the eggs, and pouring two cups for himself and Jyn. "Mom likes to sleep in," he said, handing her a mug. He scooped bunn out of the steamer with his bare hand, making a little mound in the center of a bowl and then sliding a fried egg on top.

Jyn watched Hadder eat first—breaking the bright green yolk of the egg and mixing it with the sticky bunn—and then copied him.

"None for me?" Akshaya asked, yawning and stretching as she entered the kitchen.

Hadder jerked his head toward the griddle.

"It wasn't that long ago when my son cooked for me," Akshaya said in a falsely bemoaning tone, "but now there's a new pretty girl to distract him."

"Yup," Hadder agreed cheerfully.

Jyn put her spoon down. "I was thinking," she said. "I need a job. I could try to learn how to fix your droid. . . ."

Hadder laughed. "You think Beethree even *can* be fixed?" he asked. "That hunk of junk has been broken for years."

"Or I could copilot," Jyn offered. She wasn't sure how much help she'd be if she actually had to pilot, but she was a fast learner.

"No," Akshaya said. "You're too young."

"I'm sixteen," Jyn said. She paused, thinking. "I could—"

"No," Akshaya said in a harsher tone of voice than Jyn had ever heard her use before.

An uneasy silence stretched out, and even affable Hadder looked down at the table. Jyn wasn't sure what she'd said that was so wrong, but it was clear she'd overstepped somewhere.

"Docs," Akshaya said finally. "You get me scandocs and clearance codes that help me avoid those blockades, and we'll call it even."

"You can forge Imperial clearance codes?" Hadder asked, gaping at Jyn.

"Helped me avoid a fine," Akshaya said. "We're not exactly scraping credits together, but that was a nice little bump."

"Maybe we can save up enough to replace Beethree," Hadder said.

"Yeah, that droid really isn't worth fixing." Jyn laughed. "You'd be better off using it for target practice."

Akshaya and Hadder exchanged a look. "Target . . . practice?" Akshaya asked.

Jyn felt her cheeks burn. She had said the wrong thing. Again.

"Well," Jyn said, scooting her chair back. "I'll get to work. I'll put together a packet of different codes and scandocs that may be helpful, and—"

Akshaya cut her off. "Jyn," she said. "I'm not leaving again for a few days. You can take it easy."

"I—" Jyn started, but she wasn't sure what else to say.

"I, on the other hand, need to oversee the cargo dispersement," Akshaya said, standing up. "I'll see you later."

Jyn watched her go, then turned back to Hadder. She felt . . . adrift. What was she supposed to do if she wasn't working? She couldn't train as she had with Saw.

"Why doesn't she want a copilot?" Jyn asked Hadder. "I'm not that young."

Hadder just shook his head sadly. "That's not it. It's Tanith." He looked like he was going to say more, but instead he ran his fingers through his dark hair. Jyn watched as the silky locks fluttered around his ears. He needed a haircut, but maybe he liked it that way, chin length and just enough in the way that he had an excuse to keep running his fingers through it. It was very distracting.

"Who's Tanith?" Jyn asked, pressing him for more information.

Hadder's gaze was distant. "She was my sister."

Jyn noted the way he said this, as if she was gone.

"She died when I was seven," Hadder said, confirming her suspicion. "You don't have to say you're sorry or anything," he added quickly. "It happened a decade ago."

Jyn didn't tell him that she hadn't been intending to say she was sorry. She would never give pity to someone she liked. Instead, she said, "I lost my parents when I was eight."

Hadder looked at her. She had questions for him, and he had questions for her, but neither was sure what to say.

Hadder broke the silence first. "Have you been on the run since then?"

"Since I was eight?" Jyn laughed. "No, someone else took me in." Her smile faded and she grew completely still. *The group has been utterly crushed,* Lieutenant Colonel Senjax had said, *every single member who implemented the attack has been caught and punished.* Was Saw even still alive? Her mother's death was long before, distant enough that she could speak of it without emotion. But Saw's possible death . . . that was too recent.

Hadder stood up abruptly, his chair scraping against the floor. "Come on," he said.

Jyn followed him to the bedroom she'd slept in the previous night. He went to the little shelf and pulled out the wooden box. Jyn had noticed it before, but as it wasn't hers, she'd tried to ignore it. Three hypo-injectors lay at the bottom of the box, rolling around as Hadder handed it to Jyn. She looked at him curiously, but he nodded, prompting her to inspect the needles. They were empty.

" 'Haidera serum,' " she said, reading the label and stumbling over the first word. Where had she heard about that before? "Oh," she breathed, her eyes widening.

Hadder nodded grimly.

"This was your sister's room," she said, looking around at the small space with new eyes. "And she had bloodburn."

Bloodburn was a rare disease, mostly affecting younger people who spent a lot of time in space. It was incurable and often fatal, but haidera serum injections could help.

"That's not what killed her, though," Hadder said.

Jyn put the empty hypo-injector back in the box. She was only dimly aware of bloodburn, but she knew how addictive haidera serum could be and how easy it was to overdose.

"Mum has it in her head that it's her fault. After Pop died, Tanith started working with her on the ship. Then she got sick, and . . ." His eyes flicked back to the box. "And she's convinced that bloodburn runs in families. Nothing I've ever been able to say has swayed her to believe I'd be safe to fly."

There was so much longing in his voice, such deep desire that Jyn was certain there was nothing Hadder wanted more than to fly like his mother, and that was the one thing he was forbidden to do.

CHAPTER TWENTY-EIGHT _

"I do have a bike though," Hadder said. "Want to see?"

He led Jyn to the hangar his mother used. A combination of droids and people were unloading the freighter with mag-lifts. Hadder waved at them cheerfully as he led Jyn to the back of the building, where a speeder bike was propped against the wall. It was a patchwork affair, cobbled together from different parts. "You made this?" Jyn asked.

Hadder nodded proudly.

"If you have skills like this, *you* should be the one to work on that broken droid."

"Oh, I have," Hadder said. "That hunk of junk is beyond help. It's futile. Mum probably just didn't want you to think you were getting charity. You don't look like the type to like charity."

Jyn glowered. She *didn't* like charity, and she didn't like the fact that both Akshaya and Hadder were apparently perfectly fine with deceiving her into taking it.

Hadder, however, was completely oblivious to Jyn's scowl. "Come on," he said, throwing a leg over the speeder and scooting forward in the seat for Jyn to join him. She climbed aboard behind him. He flicked the repulsorlift, muttering, "Come on, come on," under his breath as the engine warmed up. The speeder wobbled as the repulsors kicked on, and he adjusted the capacitor dials. "Ready?" he asked. "Hold on." Jyn tentatively wrapped her arms around his waist.

With a lurch, the speeder bike zoomed forward. They raced through the tall, blue-green grass, the long strands whipping against their legs. Hadder whooped in glee, leaning forward into the cool wind and pulling Jyn with him. Jyn looked behind her at the trail they cut through the grass, but Hadder's eyes were focused on the horizon. He pushed the bike harder and harder, and Jyn knew he was imagining what was just beyond the horizon.

She let herself fall into the joy of it, the speed, the wind, the reddish light as the sun dipped down, the startled vulpors that leapt through the grass, their long, silky tails swishing as they chittered angrily at the speeder. The faster they went, the more Jyn let herself pretend there was nothing more than that moment, there, nothing but speed and wind.

Her fear and anxiety melted away. She let her hands slip from Hadder's waist, trusting him to keep the bike steady. She raised her arms up, tilted her head back.

She closed her eyes.

She was flying.

Hadder kicked at the controls, and the speeder started to turn, circling around. Jyn gasped, her heart lurching. She grabbed Hadder as the bike spun out of control. He whooped with laughter as he let go of the handlebars, twisting to hug her as they slid off the bike together. The speeder went a few meters without them before petering out, and together Jyn and Hadder hit the tall blue-green grass and rolled, the momentum forcing them to wrap their arms and legs together as they whirled through the grass. When they finally slowed to a stop, Hadder was on top of Jyn.

She pushed him off. "What did you do that for?" she asked, standing, feeling a little wobbly after their unexpected dismount from the bike.

Hadder grinned. "It just seemed like fun," he said.

"We could have broken our necks!"

Hadder stretched out in the grass. "Yeah, but we didn't. Besides, we weren't going *that* fast."

Jyn couldn't help laughing at him.

"Mum'll be at the refinery until late," Hadder said. "We don't have to go back in." When Jyn didn't move, he added, "You always look as if you're about to run away. You're allowed to just . . . I don't know. Sit?"

Jyn shook her hands, trying to dispel the nervous energy that was already winding its way inside her. She reminded herself that she *liked* being on the move. She had loved the spontaneity of Saw's missions, how she'd never known if he'd knock on her door with a blaster and orders to fly halfway across the galaxy or if she'd spend the day training. She didn't know what to do with herself when she had neither a mission nor the expectation of one.

Hadder sat up and patted the patch of grass beside him. Jyn sat down tentatively. Hadder broke off a blade of the long grass and handed it to Jyn before popping one in his own mouth.

Jyn shifted uncomfortably, not used to Hadder's intense gaze. "What?" she asked more aggressively than she'd intended.

"Your eyes are strange," Hadder said pleasantly.

"You do realize that's not a compliment?"

Hadder grinned. "Yeah, it is. They're unique. I like that."

Jyn tried to look away, but she could still feel his gaze on her.

"It's like they shift color in the sunlight," he continued, oblivious to her discomfort at his attention. "Like there're holos in them or something."

"My father used to say that it looked as if there was stardust in my eyes," Jyn said. "He called me that sometimes. Stardust."

Hadder repeated the word softly. "Yeah," he said. "I like that." He paused, and Jyn felt him look away, up toward the sky that was settling into dusk. "So what happened to your father?" he asked.

Jyn shrugged, not answering him. It was easier to say he was dead, but she didn't want to speak the lie in that moment. Without realizing what she was doing, she started to fiddle with her kyber crystal necklace.

"Nice rock," Hadder said casually.

She dropped the crystal as if it had burned her, letting it fall against her chest, then quickly tucked it back under her shirt.

Hadder stared at her. "Don't take this the wrong way," he said, "but you're kind of weird."

Jyn rolled her eyes, but she was smiling. "How am I supposed to *not* take that the wrong way? What other way could there be to take that?"

Hadder's grin was lopsided. "You want me to not think you're weird? Answer some questions."

Jyn chewed on the end of the grass. "Fine," she said begrudgingly. She could always lie.

"What happened to your parents?" Hadder asked.

"My mother's dead."

"And your father?"

"As good as." Without meaning to, Jyn's voice had taken on an edge, sharp as the knife she still hid in her boot.

"Did he leave you on Tamsye Prime?" Hadder asked.

"No," Jyn said, her eyes focusing on the horizon. "My father didn't leave me on Tamsye Prime. Saw did."

"Saw? Who's he?" Now Hadder had an edge to his voice. Jyn shot him a look, trying to figure him out. He sounded almost like he wanted to protect her, which was ridiculous. He hardly knew her. And she didn't need protecting.

"He's who I was living with. Kind of like family. We worked together."

Hadder squinted. "Which is it? Someone you lived with like family or a business partner?"

"Can't he be both?" Jyn asked.

"No," Hadder said in a way that made Jyn feel like she was slow. "If someone's your family, they're not your employer or just someone you share a house with. They're . . . important." He seemed to be struggling with the right words to make Jyn understand.

Jyn thought of Saw. What had he been to her? He had been . . . everything. The only one she thought she could trust. But what had she been to him? He'd left her on Tamsye Prime. *He had to,* she told herself, remembering Reece. But he hadn't come back for her. She thought of the sure way Lieutenant Colonel Senjax had spoken of the defeat of the rebels. She thought of Saw's injuries, the way he had coughed blood.

"Doesn't matter," Jyn said, swallowing her emotion. "He's probably dead now."

"Oh." Hadder didn't speak again for a while, but then he said, "So you just got on the nearest ship and left."

"Pretty much."

"I want to do that basically all the time." Hadder sighed. "But the only real ship on Skuhl that's not a planet hopper is Mum's, and the point is to get away. Like you did. Just get on a random ship and see where it takes me."

Jyn gaped at the boy. Did he not get it? She hadn't just hopped on Akshaya's ship for *fun*. She'd been betrayed, hungry, alone, desperate. She'd had nothing, *no one* left. Nobody got on a ship going anywhere if they had ties binding them to someone else. Nobody willingly became adrift.

"What?" Hadder asked when he noticed Jyn's face.

She shook her head. It wasn't his fault he didn't know what it meant to lose everything. "Just thinking how stupid you are," she said in a casual voice, leaning back.

"You're weird, and I'm stupid." Hadder copied her, flopping down on the grass. "We're quite the match."

CHAPTER TWENTY-NINE_

Before Akshaya left at the end of the week, Jyn uploaded new clearance codes and scandocs into the ship's mainframe.

"One day, I want to know how you got to be so good at forging Imperial documents," Akshaya said.

Hadder stood nearby. "Well, I'm glad this little scam artist is working on our side," he said. "I don't like how close the Empire's gotten to your trade routes."

"You know the Empire is after ore," Jyn added. "You'd be better off transporting something else, something the Empire didn't want."

Jyn met Hadder's eyes, and she knew he agreed with her. But Akshaya laughed. "One day you kids'll understand that we're basically ants down here on Skuhl. The Empire's a giant. And giants don't care about ants, which means we can do whatever we want."

Jyn opened her mouth to protest, but Akshaya pulled her into a hug. "Thanks," she said.

When she stepped back, Jyn shuffled nervously on her feet. "So," she said slowly.

"So?" Akshaya asked.

Jyn looked down at the ship's main controls. "These should last you a good long time," Jyn said. "I made a few variations for you as well, and . . ." Her voice trailed off. Hadder shot her a confused look, but Jyn knew from the sadness in Akshaya's eyes that she understood.

Jyn had been hired to do a job. And she'd completed the job.

She couldn't look at Akshaya or Hadder. "Do you . . . have more work?" When neither Akshaya nor Hadder said anything, Jyn babbled on. "If not, that's fine. Totally fine. I understand. Maybe I could just hitch a ride to a planet that has some jobs. . . ."

Her voice trailed off again.

"Of course we want you to stay, weird girl," Hadder said, rolling his eyes.

"I'll need new codes periodically, I'm sure," Akshaya added. "Unless you want to go?"

Jyn shook her head, not trusting her voice.

⬥⬥⬥

They fell into an easy, steady routine. Akshaya was typically gone two weeks out of a standard month, first picking up small shipments of ore from the mining planets too tiny to attract Imperial notice, then distributing the refined ore to shipbuilders and other

236

manufacturers. When she was on Skuhl, Hadder made the meals and helped Akshaya with scheduling and bills while Jyn checked the codes and updated them. When Akshaya was gone, Jyn and Hadder had free rein to do as they pleased.

Which, lately, had meant flying.

Jyn had to admit that she was the bad influence. Akshaya's hangar housed the main freighter, but there was a small planet hopper there as well, one used for quick runs in the local system. Jyn made herself feel better about taking the planet hopper out by saying she and Hadder never broke atmosphere; they *technically* never left Skuhl. But she wasn't sure how long Hadder would be satisfied with playing in the clouds. Every time he sat down in the pilot's chair, his spine straightened, his eyes focused on the horizon, his hands took the controls as if they belonged nowhere else. When Hadder started up the planet hopper, he always breathed a little sigh of relief, as if he'd been waiting for that moment, and nothing more.

He had learned to fly, he told her, from his sister. After their father died, Tanith had found solace in flight, and she had taken Hadder along. When addiction claimed Tanith, however, Hadder's mother had emerged from her grief with an even stronger fear of losing her son. She'd taken over the transport business and grounded him on Skuhl for good.

The repulsorlift hummed, and they hovered over the hangar floor before Hadder eased the planet hopper out of the bay and shot into the air so fast it left Jyn breathless. "What I don't get," Hadder said as they soared over the little town, "is why Mum is so convinced I'll get bloodburn. It's so rare. The chances are miniscule, honestly."

Jyn didn't answer. She understood Akshaya's motivation. If she had her mother back, she'd want to hold on to her for as long as possible, too.

"Once I'm eighteen," Hadder mumbled. His hand hovered over the hyperspace controls. Most small shuttles like the planet hopper didn't have a hyperspace drive, but this one had been retrofitted by Hadder's father before he died. Hadder had never tried to leave Skuhl's orbit, but Jyn noticed the way his hand always lingered near the drive's sequence commands.

Hadder sighed and shifted in his seat, flipping a lever and sending the little shuttle into a stomach-churning spin. Jyn laughed and pushed his broad shoulders until Hadder reluctantly brought the planet hopper back into a steady arc.

Jyn propped her feet up on the dash. Hadder didn't need a copilot, not anymore. She glanced sideways at him, and for a moment, she let herself imagine that this was her future. She and Hadder could be a team. Maybe they could expand Akshaya's operation, going farther into the Outer Rim for shipments, exploring new planets.

Hadder turned the shuttle around, aiming for the ground. "What are you doing?" Jyn asked. This was the shortest trip they'd made.

He looked more depressed than she'd ever seen him. "It just . . . it feels like I'm on a leash," he said. "You ever feel that way? Like you can't do what you really want, like you have to be someone for someone else, and that means you can't be you? That you can never have what you really want?"

I have seen so much blood, Jyn wanted to say. *And I remember the face of everyone who's died because of me.*

Instead, Jyn stood up and moved behind Hadder. He shot her a curious look, but Jyn didn't look down at him. She put her arms over his shoulders, her hands clasped around his on the controls. She looked straight ahead, through the viewport and into the sky, and after a moment, Hadder looked up and out too. Jyn leaned forward, her body against his back, and gripped the controls through his hands, pulling them back. The shuttle's nose tipped upward, higher and higher. Jyn could feel the joy thrumming through Hadder as the shuttle pushed through the thinning atmosphere, the bright blue sky turning to white, flames licking the ablation shields. Her grip tightened around his, her eyes growing wide with excitement.

The little shuttle burst out of the atmosphere, and the entirety of the universe stared down at them.

Space was black in a way Jyn could never quite describe. When she flew with Saw, that's all she ever noticed about space—the great black emptiness of it all. But this time, her arms still around Hadder, she could see only the stars, the innumerable stars, white pinpricks of light dancing beyond their grasp, each one a promise of a new world, a new adventure, a new hope.

"If you want something, take it," she said, her breath a whisper in Hadder's ear. "If there's one thing I've learned, it's that you have to live each day as if it's your last." It sounded so trite, but she knew it to be true. Each choice could be the last one. *And I choose this,* she thought. *I choose the stars and peace and you.*

She felt him grow very, very still. Something inside her thudded, hard, and Jyn jerked back as if Hadder's skin was made of flame. She collapsed into the copilot's chair, careful to keep her gaze on the stars outside, not on the way Hadder looked at her.

CHAPTER THIRTY_

Neither of them wanted to go back to the planet's surface. As the shuttle aimed for Akshaya's hangar, they didn't talk. It wasn't until Hadder cut the engines and stood to leave the planet hopper that he turned to Jyn, eyes gleaming.

"That. Was. *Awesome*," he said.

Jyn couldn't help grinning back at him.

Hadder bubbled with pent-up excitement. "I mean, I've been up there before. That wasn't my first time. Before Tanith died, Mum used to let me go on some of her runs. But I've never been at the controls before. I've never . . ." He ran his fingers through his hair, then swooped down, grabbing Jyn in a hug so fierce he lifted her off her feet. "Thank you," he said, looking right into her eyes. When he let her go, Jyn staggered a little, unsteady without his touch.

"We have to go celebrate," Hadder said. "I'm taking you out to dinner."

"Yay, more bunn," Jyn said without enthusiasm.

Hadder laughed. "I'm not that bad of a cook," he

said. "But I meant, I'm taking you out. Not that I'm cooking. Come on," he said, grabbing her hand and leading her off the ship, out of the hangar, into the little town, and straight to the diner.

A local band was playing, and more than half the diner was singing along to songs Jyn didn't know. She sat at the table Hadder procured for them against the wall, far from the band. She looked out over the loud, tipsy crowd. Living on the outskirts, Jyn hadn't really run into that many people. But there was a whole refinery on Skuhl, as well as some trade with bunn and other goods. The diner served as a restaurant and watering hole for the locals, an inn for the visitors, and a meeting place for all of Skuhl.

"I'm always surprised there are so many different kinds of people here," Jyn commented. Coruscant had been populated with every species imaginable, but most worlds she'd been on since had been fairly homogenous.

"It's like Mum says," Hadder replied, "the giant doesn't notice ants. Skuhl is an anthill." And, he didn't need to add, there were plenty of ants in the galaxy.

Hadder insisted on ordering something special for them. "No bunn," he promised, telling the Chagrian who owned the place that they wanted two soup-soofs.

When the food arrived, Jyn looked down at her dish. "This is . . . edible?" she asked, sliding her fork through the brownish foam the Chagrian had delivered to their table.

"Trust me."

She did.

She shouldn't have.

The soup-soof wasn't the worst thing she'd ever eaten, but it was close. She'd take mystery meat from Saw's cabinet any day over the oddly textured pillow of squishy saltiness that coated her tongue with a strange, fatty aftertaste.

"Come on, it's not that bad!" Hadder laughed.

Jyn pushed her plate over to him. "You're making me bunn when we get back home," she informed him.

A smirk slid across Hadder's face.

"What?" Jyn asked.

"You've never called it home before," he said.

Jyn started to make a joke—she couldn't let Hadder get too smug—but then she froze. She recognized a face in the crowd, someone she hadn't seen in ages. Not since Inusagi and the massacre. The stocky man with broad shoulders, the one who had just grunted the code word at her and taken the invitation. She remembered the way he had looked as he fired the flechette launcher, the firm set of his jaw as he watched the destruction of life unfolding before him.

"What is it?" Hadder asked immediately.

Jyn shook herself. "Nothing."

Hadder turned in his seat to see what she was looking at. The band had taken a break, and the crowd around them had dispersed, exposing a table on the other side of the room where a handful of people were playing sabacc in the shadows. "Do you know those guys?" he asked in a low voice.

Jyn ripped her gaze away. "One of them," she said. "Let's go."

Hadder left some credit chips on the table, and together they walked out into the street. Jyn felt the nervous energy build in her, her hands gripping and ungripping. Hadder was on edge, too; he kept glancing behind him. The refinery's second shift ended, and a flood of people poured onto the street, blotting out the diner's main entrance.

"He was someone Saw worked with once," Jyn said as they pushed their way through the crowd, going against the flow. "I met him during a . . . job on Inusagi."

The bells attached to the poles lining the streets jingled, and Jyn jumped. Their metallic tinkling was nothing like the zing of the flechettes, the scent of the flowers totally different from the sakoola blossoms stained with blood.

She glanced over her shoulder. He was following them.

It's a coincidence, Jyn told herself. But every nerve in her body was rattled.

She slipped her hand into Hadder's. He looked down at her, surprised, but Jyn kept her gaze straight ahead. When they passed a cross street, Jyn yanked him into the alley. Hadder started to say something, but Jyn put her finger on his lips, silencing him. She waited.

The crowd from the shift change had thinned out, but Jyn's focus was razor sharp. A sound of heavy footsteps grew louder. Hadder reached for Jyn, but she shook him off, lunging in front of the man as he rounded the corner by the side street.

"Why are you following me?" she demanded.

"It's not for your looks, if that's what you're worried about, sweetheart," he sneered.

Jyn decked him so hard his head snapped back. Still dazed, he didn't struggle as she grabbed him by the collar and spun him against the hard stone wall. "Why are you following me?" she repeated, biting off each word.

The man knocked Jyn's hands aside and shoved her hard. She stumbled back, and Hadder leapt forward. "Leave her alone!" he shouted. The man actually laughed at Hadder's show of bravado. When Hadder swung at him, he dodged easily, wrenching Hadder's arm back and using the boy's body as leverage as he kneed his stomach. The second Hadder fell to the ground, groaning, the man stepped over him, advancing on Jyn.

She waited.

"Little spitfire, you," the man said. "Don't you remember your buddy Berk? Inusagi?"

"I remember," Jyn said, although she'd never been told the man's name before.

"Bygones be bygones," Berk said, turning back toward the main street.

Jyn shifted, blocking his exit. "You never answered my question."

"I get paid; I do a job. Ain't no harm to you. Now leave off."

"Someone's *paying* you to spy on me?" Jyn asked, her mind churning. Could it be . . . her father? Her father, who still worked for the Empire. Maybe he wanted out. Maybe he just wanted to know she was okay. Maybe he actually did care about her.

Berk shoved Jyn's shoulder, trying to move around her. She grabbed his arm, twisting him back. With a grunt of dismay, Berk forced Jyn around, trying to bodily move her aside, but Jyn was smaller and faster. She used his grip against him, dropping down and sliding a leg out so Berk fell like a stone. His head thunked against the pavement, and Jyn, still holding his arm, yanked back. "You little—" Berk growled, but Jyn didn't let him finish his sentence. She spun around, landing a knee in his chest so his breath was knocked out of him. In one fluid motion, she slid the knife from her boot and pressed it against his throat.

"Who's been paying you?" she asked in a low voice, her face centimeters from his, the blade a thin line between them.

"Saw, all right?" Berk spat. "Saw wanted to make sure you landed on your feet after the mess on Tamsye Prime."

Black spots danced behind Jyn's eyes. *Saw?*

Berk used Jyn's shock to shove her off him.

Saw's alive, Jyn thought, relief flooding through her. *And he sent Berk to find me.*

"Where is he?" Jyn asked, reaching for Berk again. He jerked away. "Take me to him!"

"He's not *here*," Berk sneered.

"When's he coming for me?"

"Ain't coming," he said. "Told me, 'Don't let her see you.' Just wanted to see if you were still alive, I guess? 'Sides, he has a new base now. Better. Bigger crew."

Not coming, a voice chanted in Jyn's head. *He's not coming for you.* A part of her had known this from the moment he'd told her to hide. Saw's paranoia had been growing slowly for years, and he had never been more paranoid than when it came to something associated with Galen. As soon as Reece had figured out Jyn's true identity, there was never any way he'd take her back.

"I'll tell him you send your regards," Berk snarled, walking away.

"He left me to die!" Jyn screamed at Berk's retreating back. "So I'm as good as dead to him. You tell him *that*!"

"Jyn?" Hadder asked, crawling over to her. "How did you—That was amazing!"

Jyn stared down at the knife in her hands. The one Saw had given to her. She dropped it as if it were covered in acid eating at her skin.

"Jyn?" Hadder asked again.

Saw was alive. And he didn't want her back.

CHAPTER THIRTY-ONE_

Jyn wrapped Hadder's injuries when they got back to the house. It was strange to spread out the medkit on the kitchen table, but that room also had the best light. "This will be sore for a while," she said, examining the purple-black stain of a knee-sized bruise blossoming on his stomach.

"Yeah," Hadder groaned. "At least he didn't kick any lower."

Jyn snorted. "Small mercy."

"Not small!"

Jyn shot him a smile, but it was gone the second she looked away and started cleaning up.

"You don't have a scratch on you," Hadder said.

Jyn didn't answer.

"You knocked that thug flat on his back," Hadder continued. "You knew exactly what to do."

"It was part of my old job." Jyn put the medical supplies away in the cabinet by the door. "My old life."

"What did you used to do?" Hadder asked. Then he immediately said, "I don't want to know. No, I do.

Maybe?" He took a deep breath. "Was it very bad?"

She met his gaze. "No," she said, thinking of doing something good, of fighting back. "Yes," she said, remembering Inusagi and Tamsye Prime.

"What did that guy want?" Hadder asked. "He said he was following you because of . . ."

"Because of Saw." Jyn slammed the cabinet shut.

"That's who you used to live with," Hadder said slowly.

"I know."

"You don't have to get mad at me."

"I'm not mad," Jyn snarled.

Hadder put both his hands up. "Okay, okay," he said. "Please don't kick my ass." When Jyn didn't move, he added, "That was a joke." And then, "But still, I'd appreciate it if you didn't."

Jyn finally cracked a smile. "I won't." She lunged at him, and he flinched. "Maybe."

"So," Hadder said slowly as Jyn sat down beside him. "Saw."

"Saw."

"Who was he? I mean, really?"

He used to call me his daughter, Jyn thought, *and then he left me behind.*

"You don't have to tell me anything," Hadder continued when Jyn didn't answer, "but I need to know—is this a problem? Are thugs going to start hassling Mum?

Because it has been made clear that I need to work out more and maybe learn how to throw a punch if that's going to be the case."

Jyn shot him a sideways smile. "I'll protect you," she said.

"Oh, whew." Hadder swiped at his brow. "I'm more of a lover than a fighter, you know, and I'm quite comfortable hiding behind you. Glad we sorted that out."

Jyn sank farther into her chair. "Saw took me in after I lost my parents," she said, looking straight ahead. She would never be able to get through this if she saw sympathy in Hadder's eyes. "He worked . . . against the Empire."

"In some sort of rebel group?" Around Skuhl, rebels were spoken of in an almost mythical way, a band of warriors who dared fight the Empire. The people of Skuhl had absolutely no concept of what fighting the Empire was really like, but to be fair, they didn't know what the Empire was really like, either. They existed in an almost childlike state where everything was black and white, a story to tell over drinks or by the bonfire, nothing more. None of the players were real; they were all just characters. Not people.

"Sometimes for groups," Jyn said. "Sometimes for himself. Saw didn't care who he fought beside, just who he opposed."

She risked a glance at Hadder. He was eating up

every word, as eager as she had been when she was a kid watching *The Octave Stairway* on the viewer.

"The last mission . . ." She looked away again, forcing her eyes and her mind to lose focus. "It went bad."

"Bad?" Hadder asked.

Jyn closed her eyes. She could see the line of green light as the Star Destroyer's beam sliced into the factory. She could taste the blood and dust in her mouth; she could smell the burning metal.

She could hear the screams.

"Bad," she confirmed.

"Tamsye Prime," Hadder whispered.

Jyn nodded.

"You were a part of the anarchists who attacked the factories?"

"It was the Empire," she said. She saw doubt in his eyes, and it killed her inside. "We were just there to look. A scouting mission. The Empire . . . it was done with the factory. And it had a message to send."

She watched as the truth settled on Hadder like a blanket around his shoulders. But she also knew he didn't understand, not really. And thanks to the Empire's lies, very few people in the entire galaxy knew what had actually happened on Tamsye Prime. The Imperials in the Star Destroyer. The pilot whose name she had never learned. Codo. Saw. Her. With Hadder's strength keeping her upright, Jyn felt strong enough to carry the weight of an entire planet's mourning.

Something changed after that night. Hadder joked that Jyn was strong enough to take him out, but the few times they ventured into town, he was on edge, looking over his shoulder. Looking out for her.

He must have told Akshaya about what had happened when she returned from her run; Jyn noticed the way Akshaya lingered by her door, as if she wanted to speak but wasn't sure of the words. She started painting more mandalas on the walls and floors of the little house, something Hadder said she hadn't done since her daughter died.

"They're beautiful," Jyn told her, but there was a twinge of guilt in her voice. She knew she worried Akshaya, and she didn't like bringing a shadow over the bright home.

"They're relaxing," Akshaya said, carefully drawing out a series of rays from a center circle on the floor. She didn't look relaxed. She was so focused on the drawing that her brow was furrowed, her gaze a laser beam trained on each line.

Jyn could understand this. She remembered just before her family moved from Coruscant to Lah'mu.

Mama had been full of frantic energy, just like Akshaya was now. Mama had cleaned everything, had taken Jyn to the park, had meticulously talked over her plans, softly, under her breath, so low she didn't know Jyn heard. Mama's plans were Akshaya's mandalas. Her love was boiling inside her and had to come pouring from her fingertips or it would overwhelm her.

Jyn watched her for several long moments. Hadder came in, interrupting the silence and his mother's concentration. "Dinner's ready in a few minutes," he said.

"I'll clean up," Akshaya replied, and Hadder left. Akshaya watched him go, her eyes soft. For the first time since she'd started working on the floor, she actually *did* look relaxed.

"I don't suppose you want to learn how to make mandalas?" Akshaya asked. "You're welcome to, you know. There's that whole wall in your room."

"I—uh." Jyn paused. She actually wouldn't mind learning how to draw the intricate designs, but she was afraid of ruining the blank wall.

"In case you change your mind," Akshaya said, pressing three paint sticks into Jyn's hand.

Jyn felt awkward lingering in the room, so she went back to her own. She sat down on the bed and stared at the blank wall. Akshaya had given her black, orange, and red paint sticks. She twirled the black one in her hands, contemplating a design she could cover the whitewashed wall with. She wondered if Akshaya's daughter had drawn mandalas on the wall and Akshaya had painted over them after she died. Or maybe her daughter hadn't bothered painting the wall at all. Maybe Akshaya wished she had, and the white wall reminded her of everything that couldn't be.

Jyn stood, the black paint stick in her hand, and she held it over the white wall. *A long swoop,* she thought, tracing a line with her eyes, *and rays made of red spiking out of it . . . tiny orange dots in between . . .*

But even though she could see the picture spreading out before her, she didn't touch the paint stick to the wall. She put them all in the box on the shelf, along with the empty hypo-injectors.

That night, Akshaya complained again that she'd lost another planet in her regular shipping run. "We're being bought out left and right," she said as Hadder scooped out bunn for their evening meal.

"The Empire?" Jyn asked quietly.

Akshaya didn't answer, which made Jyn certain her guess was right. "We're not that far away from Tamsye Prime and other Empire-run systems," Jyn said. "Just because Skuhl is in the Outer Rim doesn't mean it's going to be ignored."

"We're ants," Akshaya said, sighing heavily. "Giants don't notice ants."

"But—"

Akshaya shoved her chair back abruptly. "Come with me," she said, heading to the back door. Hadder and Jyn shared a confused, worried look, but they followed Akshaya outside.

Akshaya had her head tilted back, staring up at the stars. "What do you see?" she asked quietly when Hadder and Jyn approached. She was calm now, too calm.

Jyn looked up. "Stars," she said, confused.

"Stars," Akshaya repeated. "Where's Tamsye Prime?"

Jyn scanned the sky. All the white dots, impossibly far away, looked the same.

"Where's the Empire?" Akshaya continued. "Do you see it? Because I don't."

It doesn't work like that, Jyn thought. *Just because you don't see something doesn't mean it's not there.*

But Akshaya didn't look away from the stars. She kept staring, so Jyn directed her gaze back up, too. And she didn't see the Empire. But she thought she may have seen some of what Akshaya saw.

Up above, the stars seemed to stretch on forever. There were no clouds, no moons visible yet, just a million tiny dots of light. If she tilted her head back far enough, she could pretend the horizon wasn't there, only space.

There was something comforting in pretending

that there was nothing at all in the universe but her and the stars and the silence.

"Right, stars are far away," Hadder said. "Meanwhile, dinner's getting cold."

⬦

As the weeks turned into months and there was no sign of Berk or any of Saw's other contacts, Jyn almost let herself forget about the past. She continued working on new codes and permissions for the ship's ID chips to help Akshaya bypass any Imperial security but otherwise left behind everything she had learned from Saw.

Except the knife. Every morning, without fail, she weighed it in her palm and forced herself to remember the feel of the hilt in her hand, the pressure it took to break skin. And then she slipped it into her boot, making sure she could easily reach it if she needed to.

CHAPTER THIRTY-TWO_

"Where are you taking me?" Jyn asked.

"Don't you trust me?" Hadder turned, letting the ship veer south.

It had been more weeks than Jyn liked to count since she and Hadder had last been in the air. Akshaya was starting to have trouble with the shipment runs as more and more Imperial checkpoints were scanning ships and cargo in the area, which meant she was grounded, grumpy, and too present for them to sneak away on the planet hopper.

"Don't worry," she would tell Jyn every time the Empire came up. "We're ants, remember?"

Which wasn't really that much comfort to Jyn.

But Akshaya had gotten a new shipment order earlier that week, and she'd left on her run. And Jyn had known as soon as her freighter broke atmosphere Hadder would find a reason to take out the planet hopper.

"I trust you," Jyn said now, propping her feet up on the console, "to use any excuse you can find to leave

Skuhl. Which is why I have no idea why we're still planetside."

Hadder hummed to himself smugly. Jyn looked around for something to throw at him, but before she could find anything, the ship's nose started to dip. Jyn leaned up, looking out over the landscape.

"It's more grass," she said, unenthused.

"I didn't say it wasn't," Hadder said, initiating the landing sequence.

"You're being all secretive about where we're going, but it's just another field. With more grass."

"Isn't Skuhl lovely?" Hadder said, flipping the switch that lowered the gangway.

Jyn still felt anticipation curling inside her when she headed off the planet hopper, but as she looked around, she couldn't help being disappointed. Just as she'd seen from the cockpit window, there was nothing there but exactly the same type of field she'd seen every morning when she stepped outside her home.

"This way," Hadder called. He had a bundle of cloth under his arm.

Jyn followed him across the gently rolling field. A blue-green pond glittered in the blue-green grass, and Hadder spread out a blanket for them.

"We came all this way for a picnic?" Jyn asked, plopping down on the blanket.

"Such a pessimist." Hadder shook his head, smiling,

as he laid out their feast—sticky handfuls of bunn coated in seeds and a small steamer basket of dumplings.

Jyn claimed the dumplings, stuffing two into her mouth at the same time and chewing as she poured juice for herself and Hadder.

"Classy," Hadder said, smiling as he poked one of Jyn's stuffed cheeks.

"So why are we really out here?" Jyn asked after she swallowed.

"I've been thinking of joining a group that fights the Empire."

If there was anything Jyn hadn't expected, it was that.

"They'll let me fly. Mum still has the ridiculous notion that I'll get sick and die if I go out, but I'm old enough now. I've heard talk about a recruiter in the system. I could find him. Join up."

Jyn's stomach churned. It was hard for her to imagine Hadder fighting the way Saw did, but she could absolutely see him in a Z-95, shooting down TIEs.

"What do you think?" Hadder asked.

"Why are you asking me?"

Hadder looked at Jyn, surprised that she was confused. "Don't think I forgot the way you handled yourself in that alley. You never talk about your past, but I know you were a freedom fighter. What do you think about them? Should I join up?"

Jyn pretended not to care. "Do what you want," she said.

Hadder set down his plate and moved closer to Jyn so he was facing her, his fingertips centimeters from her knees. "I'm asking what *you* think," he said. "Could I make a difference?"

Jyn nodded mutely.

His eyes slid to a spot behind her, to the horizon and the sky. "Mum would hate it, but I could fly with them," he said, mostly to himself. "She's so in love with this idea of not being noticed by the Empire, but we both know that's not going to last." His eyes met hers again, and she saw something in them, something steely and fierce, and she knew if he joined this partisan group, he would be more than a pilot. He'd be a hero. "We can't sit around, hoping we're not stomped. We have to do what we can."

Jyn's eyes burned, but she didn't let herself look away. She had believed for how long now? More than a year. She'd been with Hadder and Akshaya more than a year, and she'd let herself believe, like Akshaya believed, that they could be safe and hidden and left alone. And together.

Hadder moved even closer. His hand was on her leg, his face so close she could feel his breath on her cheek. "If I joined the rebellion, would you come with me?" he asked, his eyes searching hers.

She swallowed, hard, and emotion boiled inside her. "I can't," she whispered. "I—"

A rare frown marred Hadder's face. "I thought—with your past . . . ?"

Jyn's eyes burned. "I don't want to go back to that. This is different, and that's *good*."

"You're sure?" Hadder asked. "You don't even want to talk to my contact?"

Something crackled in Jyn's heart—fear. "Your contact?" she asked in a cooler tone.

"Just someone I met at the diner. He was putting out feelers for people who may want to fly."

"Fighting the Empire is about more than flying," Jyn said. She drew away.

He closed the distance between them, pressing his lips against hers. The kiss startled her, but it felt natural, as if they'd been doing it for years. When he pulled back, he said, "If you're not going, then I'm not going. I'd rather have you than the chance to fly."

"I can't take that away from you," Jyn said.

"And I can't take myself away from you."

He kissed her again, harder, and she could taste the longing within him, the feelings he'd tried to keep in check. And she understood why he'd wanted to take her outside the town and away from their home to say this, to do this. They could be honest out there, under the open sky, in a way they never could with a roof over their heads. They could pretend they belonged to forever just as much as they belonged to each other.

A long time later, Jyn lay beside Hadder, watching as the clouds drifted farther apart. He played idly with her hair, rubbing the silky ends between his fingers.

A rustling in the grass nearby caught Jyn's attention, and she rolled over on the blanket, watching as a tiny brown creature crept forward. No bigger than her hand, the little mouselike animal had pale brown fur, a tiny pink twitching nose, and big black eyes, with a cute furrow in its brow that made it look comically worried.

"Hello, there," Jyn whispered lazily.

Hadder looked up, and his movement made the little animal dart several centimeters away, standing on its hind legs and scrunching its nose in concern.

"A bulba," Hadder said.

They watched as the bulba regained its courage, racing up and then halting again, tentatively touching the edge of the blanket with one tiny paw. Its long tail, covered in fine fur that ended in a tuft, curled around its body. Hadder reached over to the basket, plucked a handful of bunn from their reserves, and held it out for the bulba. It sniffed warily, then nibbled at a few grains. In moments, the bulba allowed Hadder to scoop his hands under it and lift it closer so Jyn could see.

"It's adorable," she said as the bulba stuffed grains of bunn into its cheeks.

"See this?" Hadder ruffled the fur on the bulba's back. The little creature shuddered but didn't pause eating. Jyn saw a tiny green vine stained with pink on the edges tangled in the fur along the bulba's spine.

"Bulba mothers always make a nest out of a dying vine that grows here," Hadder explained. "The seeds on the flowers of the vine plant themselves into the thin skin of the babies. They create a symbiotic relationship—the vines take root inside the bulbas. We had to dissect them in class. Bulba bones are incredibly thin. Here, feel."

Hadder dumped the little creature into Jyn's hands. It was practically weightless; her thin scarf was heavier.

"The roots wrap their way around the bulba's bones, giving them strength. Without the plant, this little guy wouldn't be able to live."

"Wow," Jyn said.

"It's a true symbiotic relationship. The plant's seed grows inside the animal, giving the animal life, because without it, it would never be able to survive. Once the bulba dies, new vines grow from its body, and bulba mothers turn their flowers into nests, which leads to a new generation being born and new seeds being planted."

Jyn stroked the fur of the bulba, feeling the tendrils

of the vine growing from its back. Its skin rippled in pleasure, and it chittered at her.

"I've been here almost a year, and I had no idea this little creature existed," Jyn said. She lowered her hands to the quilt, and the bulba scurried away once it was certain they were not going to give it any more food.

Hadder shrugged. "They're just rodents."

"They're amazing," Jyn insisted. "We spend so much time pushing the edges of our galaxy, jumping on ships to explore new planets, but we know almost nothing about each individual world. There is so much about each planet that's unique, that's special, and we ignore it because we're so busy trying to throw ourselves into space."

"To be fair," Hadder said, sweeping Jyn's hair off her shoulder so he could kiss her neck, "I'm much more focused on throwing myself at you."

Jyn playfully pushed him aside. "If you were so interested, why didn't you say anything sooner?"

"Because if you didn't want me, you would break my heart and potentially my body."

Jyn leaned in closer, her lips centimeters from his. "Who's to say I won't do that anyway?"

Hadder fell back onto the blanket. "You can do whatever you want to my body," he said, his hooded eyes gazing up at her.

So she did.

CHAPTER THIRTY-THREE_

It was dark by the time they got back. And Akshaya was there. Waiting in the hangar.

"I didn't take the ship offworld," Hadder said the second he saw his mother.

Akshaya cocked an eyebrow, and Jyn knew that for once she wasn't worried about his flying. Akshaya's gaze settled on Jyn, and she looked at her with evaluating eyes. Jyn hoped that she measured up.

"Why are you back so soon?" Jyn asked.

Akshaya's shoulders sagged, and she turned around, heading back to their house. Hadder shot Jyn a worried look as he hurried to catch up.

"Mum?" he asked.

She waited until they were all back inside before she spoke. "The Empire's cracking down. More than half the mines I usually ship for are now Imperial run."

Jyn sucked in her breath. She had suspected as much based on how little work Akshaya had been doing lately and how close they were to the Tamsye Prime system, but she had let Akshaya's confidence lull her into complacency.

"I wasn't able to bring back enough ore," Akshaya continued. Her eyes were red-rimmed and tired. "And there were Imperial officers at the refinery when I came in with what little I had for delivery."

Every nerve in Jyn was vibrating. She wanted nothing more than to run, right now, straight to a ship, straight to space. But she had Akshaya now, and Hadder.

She wasn't going anywhere. Not without them.

"I know some places," Jyn said in a small voice. "With your ship and my passes, we could . . ."

Akshaya was already shaking her head.

"Mum, we're not children," Hadder said. "We can fly. We're not going to die like Tanith."

"It's not that," Akshaya said. "We can't let the Empire run us out of business. I talked with Dasa at the refinery. She's not going to sell the operation. I'll just need to find new trade routes, different mines to work with."

Hadder was all nervous energy, stomping around the room. But Jyn was perfectly still. "The Empire doesn't work like that," she said.

Hadder kept pacing, but Akshaya's attention shifted to Jyn.

"If the Empire wants the refinery, it will have it," Jyn continued. "Not selling is not an option."

"The Empire's not the best," Akshaya admitted, "but they have to follow their own laws."

"No, they don't," Jyn said, but Akshaya ignored her.

"I'm going to the diner," Hadder announced, turning on his heel. Akshaya looked surprised but let her son leave the house.

"They don't," Jyn told Akshaya again, forcing her attention back to her. "The Empire . . . you're right. You were right all along. The Empire is the giant. And they're about to stomp on our anthill. The best thing we can do is leave."

Akshaya walked over, reaching for Jyn. She framed her face in her hands, her long cool fingers slipping into Jyn's hair. "This is *our* home," she said, as if that was reason enough. She pulled Jyn closer, kissing her forehead, and then she, too, left the room.

Jyn touched her face where Akshaya's hand had been. She had not missed the subtle emphasis on the word *our*.

And it broke her heart.

◈

Hadder didn't come back in the next hour, or the hour after that. Jyn wandered into the night to find him. Skuhl was silent, the stars stretching out forever and forever over the blue-green grass wafting in the wind. The bells lining the street jingled, and the only other sounds in the dark came from the diner. When Jyn pushed the door open, the warmth, light, and noise spilled out into the peaceful street.

It took her a moment to locate Hadder. He sat at a table in the corner, talking with a Twi'lek whose back was turned to her.

Jyn sat down in the empty chair at the table. "Xosad," she said, nodding to the Twi'lek, not letting on how surprised she was to see him again.

"Ah. The infamous Jyn."

Hadder looked from Xosad to Jyn, a little startled, but he hid it well.

"Infamous?" Jyn laughed. "I don't think so."

"Never thought I'd see you away from Saw's side." Xosad's voice was friendly, but Jyn knew that he was fishing for information. Saw was still out there, still doing missions, and she wasn't. He wanted to know why.

She wasn't going to tell him. "So you're the one encouraging people to fight the Empire." It wasn't a question.

"Clearly you've met," Hadder said somewhat nervously.

"Which group are you working for?" Jyn kept her voice cool, distant. A part of her wanted him to say that he worked for Saw. Another part of her feared that answer.

"The one Idryssa joined," Xosad said. "It's growing. A true alliance of fighters."

"Do you want some time alone?" Hadder asked. He moved to get up, but Jyn dropped a hand to his knee. He stayed sitting.

"Why?" Jyn struggled to maintain her even tone. What she really wanted to know was if Saw had joined this alliance, too, if all her old contacts had. Had Saw found a new family under their banner?

Xosad leaned back, choosing his words carefully. "I joined the rebellion," he said, "because I have seen the fulcrum upon which the fate of the galaxy is balanced. And the Empire weighed heavily on one side, and only the rebels really stood against it. I figured I could help restore that balance." He searched Jyn's eyes. "I have seen the *fulcrum*," he said again, stressing the last word, as if it had some deeper meaning. He waited, his lips barely parted, anticipation clearly painted on his face.

Jyn could tell that Xosad expected or at least hoped for some sort of specific response from her, but she had no idea what he wanted to hear. "Did Saw join as well?" she asked, not bothering to hide what she really wanted to know.

Xosad's shoulders sagged; he was disappointed by her answer. "He did some work with us, but he's still fighting his old battles, his way." He narrowed his gaze. "But you're no longer fighting Saw's battles with him," he said. "The rebellion is growing. There's good, solid leadership there. And people eager to join . . ." His eyes flicked to Hadder.

"I can't," Hadder said slowly.

Jyn looked around. The diner was loud, but it felt . . . wrong. "You're not very good at being subtle," Jyn said. Too many people were watching them but pretending not to. She stood. "Come on," she told Hadder.

"He's not your lap dog, trotting after you because you whistle," Xosad said, his voice low. He clearly had thought he'd made some headway with Hadder, then hoped to recruit Jyn as well. To watch them both dismiss him was a blow to his pride.

"Actually," Hadder said cheerfully, "I'm quite happy to follow her."

Jyn smirked at Xosad.

"Such a shame," the Twi'lek called loudly as they reached the door. Jyn froze. "All that training. You could kill any man in here and yet you just let yourself waste away in this provincial little—"

Jyn didn't let him finish. She whirled on Xosad, one hand gripping his lekku, pulling down enough that he had to crane his neck, her thumbnail digging into the soft flesh. He flinched, but otherwise didn't let anyone know she was hurting him. "You talk too much," she growled. "You always did. The Empire is watching this provincial little planet, you empty-headed moof-milker, and if you think they don't know exactly who you are and who you're reporting to, you're an even bigger fool than I thought."

She stood up, then flicked his lekku, pushing it off his shoulder. Xosad glowered at her but didn't respond to her show of disrespect.

Jyn stormed out of the diner, Hadder following at her heels. "You always have such interesting friends," he commented as she stomped down the sidewalk. "It must be your pleasant personality, the way you're constantly reaching out to new people with a smile and a laugh."

Jyn couldn't help chuckling. Under the light of the three full moons, she grabbed him by his lapel, pulled him closer, and kissed him.

"Oh, my delicate sensibilities," Hadder muttered, his lips a breath away from hers as she rested her forehead against his. "You are quite the corrupting woman."

"Shut up, you," Jyn muttered, pulling him in for another kiss, softer this time, gentle enough to let her pretend she wasn't afraid.

CHAPTER THIRTY-FOUR_

It started with stormtroopers. Their pure white-and-black uniforms shone sharply against the sleepy little town. They took over the diner. The Chagrian owner—his name, Jyn learned, was Gowayne—tried to protest the loss of his establishment, but then one day he was simply gone.

Dasa, the owner of the refinery, was an older human woman. She and Akshaya started talking. And then more people joined. The foremen, some of the workers.

"Please don't let them come here," Jyn begged. "Meet somewhere else. Let *them* meet. We should go. We have your ship."

Akshaya kissed Jyn on the forehead. "When the giant stoops down, even ants can win," she said.

"That makes no sense!" Jyn called after her as Akshaya went into the main room of their house, where the small group of dissenters met. "You realize that, right? That makes no sense!"

Hadder took her out on the planet hopper so they didn't have to be present while the refinery workers met. Jyn could tell he didn't like doing it—the only time he ever expressed a reluctance to fly. He wanted to sit by his mother; he wanted to feel like the words they said in secret mattered.

"The Empire thinks they can come in and just buy Dasa's refinery for almost nothing," Hadder growled, swiping at the long blue-green grass as he cut a swath through it. "Skuhl can't be bought."

"That's what I'm afraid of," Jyn muttered.

"Xosad hasn't left, you know," Hadder said, shooting Jyn a look.

"What's that supposed to mean?"

"He said he had friends. He said they could help."

Jyn wondered what Xosad's little rebel group was like. Idryssa had spoken of senators on their side, of larger players who could really make a difference. "I guess we'll see," Jyn said.

When they flew back to town that evening, a pair of assault tanks stood on either side of the main street and a walker guarded the spaceport, its two long legs bent backward and the command viewports protruding like eyes from the armor plating. Another walker rumbled toward Akshaya's hangar. Hadder landed the planet hopper and jumped out. Jyn stayed behind, hooking up her datapad to the mainframe of the ship's computer. She could hear Hadder's voice rising in volume; by the time she stepped out of the ship, he was shouting.

"You can't do that!" he bellowed. He caught sight of Jyn. "They say our ships are grounded."

"Come on," Jyn said gently, touching Hadder's arm.

"If you have an issue with Imperial policy, I can take you to see my commander," the stormtrooper said, his voice mocking.

Hadder opened his mouth, but Jyn pressed her fingers into his arm. "Come. On," she repeated, more firmly this time.

He followed her. "I don't know how you can stand to do it," he said, hissing angrily. "You could have taken him out. I know you could. You could be fighting back."

He didn't say it, but all Jyn heard was, *You* should *be fighting back.*

They stopped outside Akshaya's little house. Jyn stared into Hadder's eyes, hard, trying to see the things she had lost in them. "You don't understand," she said finally.

Hadder let out a huge breath, and all his anger and frustration left with it. "You're right," he said simply. "I don't."

That night, there was no meeting.

Dasa was gone. The foremen were gone. Imperial technicians now ran the refinery.

"I have all the critical documents from the ship," Jyn said, holding up her datapad. She downloaded information into two different port chips and slid one over to Akshaya. "I've forged clearance slips for the freighter and the planet hopper," she continued. "It won't be perfect, but it should enable you to at least confuse whatever blockade the Empire's set up around Skuhl and give you a chance to escape. We'll split up. You take the freighter; I'll take the hopper." The planet hopper only had a simple hyperdrive that couldn't handle more than a small jump, and without a navicomputer she would have to input the coordinates with the port chip. Jyn was still no pilot, but she knew enough about the little ship to get where she needed to go, and she knew Akshaya would never agree to be separated from her son.

Akshaya stared down at the chip. "They're not gone," she said finally. "Dasa and the others."

Jyn looked at Hadder, at the empty kitchen.

"They're not here," Akshaya conceded, "but they're not gone. I'm sure the Empire has them on a ship, for negotiations. Or something," she added lamely.

"Why are we splitting up?" Hadder asked Jyn.

"We need to start over. It'll be easier to do with two ships instead of one." Jyn slid her datapad over to him, showing him the system she'd preprogrammed into the port chip, along with their forged clearance codes. The Five Points system was close enough to Skuhl for the planet hopper to handle but had no mining or refinery resources that would interest the Empire. Furthermore, the entire system was littered with space debris, forcing ships to limp along from planet to planet in a series of short and inconvenient sublight speed routes. It was the perfect place to hide. There were five inhabitable planets, but Jyn had set the coordinates to the space station in the center. They could decide where to go from there.

Hadder took the port chip that his mother refused. He nodded at Jyn grimly.

"Tomorrow," Jyn said.

"We'll be ready," Hadder replied, even as his mother tried to say it wouldn't be necessary.

◈

Most of what Jyn needed she wore—the knife Saw had given her in her boot, the kyber crystal her mother had given her around her neck, the scarf to keep it hidden. Her satchel, stuffed with a few changes of clothes, a medkit, ration cubes. Only what she could carry.

It was too similar to Lah'mu. All of it. The storm-troopers. The fear. It was a nightmarish repetition of when her first family, her last home was taken away.

She planned to leave at dawn.

She hadn't planned on the stormtroopers attacking at midnight.

The door was kicked in. Jyn, already dressed, scrambled up. She cracked open her bedroom door.

"What is the meaning of this?" Akshaya cried, running forward. Hadder followed.

"We have reports that you are harboring a person of interest to the Empire," the stormtrooper said, his voice ringing.

"Are you saying my son is of interest to the Empire?" Akshaya asked, drawing Hadder closer to her.

"Someone of the name Jyn, last name unknown. Possible ties to a terrorist cell."

Jyn gently closed the door of her room. The only window was set high in the wall, and narrow, but she could squeeze through it. Akshaya was buying her time. She heard Hadder and Akshaya arguing with the stormtroopers, but before she was all the way out the window, she also heard the sound of smashing furniture and more doors being broken down.

Jyn threw herself out of the narrow window, landing

on the ground outside with a thud. She sucked in her breath but didn't make another sound. Stormtroopers were patrolling the perimeter of Akshaya's house and the hangar.

Through the open window, Jyn heard a stormtrooper reporting in. "She was here."

Jyn crouched under the window. How much did they know? It must have been Xosad. He had been so *obvious* that he was recruiting for an anti-Imperial group. And his little outburst as she left—definitely overheard. Maybe they thought she was working with him and his freedom fighters.

Or maybe they knew. . . .

She clutched her kyber crystal necklace through her shirt. They didn't know. They couldn't.

She heard footsteps—heavy, armored footsteps—making their way around the house.

No time to think. No time for regrets. She couldn't just sit and wait to be found. There was no Saw to save her this time.

Jyn leapt up and darted through the long grass toward the hangar. The walker was still positioned near the entrance, but it was powered down and, Jyn hoped, empty. She ran through its legs, making straight for the door.

"Hey! Stop!" a stormtrooper shouted.

Blaster fire marred the door seconds after Jyn dove

through it. So much for reaching the ship unnoticed.

Jyn hoped Akshaya and Hadder would take the opportunity she was about to give them. And she hoped whoever controlled the walker was still asleep.

The hangar door burst open as Jyn dashed up the gangway of the planet hopper. She yanked the port chip out of her pocket, then initiated the launch sequence of the ship. Blaster fire scarred the boarding ramp as she raised it. Jyn flicked on the rocket boosters, spraying fire. She couldn't hear the screams of the stormtroopers that had been rushing her, but she imagined them being cut short by the blasts.

Jyn didn't bother turning the planet hopper around. It had minimal charges that could be used to break up asteroids; Jyn fired them straight into the hangar wall, clearing a hole through the building. She rode high and hard, heading straight into the sky.

Jyn allowed herself one look down. Akshaya's little house was on fire.

But they made it out, she told herself. *They did.*

The walker lurched to life.

Jyn cursed under her breath as the walker's main cannons swiveled around, aiming straight for her. She spun the little shuttle in a loop, swerving out of range of the blast but almost losing control of the ship in the process. Hadder's quick flight lessons hadn't prepared her for a true space chase.

"That was close," she muttered under her breath.

Jyn looped back around, desperately scanning the ground for signs of Akshaya and Hadder. There. *There.* They were surrounded by stormtroopers, the cluster of their armor shining like a bright white patch amid the tall grass. Jyn swooped the planet hopper down, aiming straight for the ground. The stormtroopers tried to fire their blasters at the ship, but when Jyn didn't slow, they scattered like leaves on the wind. Akshaya and Hadder stood their ground, confident that Jyn wouldn't hit them. Jyn pulled the ship up moments later, and she grinned as she saw Hadder and Akshaya run straight for the hangar and the freighter.

The walker stomped through the grass toward Jyn. Aerial reinforcements would be there in moments, she knew. She could only try to draw away their fire.

She swerved down, moving in zigzags across the sky, maneuvering so it was hard for the slow cannons of the walker to follow. The scanner on the console started beeping, alerting her of more ships approaching. Jyn cursed again, loudly, her heart thudding in her chest, but a small part of her relished this, the chase, the danger. The fear made her feel alive.

An explosion on the ground filled the cockpit window with light. Through the smoke and flames of the overturned walker, Akshaya's freighter soared into the sky. The freighter had no cannons or guns, so Akshaya had simply rammed the Imperial machine.

"Hopper to freighter, hopper to freighter," Jyn said, flicking on the comm switch.

"The ship has a *name*." Hadder's voice came over the intercom, as casual and carefree as always. "*Ponta One* here."

Jyn whooped at the sound of his voice. "Let's get out of here, *Ponta One*," she said.

"Copy that, love," Hadder responded. She could hear the excitement in his voice, the thrill.

And then the TIEs arrived. Five of them, black against the night sky. The scanner came alive, sounding warnings.

"Straight to the port chip's location," Jyn shouted into the comlink. "Break atmosphere, jump to light-speed as soon as you can. Copy?"

"Copy." Akshaya's voice was strained, distracted. Jyn's planet hopper had less power than the freighter, but the freighter hadn't had a chance to get up to full speed, and it wasn't as nimble or easy to turn. Jyn swooped in, drawing fire from the TIEs, leading all the ships higher and higher.

Something silver and yellow flashed through the sky, zipping faster than the planet hopper could ever hope to go. Jyn grinned. She recognized the Y-wings from holos Idryssa had shown her. Xosad may have been in one of those ships, his so-called rebels in the others. At least five, drawing fire away from the civilian ships and Skuhl. A dogfight broke out, distracting the TIEs.

The Empire tried to hail both the planet hopper and the freighter, but Jyn didn't reply and the open comlink told her Akshaya didn't, either.

Laser fire streaked past Jyn's cockpit, a bright light against the blackness of space as she burst out of Skuhl's atmosphere. Beeping rang through the open comlink. Moments later, the TIEs and Y-wings streaked up and out, swarming like wasps, a blur of light and metal, yellow and black.

"*Ponta One*, you okay?" Jyn screamed into the mic.

"Go, go, go!" Hadder's voice urged her forward.

"It's getting hot out here," Akshaya said. A plasma blast fired close to Jyn, too close for comfort. She couldn't tell if it had been a stray shot from one of the Y-wings or a failed shot from a TIE, and she didn't want to stick around to find out.

Behind her, something exploded. The force of it pushed her little shuttle faster, but she was already slipping into hyperspace, the blue-gray light filling the cockpit window.

She had escaped.

MONTH 04_

Jyn's cellmate, Zorahda, curled up in the tightest ball she could manage. Her soft white hair was matted and dirty, and her big yellow eyes were on Jyn.

Jyn rolled over, but she could still feel Zorahda's gaze.

"What?" Jyn hissed at her cellmate.

Zorahda blinked. "How do you know?" she asked.

"Know what?" Jyn said in a low voice.

They waited while a stormtrooper patrolled the hall, his boots thudding on the metal floor. Jyn counted his steps until she couldn't hear them anymore.

"Know what?" she repeated.

Zorahda's look was sorrowful. "When to give up."

Her voice pitched a notch higher as she looked down at her own body, her knees pushed against the top of the cubby, her legs bent stiffly, her back curling just to fit her massive frame into the cramped space. "I'm *old*," she said. A sob choked her voice. "And my sentence is long."

Jyn knew she should say something. Words flooded her mind—words of her mother, talking about the Force; of her father, saying all he did was for her; of Saw and his impossible battles; of Akshaya and her impossible hope.

But all those words belonged to other people.

And now, in the dark, as she watched the hope die in her cellmate's eyes, Jyn found she had no words of her own to give.

❖

The next evening, Zorahda and Jyn were assigned to the same work detail, inserting stabilizers in the craggy canyons west of the prison. The Empire was going to build another factory, but the planet had been experiencing minor groundquakes. Jyn didn't like the job, but she did enjoy being outside.

Their transport took them twenty klicks south of the main prison compound, to a series of canyons that looked like the cracks in the crusts of bread Jyn's mother used to bake. The stabilizer units had to be inserted into the rock face at a horizontal angle, as deep as Jyn and her fellow prisoners could get them.

The stormtroopers stood watch as she and her fellow prisoners lowered themselves into narrow canyons, the crevices in the rock rough and jagged. They were never allowed any type of safety rigging. But Jyn was glad for Zorahda. Lunnixes were meant to be outside; being cramped in their tiny prison cell or behind factory walls surely didn't help her cellmate's depression. Not that there was much light from the sun; Wobani was covered in a thick cloud of space dust that rarely provided a glimpse through the atmosphere.

Jyn was grateful for Saw's training as she lowered herself, her tools strapped to her back, into the crevice. She kept her back against one wall and her feet in front of her, slowly inching down as far as she could, about twenty meters. The climb up would be worse; she knew from experience that her legs would cramp and her back would twist as she applied force to her tools against the hard rock wall.

She heard grunting nearby and saw Zorahda just a few meters from her, climbing down the canyon wall. She nodded to her cellmate; it was rare they were positioned so closely together.

Zorahda didn't nod back. She leaned as far against the wall as she could, staring up and up into the sky.

"You, there! Lunnix! Get to work!" a stormtrooper

shouted from the top of the canyon, pointing his blaster into the crevice.

"It never ends, Jyn," Zorahda said without turning to her.

Jyn could not deny the truth.

"You too! Work!" The stormtrooper swept his blaster toward Jyn, then back to Zorahda. "No talking!"

Jyn took out her laser pick and started scanning the rock face. The laser cut deep into the surface of the stone, then beeped in Jyn's hand, and she read the information. Jyn set up the impact hammer drill to start digging into the hard rock. The tool vibrated her very bones, and bits of rock flew back, cutting into her exposed skin. As soon as the hole was big enough, Jyn slid the stabilizer unit into the rock.

She started the tedious work of climbing back up the canyon. Jyn had to concentrate on her footing, and her back was slick with sweat. Dust caked her skin, streaking and then drying in the cooling air. By the time she reached the top, lugging the impact hammer drill behind her, she was bone weary. The light was fading, casting long shadows over the broken surface of the planet. Terms like *day* and *night* didn't really matter on Wobani; the prisoners worked fifteen straight hours and then ate and slept for eight more. Usually their shifts coincided with the sun, but sometimes they worked alongside droids at night.

"Hurry up, down there!" a stormtrooper called, leaning over the side of the canyon, where Zorahda was. Jyn moved closer.

Zorahda was still in the crevice, her laser pick loose in her hand. She hadn't even taken out her impact hammer drill. If she didn't hurry with her work, she'd receive a mark for top level.

Zorahda's yellow eyes looked up. Jyn thought maybe she was glaring at the stormtrooper and then maybe that Zorahda was looking at her, but she realized that the Lunnix was really just looking at the thick clouds in the sky, as if they had entranced her.

"Prisoner! To work! *Now!*" the stormtrooper shouted. Another stormtrooper moved forward, his blaster raised, his head cocked as he listened to orders from the warden.

"Zorahda!" Jyn yelled.

"What's the point?" Zorahda asked, looking back down at the rock in front of her.

"There is no point," Jyn whispered. The answer came to her immediately, slipping from her mouth before she could bite back the words, but it was true, perhaps the truest thing she'd ever spoken. There was no point. Not to the Empire that was mercilessly cruel for no reason. Not to the people who stood against the Empire, causing just as much destruction and death as the government they opposed. There was no point to loving family who left or men who died.

Lie, a voice whispered in Jyn's head, the word niggling through her brain. *Lie to her.*

Zorahda looked up, and Jyn could see in her cellmate's yellow eyes something that she hadn't seen there before. Determination. And with horror, Jyn realized just what Zorahda was determined to do.

Tell her there is still hope, the voice in Jyn's mind whispered. *Lie.*

Jyn opened her mouth, but no sound came out. Instead, the stormtrooper closest to her yelled into the canyon, "Get to work!"

There was a little sad smile on Zorahda's face. "No," she said simply, and she raised the laser pick to her own eye and depressed the trigger. For one brief moment, red light filled the Lunnix's skull, turning her other yellow eye orange.

Then there was no more light, but there was much more red.

Zorahda's blood splattered across the canyon wall behind her, smearing in her white fur as she slumped deeper into the canyon, her lifeless body wedging between the narrow stones.

"Right," the stormtrooper said flatly. "You, there, go down and get her gear." He pointed to Jyn.

Jyn's eyes blurred. It was this—this lack of human-ity, lack of respect for life itself—*this* was what had killed Zorahda.

"I said go." The stormtrooper pointed into the can-yon, at the red-smeared rock face.

Jyn's hands curled into fists.

But then her fingers grew slack.

She hadn't even been able to lie to Zorahda when she knew it may have saved her life. She couldn't lie to herself.

There was no point.

No hope.

Nothing at all but this: orders, and following them.

Jyn dropped her own tools and lowered herself into the canyon. As the other prisoners ate their allotted ration cubes and drank from the filtration canteens, Jyn sweated and grunted and worked her way down the wall. She tried to avoid the blood. When she reached Zorahda, her hands shook from exhaustion and emo-tion as she pulled the impact hammer drill from the Lunnix's shoulders and then reached for the laser pick still wrapped in her hand. Jyn blew out a shaky breath, unable to see properly through her tears.

She looked up.

And—for the first time since she had landed on Wobani—the thick clouds of space dust parted. For just a moment, she could see past the planet's atmosphere, into the night sky sprinkled with stars. They looked deceptively close.

But she knew it was simply a trick of the eyes. The stars *weren't* close together. Hyperspace made the distance seem negligible, but the truth? The truth was that the stars were separated by light-years. Each star was its own system, each planet its own world, each person in their own individual prison.

There was nothing connecting anyone.

Jyn's necklace pressed against her collarbone, reminding her of her mother. She closed her eyes and allowed herself a moment to remember Lyra Erso. The strong set of her jaw, her flashing eyes. She had promised Jyn that there was meaning to this life.

The Force, she had said, *connects us all. All living things. We don't always feel it, but we're connected.*

Jyn knew that her mother had meant for those words to give her comfort.

Hope.

But they were hollow, as dead as Zorahda. Jyn shook her head and got back to work, climbing up the canyon wall and leaving behind her cellmate.

There was nothing connecting anyone. The distance between stars was filled only with silence.

CHAPTER THIRTY-FIVE_

Jyn's planet hopper emerged from hyperspace with a stomach-dropping lurch. She didn't need the alarms blaring throughout the ship to know that something was wrong. She silenced them and flipped on the comlink for Akshaya's freighter.

Static.

They may have been delayed jumping to lightspeed, or the explosion that pushed Jyn's shuttle as she entered hyperspace may have set them off course. But Hadder and Akshaya had the port chip; they knew where to meet up. Meanwhile, Jyn had to dock as soon as possible, preferably before whatever had damaged her shuttle could leave her stranded.

Jyn checked out the ship's analytics; she was definitely leaking fuel. Not a good situation.

The Five Points system was a group of five small planets, closer together than normal. In the center was a space station, one that could not be reached by a direct hyperspace route, as the gravitational force of the star system constantly altered its location just enough to make it dangerous to approach too quickly, without the ability to alter course. Jyn set her course for the station. All the planets in the Five Points system were inhabited, but Jyn knew she'd find help more easily in the central station.

The space between the stars felt infinite. Limping to the station with no comms from Hadder and the warning lights blaring on the shuttle made Jyn paranoid. She paced the small planet hopper, praying that it held together at the seams long enough to deposit her somewhere safe. The Five Points system was far enough into the Outer Rim that the Empire hadn't quite reached there yet, but Jyn knew it was only a matter of time. The Empire spread and spread, like a Dothnian slime, creeping over every star system, infecting every planet.

If Skuhl hadn't been safe, nowhere would ever be safe.

The console in the planet hopper's cockpit was nothing but flashing lights and warnings by the time Jyn hailed the station.

"*Ponta Two* to Five Points station," Jyn said into the comm unit, hoping that at least worked.

"Five Points copy, *Ponta Two*. Our scans show ship damage." The voice sounded tinny, almost bored.

"Yeah, a little," Jyn said as another warning flashed across the main screen. "Permission to dock?"

"Granted."

Before the comlink severed, Jyn said, "Has an SC3000 freighter docked already? Its call sign is *Ponta One*. I was separated from my"—she paused—"family."

She waited on the edge of her seat. After a moment, the voice cracked over the intercom, "No record of SC3000 freighter on file, and I've certainly not seen one of those ancient rigs in a long time."

The station sent Jyn a landing code, and Jyn pointed the planet hopper to the waiting port.

"They're fine," she told herself.

There was an odd hissing, crunching sound as Jyn docked. A few port workers rushed forward, one with a fire extinguisher hose already foaming and pointing at the ship's hull. Jyn grabbed her few belongings and headed off the ship.

"Looks like you flew through hell," a port worker said as a droid linked into the ship's mainframe.

"Something like that," Jyn said. She stared at the planet hopper glumly. She'd hoped that when she, Akshaya, and Hadder remade their lives off of Skuhl, they'd be able to use the planet hopper to do smaller runs, diversify their income, or even sell it. It was worth nothing but scrap now.

"Docking fees are—" the port worker started.

"Take the ship." Jyn hated to say it, but whatever the fees were, she knew she couldn't pay them, and the ship wasn't worth it. She'd long before given Akshaya the credits she'd earned from selling the ship she'd taken from Tamsye Prime. Stupid. She should have asked for some back before they'd escaped, but it hadn't occured to her that they'd be separated.

The port worker marked something on his file. "Your comm indicated another ship was coming?"

"Yeah." Jyn squinted at the hull of the planet hopper.

"Will that ship be scrap as well?"

She shook her head. "There was an explosion as we entered hyperspace, and we were separated, but I'm sure everything's fine," she said slowly. She crept closer. The extinguisher foam was dissipating, exposing a chunk of metal that had ripped into the side of her shuttle.

"Names?" the port worker asked.

"SC3000, carrying Akshaya and Hadder Ponta," Jyn said. Her voice sounded hollow to her own ears.

The port worker noted the names. "Confirmed: no one by those identifications has docked here yet."

Jyn stepped past the droids clustered near the damaged hull. The metal embedded in the planet hopper was clearly a part of a ship, something ripped right off the side. The explosion . . . it must have hit another ship. But the metal wasn't black like the TIE fighters that had been chasing them, nor silver and yellow like the Y-wings.

The swath of burnt, shredded metal was roughly twice as big as Jyn, the steel twisted like a claw, curled into the planet hopper. And there was writing there. Half a handpainted mandala and the letters O-N-E. All that remained of the *Ponta One.*

"You'll need to register at the front desk," the port worker called to Jyn. "I'll put a flag on the names you said so you'll be alerted to your family's arrival. What was your name?"

Jyn looked up blankly.

"Your name?" the port worker pressed.

"Tanith," Jyn said absently. Saw had trained her too well to register her real name with any authority.

"Tanith Ponta," the port worker said, recording her name. "If you'll come this way."

The explosion that pushed her into hyperspace. Into safety. A ship exploding just behind her.

The *Ponta One.*

"Miss?" the port worker called. When Jyn didn't move, he approached. "Are you okay, Miss Ponta?"

Jyn nodded mutely.

He moved down the row, heading toward the arrival

station. Jyn followed, but she didn't hear any of his prattling. The droids walking across the metal surface of the docking port, the chatter of workers, the hiss of tools, the glugging of fuel lines. None of it reached Jyn. For her, there was nothing but the empty, gaping maw where her heart had been.

CHAPTER THIRTY-SIX_

The Five Points space station was designed like a fancy top, the kind Jyn had had when she lived on Coruscant. The wide center revolved around the axis like a gyroscope, and ships docked along the center pillar. After checking in with the droid at the entrance desk, Jyn was given a hundred credits—the worth of her broken ship in scrap metal, minus docking fees.

A giant banner emblazoned with the Imperial logo hung over the main entrance hall. Smaller posters called for volunteers to join the Imperial military, with information on how to reach the recruiter on the station. Jyn stared at the image of a proud stormtrooper bringing peace to the galaxy. She tried to feel . . . anything. But when she thought of the Empire—when she thought of the rebellion—she just felt numb. Their battle on Skuhl hadn't involved Akshaya and Hadder . . . and yet it had killed them.

Jyn wanted to hate the Empire. She could say all the words Saw had taught her, emulate all the old hates, but it was fake. She *didn't* hate the Empire. All she felt was *nothing*. The Empire hadn't killed Akshaya and Hadder. The Empire plus the rebels had. The damn rebels. If Xosad and his group hadn't shown up when they had, the Empire never would have knocked on Akshaya's door. And did it even matter whether the Empire or the rebels had fired the shot that blew up the *Ponta One*? In the end, Akshaya and Hadder were still dead.

And further back—Tamsye Prime. Would the Empire have destroyed the factories and towns had Saw not gone? Yes, Lieutenant Colonel Senjax had said that the Empire was done with production there, but it attacked because she and Saw had been there, because they were spying on the Empire. It was just as Akshaya had always said. The people of Tamsye Prime had been ants, ants the giants would have ignored. But Saw had made the giant stomp.

Jyn remembered one of the science experiments her mother had given her when she was teaching Jyn on Lah'mu. Lyra had held a bowl of acid and directed Jyn to pour in a chemical base; then they had watched as it fizzed and bubbled. The Empire was the acid; the rebels were the base. Separately, they were fine. When they met, they bubbled over into chaos and destruction and death.

Extremists were the problem. The rebels and the Empire, the people who couldn't exist without drawing lines and daring others to cross them. Jyn very consciously turned her eyes away from the Imperial banner. She was done with giants. She could be an ant.

She ran over her options as she was carried closer and closer to the top of the space station by the lift just past the entrance desk. A hundred credits. The clothes on her back and a small pack of supplies. At least on the station, she wouldn't need to worry about environmental hazards or dangerous animals . . . but beyond that, she couldn't really consider anything or anyone safe.

She'd heard Saw talk about Five Points before. It was a last-resort sort of place, a den of infamy where the Empire didn't rule; the gambling lords did. Bounty hunters often met there to pick up new jobs. The black market thrived.

Jyn tucked her hundred credits in a hidden pocket of her pants. They would not last long. She had to find food and a ship out of there. It didn't matter where.

The lift doors opened, and Jyn stepped into the station's main hub. Five Points was nothing compared with the city-planet of Coruscant, but it was a hundred times larger than the town on Skuhl had been. With a finite amount of space, the inhabitants of the station occupied every area. Living cubes were built all along the walls, so high that if she stood on top of them, Jyn's fingers could have brushed the ceiling. Despite that, many of the solar lights embedded in the metal ceilings were burned out—or perhaps just broken—casting the entire city into a perpetual twilight.

Someone bumped Jyn's shoulder, hard, and she scooted out of the main line of foot traffic. She leaned her back against the wall of a nearby shop, her eyes alert, watching the various types of people walking by.

"So I knew Crawfin was on my tail, yeah?" someone said in a deep voice. A large man with broad hands was talking animatedly to a Twi'lek. The Twi'lek kept her eyes on the ground, not on the man who was clearly trying to impress her. "So what did I do? What'd I do? I took my ship straight into Smuggler's Run. Knew he couldn't catch me there. Hid out, caught a hyperspace route, and here I am." The young man puffed out his chest.

"Uh-huh," the Twi'lek said, glancing at the comlink strapped to her wrist.

The couple continued down the street, but Jyn bit her lip, thinking. Smuggler's Run . . . She could use some of her credits to comm Saw. He owed her.

She snorted at her own stupidity. She could no more contact Saw than she could her father. Both men had proven exactly where their loyalties lay. Her father cared more about his science and the Empire than about her. And Saw cared more about himself.

Jyn scanned the crowd again, though, half wondering if Berk, the man Saw had hired to spy on her, was out there. Her hand went to her hidden pocket, the hundred credits. If Saw knew . . .

He left me to die, she told herself.

She could still smell Tamsye Prime, burning.

No Saw. This was just Jyn being weak. Her home on Skuhl had been destroyed by the Empire much like her home on Lah'mu had; stormtroopers had invaded like parasitic space ants, eating away at another place she had felt safe. Saw had saved her once. But she would never ask for his salvation again.

She pushed off the wall, heading aimlessly down the street, absorbing Five Points. She chanted in her head with every step the things she needed: *food, shelter, a ship off this place.* Food. Shelter. Ship.

Saw may not have been the answer to her problems, but at least his training would come in handy. At the heart of every punch and each cold night, he had been teaching her how to survive in this galaxy. Food. Shelter. Ship. *Survive.*

She needed a job. Anything would do. Well—not anything. Not yet anyway. But definitely something. She could forge Imperial freight route passes—that could work. There had to be a demand for those, considering the new blockades and checkpoints.

She felt the brush of a touch on her hip, near her pocket, where her only credits were. Instinct took over; she snatched the slimy wrist of a Caldanian and twisted it away from her. The Caldanian cried out in pain, a gurgling, low sound, and Jyn tightened her grip.

"Let go of my man," a Gigoran said. His translator was old and broken, the words barely understandable through the crackle in the speakers, further drowned out by the respirator he wore over his mouth.

What an odd pair, Jyn thought, evaluating them. The Gigoran's long, fine white fur was matted and dirty but still stuck to the Caldanian's dark-brown, slimy skin. Tendrils of the Gigoran's fur clumped around the Caldanian's elbows and in the hollow spaces that encircled his long neck.

The crowd drifted apart, leaving Jyn, the Caldanian, and the Gigoran in a pocket of space between a wall and a dead-end alley. Jyn could potentially burst past the two and into the crowd, but she was fairly certain that would do her no good. Not there. She couldn't see them, but there were surely others watching like carrion birds, waiting to see whom they could pick off next.

Jyn cracked her knuckles as the Gigoran and Caldanian grew closer. Fine. She was going to have to rely on Saw's other lessons on survival.

The Caldanian struck first, which Jyn had been fearing. Caldanians didn't have bones, just a flexible cartilage that they could change the rigidity of. The surface of their skin was also covered in a tacky mucus that could potentially slow her down. She needed to strike hard and fast, and she couldn't waste time getting too close.

Jyn pressed her fingertips together against her thumb, forming a hard point with her fingers, reared back with all her strength, and jabbed her hand straight into the Caldanian's wide left eye. He screamed in pain, dropping back. Jyn's fingers were coated with sticky mucus, but the Caldanian was too distracted and in pain to fight. The Gigoran shouted as he raced toward her, but Jyn dropped to the ground, kicking out to trip the large furry creature while reaching for her knife in the other boot. When she jumped up, the Gigoran had already spun around to face her, and the Caldanian was standing again, his eye turning blue around the rim.

Jyn flashed her knife blade, shifting it from one hand to the other, hoping it would be enough to scare off her two attackers.

It wasn't.

They rushed her simultaneously—clearly they'd fought together before—and Jyn slashed wide. She cut the Gigoran's shirt and fur, but she didn't see any dark blood splatter across his long white hairs. The Gigoran's beady eyes narrowed, but Jyn didn't have time to focus on him; the Caldanian had wrapped a slimy arm around her throat and started squeezing.

The Gigoran laughed at Jyn and pulled out a small blaster.

"We were just going to take your credits," the Caldanian snarled in Jyn's ear. "But you poked me in the eye. That was rude. Wasn't it rude, Bunt?"

"Rude," the Gigoran agreed.

Jyn didn't bother replying. She shifted, and thinking that she was trying to escape, the Caldanian tightened his grip around her neck.

Jyn stabbed him in the arm.

The Caldanian let go, howling. The Gigoran, distracted by his friend's injury, didn't shift the blaster in time as Jyn lunged for him. Blaster fire scarred the resident cube behind Jyn as she slammed into the Gigoran. She wrapped her left hand in his long white fur, yanking hard enough to jerk his head around. She balled her other hand into a fist and slammed it into the Gigoran's face, aiming for his beady eye. She felt her knuckles crunch against the Gigoran's hard skull, but she punched him again, hoping to daze him. She grabbed his wrist, pressing hard and then slamming it against the pavement until the Gigoran's fist opened and the blaster fell.

Jyn let go of the Gigoran and grabbed for the blaster. As soon as her hands were off him, the Gigoran kicked away, scooting down the alley. He made a run for the crowd, the Caldanian on his heels.

Jyn cursed under her breath. She had liked that knife, and it was still sticking out of the arm of that slimy Caldanian.

At least, she thought, *I got a blaster out of the trade.*

CHAPTER THIRTY-SEVEN_

Jyn hid in a nearby bathroom stall and pulled out her credits, counting them one by one, just to be sure they weren't gone. One hundred Imperial credits.

She noticed the Imperial cog on the front. She had thought Five Points station wasn't under Imperial control—and she was mostly right, judging from the heavy presence of gambling halls. But she'd seen a flash of black-and-white armor on some street corners, especially in the center of the station, where the more elite lived. No one wanted to be near the walls.

In the end, it didn't really matter. She couldn't go to the Empire for help—that was obvious—but she doubted they cared about her, either. She was still an ant. At the attack on Skuhl, they had come for her, but they hadn't known her last name. Just that she had ties to "terrorists." Maybe Xosad had given them her name. Maybe Berk had, or someone else in town who just didn't like her. It didn't matter—what was important was that they had been after "Jyn, last name unknown." Not Jyn Erso. And besides, now she was Tanith Ponta.

What would happen if she went back to her father? The Empire had killed her mother but just taken her father. He was their golden boy, and he seemed to relish that status. Could she be afforded the same luxuries he had been? Another apartment on Coruscant, another Mac-Vee, another chance?

Jyn shoved her hundred credits back in her pocket. Even without them, there was no way she was going back to him or that life. Not while she still wore her mother's necklace.

One hundred credits. She had to make it last. But first: food. Jyn slipped out of the reeking public bathroom stall and headed deeper into the station. She clung to the outer perimeter of the main floor, where the shops were smaller but cheaper. A bodega built between two towers of residential cubes looked local enough not to extort her too badly. She bought a can of nutritive milk that was dusty on top and a tube of dehydrated vegetable protein straws. Not the tastiest but definitely the healthiest, most filling option; this would last her the whole day if she was careful. Food was important. Hunger would make her careless, an easy target. Food and sleep were vital to survival.

Ninety-four credits left. After jamming a bland protein straw in her mouth and choking it down with the slightly chunky nutritive milk, Jyn headed to the midrim of the station. The gambling halls went from flagrantly touristy to elite houses of decadence within just a few blocks. The games played were mostly the same on the ground floor of each hall. Sabacc, chance cubes, wheels of fate. Jyn ventured into a few of the halls, enticed by the promise of free liquor and meals, but it was quickly apparent that nothing in those places was free, and Jyn wasn't willing to risk her credits on a chance. Especially since the gambling halls used their own specialized credit chips, and she was willing to bet the conversion rate wasn't that great.

Still, she logged the gambling halls in the back of her mind. There was a way to make money there; she just had to figure it out.

But first, she needed better weapons. The blaster she'd taken from the Gigoran wasn't in the best condition. Actually—she cursed—it wasn't holding a charge. A short circuit somewhere. Dangerous. It could overheat or, worse, not fire when she needed it. Jyn headed to a shop with used weapons in the front.

"How much to fix this?" she asked, plunking it down on the counter.

The Kath picked it up with a look of disdain on his scaly face. "More than it's worth," he said, tossing it back on the counter.

Jyn had figured as much. She glanced through the

shopkeeper's cases. Any blaster was out of her price range. Instead, she pointed at a set of extendable truncheons. "Those?"

The Kath pulled out the batons for Jyn to examine. She flicked them open in her hands, extending the collapsible truncheons to their full length, the solid krallian core locking into place. She whacked one in her palm, testing the weight.

"Yes," Jyn said. "How much?"

The shopkeeper stated his price in a bored but firm tone, indicating there was no chance to haggle for a better bargain.

Jyn hefted the pair of truncheons in her hands again. Quiet. Discreet. No one would ever think that a girl like her could do any damage at all with a set of weapons like this. Meanwhile, she knew the damage she could do. The truncheons didn't look like much. *Neither do I,* Jyn thought.

She paid the shopkeeper and strapped the truncheons to her back. She kept the blaster, despite its malfunction, strapped to her hip. It would be the weapon people went for, if they bothered her. It would be the thing they would watch. They wouldn't think anything of the truncheons, and that would be her saving grace.

Eighty-six credits left, Jyn thought as she left. She had never worried about credits as a child. Her parents had always had enough for her. She didn't worry about credits when she was with Saw, because they rarely had any to worry about. But now that a pocketful of credits was all that stood between Jyn and starvation, they felt hugely important.

Jyn kept walking. The problem was, she wasn't very sure what to *do*. Without Hadder or Akshaya, she had no goal. Without a ship, she had no escape.

Near the center of the station was a small park. Fake greenery sprouted from fake rocks, and recorded nature sounds wafted from cleverly hidden speakers. A group of various specics huddled near the larger rocks, their palms held outstretched over their knees, their heads tucked down. Jyn wondered how long her eighty-six credits would last. If she would ever have to supplicate by the fake rocks and hope for enough to survive another day.

As she watched, an Imperial officer strolled by. He looked down at the beggars, but then he paused, reaching into his pocket and pulling out a single credit that he dropped in the outstretched hands of a young woman with a child leaning against her. The child whispered her thanks.

After the officer had left the park, a different man cut across the path, kicking at the woman's feet. She curled into herself like the petals of a daybloom when the sun sets, pulling her daughter under one arm. She didn't lift her head.

"You should be ashamed of yourself," the man spat at the woman. "Taking an Imperial's money. Disgusting."

He glared at the woman, but when she didn't so much as look up, he growled and stormed off. Jyn watched him leave the park, agape. If, in the next week, she had to sit beside that woman and beg, she would not turn down Imperial credits. And she had absolutely no shame about that.

As she headed out of the park, she considered giving a few of her credits to the beggars. She didn't. And she had no shame about that, either.

⬧⬧⬧

A pickpocket had stolen her pouch of protein straws. Jyn didn't realize it until near the end of the day, when the lights of the station blinked, indicating that twelve standard hours of daytime were up and work shifts should change. In the bustle of people leaving their jobs and heading to their resident cubes, Jyn had been caught up in the crowd. By the time she was free, she found the small pouch of food was missing. Her hands shook as she checked her weapons, her hidden pocket of credits. Nothing but the food was taken; that, at least, was a small blessing.

Still, she had to spend another six credits for more.

The night shift seemed no different from the day

shift. The overhead lamps still burned; the businesses stayed open. But the people seemed different. Harder. Jyn started recognizing the same faces over and over in the crowd, and she realized she was being tailed. Three human men. Her nerves were flayed; her body ached with walking in circles around the station. She couldn't trust herself in a fight, not like this. She couldn't trust herself to sleep alone, either, not with the three men watching, waiting.

Maybe they just want to rob me, she thought. But she couldn't be sure.

An inn had rooms for rent, and Jyn passed over more of her meager supply of credits.

Sixty-seven left. But the men didn't follow her inside the inn, and although she had to share a shower and toilet, the room she would sleep in had a locking door. Jyn collapsed on the pallet on the floor, one hand on the blaster, one hand wrapped around her body. She didn't take off her clothes.

❖

Jyn awoke early. She stared at the dark ceiling in the cramped room. For the first time since she had arrived on Five Points, it was silent. No voices from next door, no bustle from the streets outside. Utter silence.

Her near-constant inner dialogue—*food, shelter, a ship off this place*—had quieted as well. Without the noise outside and inside to distract her, an aching sorrow swept into all the hollow places that she wanted to ignore.

Akshaya was gone.

Hadder was gone.

It wasn't the loneliness that clawed into her now. She knew loneliness; she understood that old wound. It was the deep, infuriating *injustice* of it all. The impossibility of changing what had happened. The knowledge that all she had felt for Hadder had amounted to . . .

Nothing.

Jyn curled up on her bed, pulling her knees to her chin, as if compressing her body would lessen the emptiness inside her. A sob burst out of her mouth, and she swallowed air, and then she was gasping, her shoulders shaking, desperate for breath. It felt as if her ribs had collapsed. She couldn't breathe. She couldn't think. She could only sob, muffling her sorrow with the musty-smelling pillow as she rocked back and forth, weeping until she fell back asleep, exhausted from grief.

◈

The innkeeper walked up and down the hall of rooms, banging on the doors with a heavy stick. Time to go.

Jyn scarfed down a breakfast of bread that was offered to all the nightly guests. It wasn't much—mealy and dry. But it was something.

"Stay another night?" the innkeeper said, the loose skin of her arms slapping against her torso as she walked among her lingering guests. "I give discounts."

She paused by Jyn. "Need a place, sweetheart?" she said in her low, gravely voice. Jyn wondered what her species was; she had never seen anyone like the innkeeper. Short and skinny but with loose skin all over and comically large feet.

Jyn shook her head. She needed to figure out where she could sleep, but she couldn't afford to continue sleeping there. And she didn't want to guess in what ways the innkeeper would make her pay her bills when the money ran out.

Jyn knew if worse came to worst, she could sell something. The only things of value she had were the necklace her mother had given her and her weapons. She needed the weapons.

Her hand went to her neck, fingering the leather cord the kyber crystal hung from.

The innkeeper started clearing away the bread dishes and empty cups, her scowl a clear indication that it was time to move on. Jyn kept her eyes on the HoloNet display, pretending not to notice, relishing the chance to just sit and think. Her gaze drifted to the bottom of the viewscreen, to the running ticker of local news. There didn't seem to be that much. An advertisement for a special deal on credits at one of the gambling halls. An announcement for a stormtrooper formation exhibition happening in three standard days. Notices of jobs—none of which Jyn was qualified for. She started to look away, but then she noticed a name she knew.

Ponta, report to main processing unit on level TJ56.

"Time to go, sweetheart," the old woman who ran the inn said, plunking down the dirty dishes she'd been carrying.

"Yeah," Jyn said absently, looking past the woman's shoulder.

" 'Lest you pay me for another night, get out," the innkeeper said, her voice sterner.

"I just want to read—"

"Ain't free. Go." There was steel in the old woman's voice. The ticker display had cycled around and was showing the advertisement again; it would be several minutes before Jyn could get back to the name Ponta.

The woman pushed Jyn out of the chair. "Fine!" Jyn roared. "I'm leaving."

Jyn stormed out, her mind churning. Someone named Ponta was to report to the main processing unit, where everyone who docked at the station checked in.

She felt her heart thudding with hope. Akshaya or Hadder—maybe both—was still alive.

CHAPTER THIRTY-EIGHT_

Jyn took the lift to level TJ56. There was a line at the main processing unit, despite four droids working. Jyn stood to the side, scanning the crowd for Akshaya's bright scarf or Hadder's black hair. Her eyes darted from person to person, hope surging inside her with every blink. Ponta . . . someone named Ponta was going to report to this desk.

After nearly an hour had gone by, Jyn's hope was turning to anxiety. Maybe the ticker had given a specific time and Jyn hadn't noticed it? Maybe she was at the wrong desk.

"Miss?"

Jyn's blood turned to ice as she faced the Imperial officer looking down at her. Tall and thin, the female officer had a cold look in her eyes. Her coarse black hair had been carefully braided and bound in a bun at the base of her neck, and her dark skin blended with the black uniform.

"Yes?" Jyn asked, forcing her eyes to look innocent, her hands to stay away from her weapons.

"I couldn't help noticing you've been lingering here. Are you waiting for someone?"

"Um . . ." Honesty was probably the best option; the request that a person named Ponta show up at the desk was public, so it wouldn't look strange for Jyn to say it. "I saw on the HoloNet that Ponta was supposed to report here?"

The Imperial officer's face lit up. "Tanith Ponta? Is that you?"

And every single hope Jyn had for Hadder and Akshaya's return crashed. She'd forgotten that the name she'd given when she'd landed was theirs. The processing unit had been looking for *her*.

"Yes," Jyn said, wary but too tired to think of a lie.

"How fortuitous," the officer said.

Jyn shot her a questioning look.

"Because I was the one requesting your presence." The officer swept her arm out, and Jyn had no choice but to follow her to a private office down the hall.

Stupid, stupid, stupid, she chanted to herself. The Empire had simply posted her pseudonym, and she'd *shown up*. Saw would be apoplectic to see how easily she'd done the Empire's bidding.

The office the Imperial took Jyn to was large, and furthermore, it had a window looking out at the expanse of space. A bright glowing star was perfectly framed in the square, and Jyn suspected it was actually one of the five planets in the system.

"Yes, I'm lucky," the officer said, following Jyn's gaze. "I understand why the main level of the station doesn't have portholes, of course, but it lowers morale, don't you think?"

Jyn shrugged in a noncommittal way.

"Tanith Ponta . . ." the officer said, reading the datapad in front of her. "I'm Commander Lucka Solange."

"Why am I here?" Jyn asked. She felt stupid, and that made her angry. Also, she was talking to an Imperial officer, something that always made her want to punch things.

"You arrived on a planet hopper, *Ponta Two*, yes?"

Jyn nodded, one short, sharp dip of her head. No use denying it. It was public record.

"That ship was labeled irredeemable and reclassified as scrap. Before scrapped ships are processed, I inspect them. That is part of my duties here on this station."

"I didn't know the Empire had official duties here," Jyn said. Also true. If she had known, she never would have come.

"The Empire," the commander said, "is everywhere."

Jyn had no reply to that.

"In my inspection of the remains of your ship, I couldn't help discovering that some elements were not exactly *authentic*," Commander Solange continued. "A less forgiving person might even label your ship's permissions and identification codes as forgery."

Jyn waited, fear coiling around her anger.

"Can you tell me who did these . . . alterations?" Commander Solange said, finally sitting down in the chair across from Jyn.

"No." Jyn bit off the word. The less she said, the better.

Commander Solange narrowed her eyes. "That is indeed a shame," she said. "You see, I have . . . use for such a person and her skills. But if you cannot help me, I'll be forced to arrest you for possession of forged documents."

Jyn's head spun. Commander Solange held a communicator but hadn't turned it on. She was waiting. She knew.

"And if it was me?" Jyn asked.

"Then I would be happy to send the ship on to the scrappers and conveniently forget about what I saw on board."

"For what price?" Jyn asked. There was always a price.

Commander Solange leaned over her desk, evaluating Jyn. "I saw the recording of your arrival," she said finally. "I have to say, I had my suspicions that you were skilled enough to have done the forgery. It's very good. Some bits were outdated, of course—the Empire is on to you rogues—but it was very good. And you seem young."

It took Jyn a moment to remember how old she was, and she was surprised to realize that she'd missed a birthday. Eighteen years. Keeping track of her age seemed like such a simple thing, but she'd legitimately forgotten about it.

"But I've been following you. No, not in person," Commander Solange waved her hand when Jyn looked startled. "I've been watching the feeds from the camera security droids. You know how to handle yourself. You seem . . . *scrappy* enough to handle the job I need you to do."

"What is it?" Jyn asked, impatient. She didn't like the way this commander talked, as if each word she spoke needed to be tasted and relished and a sentence wasn't complete without dropping subtle emphasis.

Commander Solange stood up and moved over to her window, staring out into space. "I *hate* it here," she finally said, more emotion in those four words than in anything else she'd said. "The people are crude savages, no one of any importance comes to this station, and it's *boring*." She turned around, meeting Jyn's eyes. "So boring, in fact, that one is reduced to visiting the gambling halls."

Jyn leaned back in her chair. The picture was becoming clearer now.

"I've fallen into a spot of trouble. I'm in a bit too deep."

"How deep?" Jyn asked.

The commander said a number that made Jyn's eyes go wide.

"Exactly," Commander Solange continued. "Too deep for me to work my way out. If I don't pay off my debts, the gambling lord will start extorting me. Or he'll report my debts to my supervisors. I very much do not want a few misspent months on this hellish station to ruin my entire career." Her voice grew angrier, and by the time she finished, she was actually snarling.

Ah, there it is, thought Jyn. *This is what makes her an Imperial.*

"I don't see how I can help you," Jyn said.

Commander Solange turned to her desk, ripping open a drawer and dumping a handful of credits on the surface. Jyn reached out and picked one of them up. It was as long as her finger and three times as wide, the front decorated with the words PSO'S PALACE and a silhouette of a Twi'lek dancing.

"The gambling halls all use their own currency. I

don't know why," Commander Solange said, waving her hand dismissively.

Jyn could guess why. It was easier to spend these credits, which looked almost like toys, than real credits. And it was probably a pain to cash out, meaning it'd be simpler to stay in one gambling hall for a night than to move around to multiple ones.

But then it hit Jyn what Commander Solange was asking her to do. "You want me to forge credits?"

The commander nodded.

"Counterfeiting these would be as difficult as counterfeiting real credits," Jyn said, analyzing the gambling hall chip.

"Not really," Commander Solange said. "There is less security on one of these. The Empire is *slightly* better at protecting its funds." Her voice dripped with sarcasm, but Jyn had to admit that she was right.

"If I'm caught, the gambling lord will—"

"I'll protect you," Commander Solange said, but they both knew that wasn't true. If Jyn was caught, she'd be on her own.

"It's too obvious if you just show up with a pile of chips and pay off your debt," Jyn said, thinking aloud.

"So make me a portion of them, and I'll win my way out of debt." Commander Solange's voice was impatient. She leaned over her desk again, closer to Jyn this time. "Will you do it?"

Jyn's hand tightened around the chip. "I'll need supplies," she said. "And payment."

"Clearing your name of possession of forged documents is payment enough." Commander Solange narrowed her eyes.

"No, it's not," Jyn said. "I want a thousand credits."

"A thousand?" Commander Solange laughed.

"That's a fraction of your debt. A fraction of what I'll be counterfeiting for you. A thousand."

"Fine." Commander Solange waved her hand again. "But do it quickly."

"I also need a place to work." Jyn spoke in a rush. She was pressing her luck, and she knew it.

Commander Solange cocked her head. "You can work here. I have business on Uchinao; I will be gone for a week. You may use my office. There's a suite there that's stocked with whatever you might need. We have a deal?"

Jyn's mouth slid into a smile. "Deal," she said, shaking the hand of the Imperial officer.

CHAPTER THIRTY-NINE_

It was little wonder why Commander Solange had been assigned to Five Points station. There was nothing there that the Empire wanted, so it didn't matter that she was utterly incompetent at her job.

Once Commander Solange had set Jyn up with all the supplies she needed, she left, stating clearly when she'd be back and that all droids and other officers had been banned from her office. As long as Jyn was quiet, she'd be fine. Jyn waited several hours and immediately turned to Commander Solange's databanks. She was no slicer, but it was easy to break through the commander's meager protections and scan the least secure files. She flashed everything to a portable datapad she stole from the commander's office. Maybe Commander Solange had thought that Jyn's forgery skills were outdated, but Jyn had just downloaded clearance codes for any ship she wanted to steal in the future.

It'd be easier to get paid than to steal a ship, so Jyn focused on the task at hand. Forging the Pso's Palace credit chips didn't prove as difficult as she'd feared.

A replicating holograph provided her with the casing image, and while the internal security of the chips was complicated, it was nothing that a little patience couldn't solve. Jyn created a pile of Pso's Palace credit chips, all of varying amounts, and even scuffed them up to make them look older and used.

As with any counterfeit, a close examination of the credit chips would prove these were false. But Jyn had had Commander Solange buy up a couple thousand legitimate chips, and when she mixed them together, it was impossible to tell which were real and which were not by sight or scan.

When Commander Solange returned, the chips were done. "Oh," she breathed. "These are marvelous."

"Remember the plan," Jyn said. It was Commander Solange's own strategy, but she didn't seem eager to follow through. "Use these to win a little. Stick to games of skill, like sabacc, and not just chance. The wheel of fate never plays outside the house's favor."

Commander Solange nodded, but she was distracted, her eyes glued to the credit chips.

"A little at a time," Jyn reminded her. "Don't blow it all at once."

"If I do, you can just make more," Commander Solange said.

"That's a bad idea," Jyn snapped back, but she wasn't sure the commander heard her. Flood the gambling hall with fake chips, they were sure to be caught. The whole scam relied on Commander Solange winning in a slow and steady way.

"Right, well," Jyn checked her own credits—real, Imperial credit chips. Commander Solange had paid her a thousand credits, as promised. "I'm gone."

"Not off the station," Commander Solange called.

"What?" Jyn whirled around. She'd intended to use the credits to buy passage on a ship—any ship.

"At least for a few standard weeks," Commander Solange continued. "I've banned your scandocs from leaving Five Points, and I've posted your picture in case you try to bypass that. Must be sure this works and that I have no future use of you." She tossed Jyn a communicator. "Just in case."

Jyn ground her teeth. There was no point arguing. This was what you got when you dealt with the Empire.

⬦

Jyn rented a bedroom from an older man near the wall of the main floor of the station. He left her to her own devices, and the rent was both cheap and accepted on a weekly basis. Vegetable protein straws and nutritive milk was a bland diet, but it kept Jyn from bleeding funds. She only had to survive a little while longer, and she could escape.

The communicator, obviously, had a tracker in it.

Jyn popped it open, pulled out the tracking device, and left that in her apartment. She kept the comlink in her pocket. Just in case.

Every day, when the lights blinked to indicate a change in the twelve-hour shifts, Jyn walked around the station. She kept her eyes and ears open. She wanted to know who had ships, who was looking for off-station work, who was going where. The second Commander Solange gave her clearance, Jyn was leaving Five Points for good. She'd be happy never to visit another station in her life.

She always circled back through the park in the center of the station. She watched the beggars, their palms open on their knees. She had more credits clinking in her hidden pocket now, but she didn't share them. Instead, she waited.

"Seat taken?" a man asked, indicating the bench Jyn sat on.

She shook her head.

"I've seen you here before," the man said.

Jyn tucked a piece of hair behind her ear. "You have?"

He nodded. If Jyn had to guess, he was about ten years her senior, with rough knuckles that indicated he used his fists often. "Pretty little thing," he said in a lower voice, leaning closer to Jyn.

She didn't move away.

"Why don't you come back with me?" the man asked. He jerked his head toward the wall. "I've got a little place nearby. Shift's about to change out."

"No, thank you," Jyn said in as neutral a tone as she could.

The man's eyes narrowed. "You waiting on someone?"

Jyn looked around the park. There was no one there but the beggars. "No," she said.

"So have a bit of fun."

Jyn pressed her lips together and shook her head again.

"What, you're too good for me?" the man asked.

Jyn held her hands primly in her lap and stared straight ahead.

"Fine," the man spat out, standing. "Coldhearted Kath," he muttered under his breath as he stormed off.

Jyn counted to a hundred in her mind. When the man didn't return, she stood up and crossed the path to where a Huloon youngling crouched in supplication. She tossed the credits she'd picked from the man's pocket into the Huloon's outstretched hands and left the park.

The evenings she spent in Moeseffa's Cantina. It was a little more upscale than the inn at which she'd spent her first night, but it was also a favorite among the people who used Five Points as a base of operations. The five planets of the system circled a single star, and the space station was positioned in the gap between Rumitaka and Satotai, making it an ideal location to reach all five with relative ease. Each planet supported life, had various minerals, and had its own loose governing system, although their power was ostensibly curtailed by the Empire. Trade was frequent, both between planets and with other systems, and everything came through the Five Points station eventually.

And it seemed everything came through Moeseffa's Cantina as well.

Jyn's practice was to go early, about two hours before the end of the day shift, and stay at least two hours into the night shift. She'd order a large blue mappa, a weak drink even before Moeseffa's crew watered it down, and sip on it for as long as possible. She kept to herself, with her scarf pulled over her head, and usually she was ignored. The few men and women who'd approached her had been able to tell early on that Jyn wasn't interested in them, and Moeseffa himself had taken a liking to his new young regular, who tipped well and never caused trouble.

The table between the door and the mini holo entertainment was the perfect spot, quiet enough that Jyn could hear people talking but distracting enough that few noticed her listening. Their eyes slid over Jyn, lingering in the shadows, to the meter-tall projections of an apparently popular band led by an attractive female Fryiaan. She was a better dancer than singer, using all four of her arms to her advantage, and Jyn appreciated just how distracting the holo was to the other patrons.

"Watassay's mining is picking up," a man said, chugging a glass of something brown and rank. "The Empire's put in a bid for the central mining system."

"Joynder will never sell to the Empire," his companion said.

Jyn snorted quietly into her glass.

"What's the Empire need all the mines for anyway?" the first man said, glowering at his empty glass. He beat it on the table until Moeseffa came by to refill it. "They've got enough ore now to build a fleet of ships, but no war to fight with them."

"Maybe they're building more stations like this one?" his quieter companion mused.

Jyn's gaze slid around the room as the day shift ended and the old drunks left to make room for the new ones. A couple near the window, an Espirion male and a human woman, spoke in low voices.

"My client is looking for something rare, an item used during the Clone Wars," the woman said in a soft voice.

The Espirion responded, muttering so low that Jyn couldn't hear him.

The woman snorted. "Credits are no object."

Jyn always paid attention when it came to jobs. Something with enough pay—or a ship big enough to hide her—and Jyn could leave whether Commander Solange "allowed" it or not. She suspected that's what she'd ultimately have to do. Commander Solange would never easily let go of her little forger.

The first hour into the night shift was a matter of waiting. People were coming off their jobs, looking to stretch their limbs and dull their minds as quickly as possible. It wasn't until the second hour—the second or third or fourth glass—that things settled back down. This night, however, there was an anxious undercurrent among many of the patrons. Jyn watched, waiting for the news to come to her.

And then she heard it.

A whispered word, sliding through the bar like Freyan creeper moss, expanding in the shadows and retreating in the light.

"The rebels."

There were recruiters nearby. On the station? Maybe. Guesses of a base being set up in Hirara. "They'll buy up contracts," one man said.

"They're just looking for fodder," another snapped back.

Jyn slammed her glass down on the table, ignoring the way the blue liquid foamed over the side. The damn rebels. Everywhere she went, they followed. Mucking it all up. Bringing the Empire down on the people who didn't want to get involved. Why couldn't people just be *people*? Why did they have to be on one side or another? If everyone would just stop caring so much, maybe the galaxy could actually find the peace everyone claimed they wanted.

Jyn thought bitterly of Akshaya and Hadder and the blast that had killed them, the shot fired from either an Imperial TIE fighter or a rebel Y-wing. It didn't matter which one had killed them. They were still dead. And damn both the Empire and the rebellion for it.

Jyn nodded to Moeseffa as she left the cantina. He shot her a worried glance—she rarely left so early—but she waved at him cheerfully to allay his fears. She was done for the night.

Her rooms weren't that far away, but Jyn stuck to the well-lit streets near the center of the station until it was time to turn off and head back to the wall. Her mind kept lingering on that word—*rebellion*. What was the point? Saw had spent his whole life fighting the Empire, and it had cost him his sister, his health . . . her. Her father had tried to fight the Empire, and it had cost them her mother. And Jyn? She didn't even want to fight anymore, and she'd lost Hadder.

She heard movement behind her. Jyn whirled around—just in time to see a dark shadow, the blur of an arm, a fist connecting with her head.

And then the world went dark.

CHAPTER FORTY_

Jyn woke up with her arms and legs bound to a chair by plastoid ties. Her tongue felt fat and dry in her mouth.

"Aaand there she is," someone with a deep voice said kindly.

Jyn forced her eyes opened. Her head ached, and the bright lights overhead lanced through her eyes.

"I didn't hit her that hard," a male Dowutin said, his voice low and guttural. He was easily over three meters tall, with arms like tree trunks.

"It's fine, it's fine," another man said. He waved his hands, and the Dowutin left the room.

The man turned to Jyn. "I am Allehander Pso," he said. He smoothed down the thin hair on his balding head, and Jyn noticed that it was actually feathers, not hair, covering his skull. When he turned, the downy wisps grew longer, and dark brown and green feathers about as long as her fingers trailed all the way down his back, under his shirt.

"Pso's Palace," Jyn mumbled.

Allehander's face broke into a huge grin. Each one

of his jade-green teeth was pointed and jagged like the edge of a saw blade. "Yes! You've heard of me!" He seemed positively delighted by Jyn's knowledge.

She nodded, wincing in pain.

Allehander tsked. "You must forgive my man," he said. "He doesn't know his own strength. He's normally gentle as can be. A big softy."

"Oh, obviously," Jyn said. She tried to lift her hands, but the plastoid ties were tight.

"Those, I'm afraid," Allehander said, "will have to stay."

Jyn looked up at him. "What do you want?" Her voice was stronger now, clearer.

"I want to talk to the person who made *these*." Allehander snapped his fingers, and a man stepped forward. He dumped a satchel of Pso's Palace gambling credits on the table in front of Jyn. Her heart sank, but she was certain her face didn't show anything more than mild confusion.

"You're the one who commissions the credits. You should know who made them," Jyn said.

Allehander laughed merrily. "Ah, sweet young thing! I believe I do know who made these, and I believe you know that they were not from my sources."

He picked one up, tapping the side with his taloned finger. "These are very, *very* well made," he said in an impressed voice. "Still, we do have to punish those who steal from us."

Jyn still didn't let her face betray her true emotions. She stared at him blankly. And it was in that moment—bound in a gambling lord's office as he withdrew an assortment of killing and torturing devices from his desk and laid them out—it was in that precise moment that Jyn realized something hugely important.

She didn't care anymore.

Her mother was gone, Saw had betrayed her, Hadder and Akshaya had burned in merciless space. *I have nothing else to lose,* she realized. Obviously, she didn't particularly want to get tortured and killed, especially not over an Imperial officer with a gambling problem, but there was an emptiness in Jyn now that pushed on the edges of her soul, expanding, forcing out her other emotions.

Including fear.

Allehander picked up a hand press, the tiny spikes twirling through the metal plate as he twisted it. When he looked at Jyn, his eyes widened a little at her complete and utter disinterest in the weapons spread out before them.

The corners of his mouth slid up in an appreciative smile. "I must confess that I did notice two things," he said, putting down the hand press. "First, you did a very, *very* good job."

Jyn wondered if he realized he doubled up on words as if that would make them truer.

"I appreciate skill," Allehander confessed. "And second, you didn't flood the market. I've checked with the other gambling lords. Only my palace had the counterfeit credit chips, and I know who commissioned them. You did a job. You could have made more, kept some, used them for yourself. But my men have searched your little apartment, searched you, and there was nothing, *nothing*. Not greedy. I like that. You do a job, and you're done."

He paced in front of her. Jyn tested the plastoid ties, not because she was trying to break out but because she was curious how strong they were. The answer was *very*.

"Useful," Allehander mused, looking at her. "You made the credits for Commander Solange, yes?"

Jyn nodded. She had no reason to keep up the act.

"When I confronted her, she and I were able to come up with something of a solution. A way for the Empire to pay her debt without knowing it."

Jyn blinked. This was a skill she had learned on Five Points, from waiting in the park across from the beggars. Men loved to talk. All she had to do was wait and listen, and they would tell her everything.

"I have some products I need to get off the station. Commander Solange has arranged for the Empire to buy them at a good price for me, one that will clear her debts. Win–win, yes?"

Because he seemed to expect an answer, Jyn nodded.

"But we need some documents altered. And I think *you* can do that, yes?"

"Will it get me off this station?" Jyn asked.

"To Rumitaka," Allehander said. "And after that, you do as you wish."

"And you'll pay me."

Allehander barked a laugh. "Your freedom will be payment enough!"

Jyn lifted an eyebrow and waited.

Allehander scowled, but then the corners of his mouth quirked up in a smile. "Oh, I like you. Fine, yes. A payment. A thousand credits?"

"Imperial, not those." Jyn nodded to the pile of forged Pso's Palace credits on the table. "They're too easy to fake."

Allehander's eyes flashed, and for a moment, Jyn thought she had gone too far. But he laughed again and waved his hand for the straps to be removed from around her ankles and wrists. "We have need to hurry," Allehander said. "Can you be ready to leave in an hour?"

"I'm ready to leave now," Jyn said.

Allehander gave her instructions to head to docking bay NC13 and board the *Amarills*-class freighter that was waiting. "My men will have everything you need to alter the documents on board the ship. You can work on them as you travel."

It was ironic that Jyn could move across the galaxy faster than she could hop between the planets of one solar system. But the hyperspace routes that enabled high-speed travel didn't stretch to the tiny planets of the Five Points system, often littered with asteroids, and the freighter would be limited.

"Commander Solange has provided clearance for our ship to land on Rumitaka," Allehander continued. "But there's a chance there will be checkpoints on the way that she is not aware of. She thinks herself more important than she is. If we run into such checkpoints . . . ?" He let his question drift between them.

"Not a problem," Jyn said. Imperial checkpoint clearances were her specialty.

"Good, *good*," Allehander said, nodding. "And if you ever find yourself in need of future work, come back to Pso's Palace," he said. "You're exactly the kind of girl I could use."

CHAPTER FORTY-ONE_

The ship was larger than Jyn had expected; Allehander had said there were only twenty units to move. Of course, he hadn't said *what* the units were, and Jyn hadn't asked. It was easier to move contraband through the space station, where only Commander Solange's corrupt eyes could see, than between planets or on more traditional trade routes.

"You Allehander's girl?" said the captain of the ship, a rough-looking man about fifty years old.

Jyn nodded.

"Get in. Mathey will get you started."

Jyn boarded the ship, and before she'd found Mathey, she felt the engines lighting. The ship shot out of the station and into the blackness of space. "They're in a hurry," Jyn said to herself.

She pushed open a door at the end of the main hallway and discovered a group of three men sitting at a table. These were not the kind of men who would visit Moeseffa's Cantina. These were the kind of men who'd guzzle whatever was left over in the glasses sent to the back for cleaning.

"You that girl?" one of them asked. He had a patchy red beard that was only just starting to shadow his chin.

"You Mathey?"

He grunted. Jyn took that for a yes. She pulled out a chair and sat across from him. The other two men stood up and left. "Gonna check on the cargo," the older one said, drawing the last word out as if it were two.

"Right, so Allehander said you wouldn't know all about the job," Mathey said. His voice crackled like it was made of ice. He pulled out a stack of identity contract pads. Jyn counted them after he slid them across the table to her. Twenty. She read the top one.

Greyjin Marscopo
Eight standard years
Servitude: Allehander Pso
Service years: Three
Status: Complete
Compensation: Passage to Rumitaka, Five Points system

"What's this?" Jyn asked.

"Indentured service records." Mathey was watching her. Waiting. Jyn could feel his eyes boring into her, hungry for a reaction.

"What am I supposed to do with them?" she asked in an even tone.

"Allehander has twenty servants whose time is up," Mathey said. "They were told they'd get a new start on Rumitaka soon as their contracts are finished."

"And . . . they're not?" Jyn asked.

Mathey's eyes were alight. "Well, it's something of a new start. Different from working at the palace." He took the top identity contract off of Jyn's stack. "You're to alter these. Each one needs to have five more years added, and assigned to the Empire, not Allehander. That's who he sold 'em to."

"Sold them. Like slaves." Jyn kept her tone carefully even.

"Exactly. 'Cause that's what they are." Mathey grinned with all his teeth, even the broken front one that was blackening on the inside.

"Ah." Jyn stared at the ident pads.

"You got a problem with it?" Mathey added, his tone mocking.

"No," Jyn said simply.

Mathey didn't look convinced.

"A job is a job," she said. "And I've been paid."

"How much?" he asked.

Jyn let her eyes linger on Mathey's dirty hair, the oil staining one cheek, his disheveled clothes. "Probably more than you," she said. She stood, gathering the ident pads, and added, "Where is my bunk?"

Mathey grunted, hooking his thumb down the hall. Jyn left him grumbling at the table, and when she entered her room, the first thing she did was lock the door.

Then she sat down and memorized the names at the top of each ident pad.

A few hours later, the door rattled in its frame. "Eatin' time," Mathey growled.

Jyn set the ident pads on her bed—a moldy pallet she had not yet decided whether or not she would actually sleep on—and stood up to join the rest of the crew for dinner.

The others were longtime partners; Jyn was clearly the outsider. The two workers were older than Jyn had thought, in their midtwenties, and Mathey talked with pride of how many people they'd killed on the streets of Satotai before he picked them up. This seemed to be their chief selling point—that they had no compunction at all about pointing blasters at people and firing at will.

The captain was known only as Captain, and his word was law.

"How long have you been a slaver?" Jyn asked politely.

Captain's eyes widened. "Not a slaver," he said. "Just transporting cargo."

"But the cargo is people," Jyn said, keeping her voice cool and even. "Therefore, definitionally . . ."

"Definitionally," Mathey said, mocking Jyn's polite tone. "Look, ain't got to have all those fancy words. Ain't got to be all high and mighty. You're in the scum with us now."

Jyn looked down at her hands. "Indeed."

At the end of their meal—a sloppy sort of stew—Jyn offered to clear the plates away and wash them. The others laughed at her, saying it was high time they had a woman to take care of them, but Jyn was mostly concerned with ensuring that the next meal she ate would be on a clean plate.

"And what about the slaves?" Jyn asked when she was done and the men were busy starting a game of sabacc.

"Cargo," Captain corrected. Jyn cocked her head but didn't point out that changing what they were called did not actually make them less human.

"What about 'em?" Mathey countered. He was like a rabid Gamorrean, always looking for a fight.

"Have they been fed?" The pot of stew wasn't good, but there was plenty of it. Jyn recited their names in her head. *Greyjin, Kathlin, Dorset, Harvey.*

"They're fine," Captain said.

"I don't mind; I can take some food down." Jyn started to pick up some bowls.

"They're. Fine." Captain's voice brooked no argument.

Laurose, Owlen, Blane, Efford.

"D'you not hear Captain?" Mathey shouted when Jyn didn't move. "Leave 'em be! They got water. It's only a week."

Jyn let the full impact of Mathey's words slide into her soul.

She left the pot on the stove, went to her room, and locked the door again.

Several hours later, there was a soft knock on her door. Jyn stood to open it and was surprised to see Captain standing there. "May I come in?" he asked politely.

Jyn stepped back.

"Already working?" Captain nodded to the ident pads spread out on the bed.

"It's not an easy task," Jyn said. "I'll need almost the whole trip to finish."

"But you can do it?"

Jyn nodded. She couldn't tell if Captain was relieved or disappointed by that.

"I wasn't always a slaver," he said finally, his eyes

still on the ident pads. "Fact is, I used to be a slave myself."

Jyn didn't speak. She had learned her lesson on Five Points well.

"Allehander Pso was my last owner. Bought me from Kiretim, who bought me from my stepfather. Evil bastard, that man."

Jyn knew a thing or two about bastard fathers.

"Being a slave . . ." Captain finally looked at Jyn. "It wears on you. I hated it. Kiretim made me wear a collar. It was a constant reminder that I was a thing. Not a person. Couldn't do what I wanted. Couldn't even dream, not with that thing strangling me." He put his hand up to his bare neck. "Allehander took my collar off. He cares about what a person's use is, not status. Saw I had a use."

"As a slaver," Jyn couldn't help saying.

A shadow passed over Captain's face. "As a pilot."

"And this . . . ?" Jyn indicated the ship.

"The cargo changes. It's not all bad."

They were silent for a moment.

"Is it worth it?" Jyn finally asked. "Is it worth helping other people be enslaved, just so you can have your freedom?" She sought his eyes, truly curious about his answer.

"Yes," he said emphatically. "Now I have to ask you

something. You gonna be a problem? It's okay to not like what you do, but you still have to do it."

"I was paid. That's all I care about," she lied.

Captain nodded once, accepting her answer. "Don't let the boys ride you," he said. "They aren't used to being reminded what they are. They give you trouble, let me know."

Jyn thanked him, but when he left, she locked her door again, making sure Captain heard the metallic click. Then she finally allowed herself to unpack. She spread out all her credits, the ones from Commander Solange and the ones from Allehander Pso, and she set them beside the twenty ident pads. She did not let herself think of the names written there again.

She knew what she *should* do, and she knew what she *had* to do.

CHAPTER FORTY-TWO

Travel through the Five Points system was tedious, a series of short jumps as they zigzagged to avoid the space debris that littered the entire system. What should have been a quick journey was drawn out at an excruciatingly slow pace.

It was three days before Mathey and the boys let her go into the cargo hold. The boys hung back near the stairs, watching, as Mathey led Jyn into the hold.

There were seven cells, with two to three people in each one, despite the fact that the cells were about half the size of Jyn's room. One bucket of water with a ladle hanging from the side stood near each door.

Jyn covered her mouth.

"Yeah, the smell's the worst," Mathey conceded. He had been warming to Jyn over the past few days. "We're going to have to wash the floor with halliol acid to clear out the stink."

The slaves had been trying to keep their areas clean, but the only thing in each cell was the bucket, and they couldn't defecate there. "Why not just let them go to the restroom?" Jyn asked.

Mathey snorted. "Ain't none of us have time to 'escort' 'em," he sneered. "You volunteering?"

Jyn's eyes watered at the stench, but she shook her head. *Don't show emotion,* she ordered herself.

Jyn had read over all the ident pads, and she knew that most of the slaves were young, between the ages of seven and eleven. There was a difference, though, between reading names and numbers and seeing their faces.

The five adult slaves were all women, and from the way they reached for the children through the bars, Jyn suspected that most of them were the children's mothers. None of them had similar surnames, but names meant nothing. Jyn knew that.

Mathey picked up a short stick that had been plugged into the wall. Jyn noticed that the nearby prisoners all scooted away as soon as he touched it, and she looked at it closer.

"Stun prod," he said, slapping it in his palm. "Don't kill 'em, but gives 'em a buzz." He drew the last word out, widening his eyes in a way that made him look mad. He lunged at one cell holding three children, and the little girl inside screamed and scrambled to the back wall, slipping on the filth covering the floor.

He laughed; he had only meant to get a reaction out of her, and it had worked.

"Leave her alone!" one of the women roared, straining to reach through the bars. "I'll kill you!" she choked out, her face turning purple with rage.

Mathey turned, hate in his eyes, and Jyn stepped forward. She stood directly in front of the woman, but far enough away that her fingers couldn't quite grasp Jyn.

"I was raised by a man who taught me to fight," Jyn said. "He was the strongest person I ever knew, and he'd never let anyone hurt me. You know what my most important lesson was?"

The entire hold was silent, even the children.

The woman shook her head. "No," she whispered.

"Don't start a fight you can't win." Jyn turned on her heel and left the cargo hold. The boys howled at the woman, rattling the bars of her cage, laughing at her screams.

That night, Jyn started cooking. "This slop is disgusting," she said. "I don't know much, but I can do better than this. For starters, let me introduce you to salt."

Captain laughed, pleased with the variety, and the boys in general eased up around Jyn.

"You don't seem like the kind to cook," Captain said.

Jyn stared down at the pot of boiling water. Her mother would have taught her to cook, but Jyn had been too young to retain any recipes. Saw hadn't cared about food as anything more than a means of sustenance.

Everything she knew about cooking, she knew from Hadder—from watching him toss spices into bubbling pans, her eyes glued to his quick hands as they chopped through glick before sending the white bits skidding through sizzling oil.

"How much longer is this journey?" she asked in a low voice.

"Eager to be off my ship?" Captain said.

"Yes." Jyn let the simplicity of her word show the honesty behind it.

Captain pressed his lips together and nodded. "Three more days," he said. "How's the forgery going?"

Jyn looked him right in the eyes. "Almost done," she said.

Two days later, and the boys were getting antsy. They kept going down to the cargo hold for entertainment, taunting the slaves by eating in front of them or jeering insults.

Jyn prepared a feast for them all. "Our last full day together," Jyn said. The ship was already in sight of

Rumitaka; they'd dock by the next morning.

"I've got a feeling that as soon as we land, you're high-tailing outta here," Captain said.

"You're not wrong," Jyn said. She was eager to pretend this job had never happened. She put the food she'd made in the center of the table, and the boys started fighting over the bread.

"What's that?" Mathey asked as Jyn turned around.

She held the stun prod, the one Captain had taken away from the cargo hold. "I've not seen one like this before," she mused. Her thumb pressed the trigger, and electricity crackled at the end.

Captain shrugged. "Mostly harmless," he said

"Mostly," Jyn agreed, and she pressed the end of the stun prod to Captain's skull. His eyes widened and his teeth chattered involuntarily, then he slumped to the table, knocked out cold.

"Hey!" Mathey shouted, throwing his chair back and lunging for Jyn. She tossed the stun prod to her left hand, rammed it into Mathey's stomach, and with her right hand withdrew the truncheon she'd secured to her back. As Mathey doubled over in pain, she walloped him in the back of his head with the truncheon, and he dropped like a stone.

The boys were stupid. They could have run, but instead they tried to fight Jyn at the same time. It took her only minutes to knock them out.

"Messy," Jyn complained, dragging Captain up out of the bowl of gravy. She held both his arms and dragged him down the ship's length. She opened the airlock chamber door and dumped his body on the floor, then went back for the others. As soon as all the men were inside the chamber, she locked the pressurized door, but she didn't release the hatch. They would wake soon, but Jyn made sure the lock was sealed and they were trapped in the chamber.

Jyn went straight to the cargo hold. The slaves inside were too weak to stand; they had lived on little more than water and the occasional ration cube for a week.

Jyn sat down at the cage holding the mother she'd spoken to a few days before. "Why did you sell your children into slavery?" she asked.

"I didn't," she said. She scowled at Jyn but was too tired to censor herself. "Laurose and Efford were born while I served Pso. Owlen became mine after his mother died."

"And you?" Jyn asked the other women. They all confirmed; their children were born into slavery. And they had all taken extended contracts with Allehander Pso in an effort to buy their own and their children's freedom. Pso's deal was to set them up on Rumitaka at the end of their service; instead, as soon as they'd boarded the *Amarills*-class freighter, Captain and Mathey had pushed them into cages, mocking them for their stupidity in trusting the gambling lord.

Jyn stood after she finished speaking to the last woman. She moved to the end of the hall and set the all-release button. The cage doors opened simultaneously.

"You're . . . letting us go?" the mother who'd tried to fight Mathey asked.

"Come with me," Jyn said. To the other women, she added, "There's food in the mess hall. Eat as much as you want." They nodded and then led the children up the stairs.

"I know you're hungry," she told the woman. "This won't take long."

"As long as the children eat."

"What's your name?" Jyn asked.

"Annjin," she said. Jyn recalled her ident pad; she'd known this woman had to be one of the five adult idents she had.

"I was hired to alter your contracts," Jyn said, leading Annjin to her room.

"I know," she growled. "That one man—he laughed about it. How dumb we were to fall for that plan. To trust a contract from Allehander Pso."

Jyn opened her door and Annjin followed her inside. All twenty of the ident pads were stacked neatly on the bed. Jyn picked them up and handed them to the woman. "I didn't alter them," she said. "The contracts are free and clear. Don't lose these."

Before the woman could say anything, Jyn led her back down the hall. Behind them, they could hear the other women and children eating, their hunger all-consuming. Annjin looked as if she wanted to join them, but Jyn was almost done.

"Where are you taking us?" Annjin asked, suspicion in her voice.

"Nowhere. I'm leaving. I suggest you go elsewhere. The Empire's waiting for you on Rumitaka." Annjin looked confused, so Jyn added, "There's a shuttle. I'm taking it. You can have the ship."

"What about—" Annjin started, but Jyn stopped in front of the airlock. Annjin stared through the porthole window, her eyes widening.

Captain and Mathey were almost lucid now; the boys at least were awake. "Let us out!" Mathey shouted.

"If we land on Rumitaka with these men as prisoners, they'll blame us," Annjin said. "Our contracts don't run out until tomorrow; we're technically still slaves until then. We'll be put on trial for revolting against our masters."

Jyn put her hand next to the release switch. Annjin's eyes fell to the large red handle. Jyn had already set up the airlock; all the safety measures were overridden.

All it would take was for the handle to be pulled down, and the four men who had locked up Annjin and her family on the slave ship for a solid week to rot in their own filth with less food than they could live on would be shot into the blackness of space.

"So," Jyn said, once she was sure Annjin had seen the release handle, "I'm taking the shuttle. I'm also taking the credits I was paid. You may want to check Captain's quarters. There may be more for you. Or you could sell the ship. I don't care. But I'm leaving."

Annjin stared at the porthole. The men had realized what the women were looking at; they were all too aware of the big red handle.

"Please don't go," Annjin said softly. "I've been a slave since I was a teenager. I don't know what to do. We could . . . we could be your crew. We could take the ship and go anywhere."

"No," Jyn said simply.

She turned around and headed toward the shuttle. It wasn't much, about the same size as the planet hopper, and fortunately it had similar controls. Jyn was no pilot—she couldn't have stolen the freighter if she'd wanted to—but she knew she could at least land the shuttle on Rumitaka. It was a straight shot with auto-pilot engaged.

Jyn had disconnected from the freighter in a

matter of minutes, pulling away from the larger ship. She watched as it soared toward Rumitaka, the planet barely in view. And she watched as the airlock opened and four men drifted out into space.

CHAPTER FORTY-THREE_

Rumitaka was a dusty planet that had very little going for it. There was a small mining operation to the south, a refinery on-site, and irrigation farms to the north. The spaceport was located near a small town. When Jyn landed, she inquired about any nearby junkers.

"Looks like a good little shuttle," the junker, a male Labbo, said, eyeing it. "What's wrong with it?" His long ears twitched, the flaps brushing his shoulders.

"It'd be better off as parts," Jyn said. "And the ident code isn't original."

The junker eyed Jyn, then scanned the ship's codes. Jyn's work was good, and in general, the ship would pass any clearance, but there was already an alert out for it. "Reckon I could keep this in storage for a bit," the junker said. "Until things are a little calmed down."

"Good plan," Jyn replied. They settled on a price, and Jyn cashed out. She could have earned more, but it was evident that she had to sell fast.

She went right back to the spaceport. She bought passage on an interplanetary transport unit and disembarked on Uchinao a few weeks later. From there, she picked up odd jobs, moving between the planets in the system whenever she got antsy.

As soon as possible, Jyn took a job on a freighter leaving the Five Points system. Between Commander Solange and Allehander Pso, she had no reason to stay and every reason to leave.

Time and distance blended together as Jyn crisscrossed the galaxy. Sometimes she thought about how much Hadder would have liked this life, seeing new planets from the viewports of different ships, but usually she tried not to think about him at all. Instead, she pretended to be the starbird she had heard about on Inusagi, the one that turned to stardust and spread across the galaxy.

It didn't matter who she was as long as she wasn't Jyn Erso. She picked up a code name, Liana Hallik, and created scandocs for the new ident that were so good they passed more than one Imperial inspection. She just hoped they were good enough to get her through the Five Points system unnoticed, when she returned there several years later.

Jyn docked at Rumitaka with the intention of reaching out to a splicer she'd met before leaving the system.

She needed credits after a run of bad luck. But instead of her contact, she ran into the old junker.

"Hey!" he called, crossing the small spaceport to where she stood. "It's been a while."

Jyn frowned, trying to add up the time. She was in her early twenties now, she supposed. She was surprised the Labbo remembered her.

"Sold that ship of yours," the junker continued, pulling up a chair. "Made a good price. Might have some work for you, if you're interested."

She shrugged. She'd learned that lesson from her travels; never appear eager. The Labbo offered to discuss the finer points in the small cantina down the road, and Jyn allowed him to buy her a drink.

When they were seated, the junker said, "Got some interest in the kind of codes you make."

Jyn closed her eyes and allowed herself one wistful moment of recalling who she had been before she went to seedy cantinas to haggle with dishonest skills. She could still remember when her life had been normal and good. *No,* she thought viciously, excising the memories. *That's not what I get. I don't get normal. I don't deserve good.*

Everything good dies.

All she needed now was credits.

"How much interest?" Jyn asked the junker.

He told her his plan, and it was smart. If the ident

codes and ship docs she forged were sold through the Labbo, her name wouldn't be directly attached. It provided her with separation, although it did mean less payment.

"I've got a group; they need past checkpoints. Want some manifests and logs that look a little more . . . mediocre," the junker continued.

"I could do that." Jyn drained her glass. "How much?"

This was the right thing to say; the junker wasn't keen on small talk and preferred business. They quickly hashed out a payment plan and work schedule. "I don't even know your name," Jyn commented. It was her second dealing with the Labbo, and it had only just struck her as odd.

"Risi Amps," he said. "You?"

"Liana Hallik." The lie came easily. She hardly ever thought of herself as an Erso anymore, and it hurt too much to think of the name Ponta.

The work Risi provided was simple enough, although time-consuming and tedious. Jyn kept careful tabs on her credits. She could eke out a better-than-average living with the illegal work, and she had her eye set on going deeper into the Outer Rim and leaving behind Five Points. Commander Solange may have been an inept and corrupt officer, but she was still an Imperial presence on the space station, far too close for Jyn's comfort. So Jyn checked every ship that came into the spaceport, hoping each time to find someone who was keen on leaving the system behind.

She didn't find anyone. The holodramas she'd viewed as a kid implied that the Outer Rim was a constant source of adventures, new species to discover, strange new landscapes, and exciting exploits on ships that darted through the systems. Instead, Jyn spent her days in the little boarder room she rented on Rumitaka, hunched over a code replicator.

That feeling of missing out, of making the wrong choice for her life by accepting this job, was strongest late at night, when Jyn carefully crafted ship logs for Risi, taking out damage reports from space battles and adding in cleared Imperial checkpoints or boring trade route runs. As she examined the records and altered them, Jyn grew certain that Risi was being paid by a subversive partisan group. Probably not the growing group of rebels that Xosad and Idryssa had joined—this one seemed smaller, a fleet of no more than six ships, she guessed. None of which was a shuttle like the one Saw had flown, or a Y-wing like she'd seen on Skuhl.

Jyn traced the outline of a Y-wing in the dust on the table she was working at in her little dormer. What would life have been like if Saw hadn't been so isolated on Wrea? If he had followed Xosad and Idryssa into the rebel group? He wouldn't have taken that job on

Inusagi, the one that still woke her up with nightmares sometimes. She might have met Hadder not on Skuhl but on some rebel base on some far-flung planet. Because if it wasn't for Jyn, Hadder would have joined Xosad's group.

And he would have still been alive.

She didn't like having a name for the feeling that had been plaguing her for so many months now.

Regret.

She swiped her hand across her doodled Y-wing. The only regret she had was ever coming across groups like Saw's, like Xosad's. Like this one. Whatever they were doing now, these runs she was wiping from the manifests, the codes she was forging to get past blockades—Jyn was not so naive as to believe that they were helping anyone but their own entitled sense of justice.

In the end, she didn't care. As long as she got paid, as long as she was safe, as long as she could eat—that was all she cared about.

That night, a loud knock on the front door of the old house Jyn was boarding in was so persistent that Jyn startled awake, even though she was on the second story. Her landlady cursed a blue streak as she clomped down the stairs to answer the door. Jyn sat up in bed, straining to hear what was being said. Her landlady was loud, protesting that someone shouldn't come in.

And then Jyn heard the boots. She was certain she would always be able to identify a stormtrooper just by the sound his boots made.

She shot out of bed and went straight to her code replicator. She wiped the data as quickly as she could. It wasn't a perfect job, but it was something. All the logs and scandocs she'd been working on for the past few days were gone. She could re-create the work, but . . .

Her bedroom door swung open. Jyn grabbed the scarf she'd taken off earlier and threw it around her neck and hair. She hoped she looked as if she were being modest in her low-cut top, and not that she was hiding her kyber crystal necklace.

"Tanith Ponta?" the stormtrooper said.

Jyn turned slowly.

"I told you, her name is Liana Hallik, not Tanith whatever," the landlady shouted. "This is a violation of privacy!"

"You're wanted for questioning," the stormtrooper said.

"Am I being arrested?" Jyn asked.

The landlady stared at her, as if it had only just occurred to her that Jyn could have lied about her name.

"No," the stormtrooper said.

"Do I have a choice in whether or not I come with you?" Jyn asked.

"No," the stormtrooper said.

"Can I at least get dressed first?"

The stormtrooper hesitated.

"It's cold outside," Jyn said, looking down at her bare arms and legs.

"You may dress," the stormtrooper said, but he didn't leave the doorway. He watched as Jyn awkwardly stepped into pants without removing her shorts and layered another shirt under a heavier coat. She shoved her feet into her boots and stood awkwardly.

"Don't rent my room out," Jyn told her landlady. "I'm coming back."

The older woman nodded vigorously, and Jyn hoped she would be honest enough not to loot the credits Jyn had hidden under the mattress.

The stormtrooper led Jyn to the spaceport. Risi Amps sat on the ground, his back against the wall, his hands held in heavy durasteel locks. He looked up at Jyn with watery eyes as the stormtrooper pushed her forward. The guards on Risi yanked him to a standing position.

It did not bode well that Risi had been arrested. He had been her go-between for the codes and logs and docs she forged for what was obviously a rebel group.

While Jyn could reasonably protest that she didn't know she'd been working for partisans, she couldn't deny that her actions—forgery—were illegal. She wasn't sure why Risi had been arrested and not her, but she couldn't help feeling nervous as the stormtrooper escorted her into an Imperial transport ship and they headed back to Five Points station.

CHAPTER FORTY-FOUR_

Risi Amps was put in a separate, locked room on the ship during the short trip to Five Points. Jyn didn't see him again until they docked on the station and two stormtroopers unlocked his room and led him silently off the ship. Another stormtrooper guarded Jyn, and after several long minutes, he led her off the transport ship as well. There was no sign of the other stormtroopers or Risi—no sign of any other ship on this level. The long expanse of ports was empty and silent, save for Jyn, the stormtrooper, and the sleek transport shuttle.

The stormtrooper walked a little behind Jyn, on high alert despite the fact that the bay was empty. It surprised Jyn; she hadn't thought Commander Solange was capable of running an efficient troop.

At the end of the bay, the stormtrooper nudged Jyn to a small private turbolift. They went up three floors, then got out on a hallway that Jyn recognized as the Imperial headquarters on the station.

"That way," the stormtrooper said, pushing Jyn down the hall toward Commander Solange's office.

Although she was wearing a heavy coat that was making her sweat on the warm station, Jyn felt a little naked without her usual access to at least some form of weapon. She felt like a nerf being led to a rancor's den.

The stormtrooper stopped outside the door to Commander Solange's office. He pressed a button, and the sleek enameled door slid open. The stormtrooper did not move to enter the room, but nodded for Jyn to do so. She stepped inside, her chin tilted up, her spine straight.

"Yes," drawled a voice on the opposite side of the room. "I can see why you thought she was a good choice, Solange."

Jyn felt a chill move down her spine, one that seemed to undermine her false bravado. "Who are you?" she asked.

The woman tilted her head, her ice-blue eyes narrowing just a tiny bit. "Speak only when spoken to," she said in an even voice that brooked no argument. Jyn found she had none to give.

Jyn examined the woman's insignia plaque; she was an admiral. Her crisp gray uniform was impeccable, making her pale skin look even whiter in contrast. Her platinum-blonde hair was braided so tightly it made

Jyn's head ache. The only real color on her, aside from her insignia plaque, was on her long eyelashes, which had been tinted red.

The admiral glanced at a file. "Our records show you gave us the name Tanith Ponta," she said in a bored voice. "But you were under the alias Liana Hallik when our troopers picked you up." She looked up, analyzing Jyn. "Which is your real name?" When Jyn didn't answer, she added, "You may speak now."

"Hallik," Jyn said.

The admiral nodded. She put the file on the desk, angling it so Jyn could see her own image, with the name Liana Hallik emblazoned across the top, followed by the ident code she'd forged when she first started using that name. As she'd suspected, the troopers had pillaged her room after taking her and assumed the scandoc she'd left there was real.

The admiral waved her hand at Commander Solange.

"We've been looking for you, Liana," the commander said. "Where have you been?"

Jyn leveled a cold stare at her and didn't answer. Where had she been? In the Anoat system, working on a Tibanna gas tanker. Bouncing around the Mid Rim for a bit—Cerea and Coyerti—before settling in Takodana for nearly a year. On a freighter that needed clearance codes and no questions asked for so long that

Jyn had forgotten the smell of fresh air by the time she switched jobs and went planetside again.

"Around," Jyn answered.

"Yes, well," Commander Solange said, frowning, "we have a job for you. There's a rebel cell in the area that we want to crush."

The admiral cleared her throat.

"That we *will* crush," Commander Solange amended. "A partisan group that is particularly vicious. They've been using the criminal Risi Amps as a source for clearance codes that have enabled them to bypass the security measures we've implemented in this system." She raised her eyebrows, and Jyn knew that everyone in the room was well aware that the codes had actually come from her.

"Risi Amps is, sadly, ill-informed of where this partisan group is actually located," the admiral commented, speaking in an impatient voice.

"Admiral Rocwyn has implemented a plan that should help us locate the main base of the partisan group," Commander Solange continued. "With Risi Amps arrested, they will need a new way to bypass our checkpoints, and we want you to give it to them . . . but we have a bit of additional code for you to add that will enable us to better keep tabs on this group. This ship is the little bee that will lead us to the hive."

Jyn thought about trying to protest that she knew

nothing about forgery, but she sensed it would be futile and only anger the admiral. "I don't have a code replicator with me," she said instead.

Commander Solange reached into her desk and withdrew a new code replicator. Jyn opened it and scanned the contents, noting the tracker program already installed on the device.

"What will my payment be?" Jyn asked.

The admiral stared at Jyn just long enough for Jyn to be uncomfortable, not long enough to reasonably break her gaze. "This way," Admiral Rocwyn said finally, striding toward the door. She didn't turn around; she expected Jyn and Commander Solange to follow her and knew they would.

Jyn followed the admiral down the white-tiled hallway and through a door with a high-security lock, guarded by a pair of Imperial privates. The room past the door was dimly lit and smelled odd, like a combination of burning and something else, something metallic.

"Hello, Bardbee," the admiral said in a pleasant voice.

For the first time, Jyn noticed a pale white creature strung up in the center of the room. The creature was diamond-shaped, the torso about as tall as Jyn but with almost translucent membranes connecting the top of the head to the tips of the fingers, and then another membrane connecting the fingers all the way to the ankles.

"The Rayeth people are very strange," the admiral said to Jyn, as if this were a casual observation. "They're amphibious, did you know?"

"Yes," Jyn whispered. She remembered the first time she'd seen a Rayeth, on Inusagi, where they'd been pleading with stormtroopers to allow them entrance to the palace. They had been so elegant and beautiful, soaring through the waters of the azure pools. When they had wrapped their thin membranes around themselves like robes, they had seemed noble and tall.

So it was especially strange and cruel to see this Rayeth exposed the way he was. His arms were stretched out to their maximum length, held painfully in place by a pair of magnetic cuffs built into the wall. The Rayeth kept straining against the cuffs, his instinct to cover his body overriding the pain of the restraints on his bruised and bloody wrists. His face was mostly flat, with a little bump and two slits for a nose and a flat, long horizontal slit for a mouth. The Rayeth's eyes were milky white, and a glue-like mucus dripped from his eyes and down his face.

He was crying.

"This particular Rayeth is proving rather difficult," the admiral continued, her voice light. "He has worked with the partisan group we've been targeting for years, and we're certain he knows the location of the group's headquarters and main operation paths. But he just. Won't. Talk." With each of these last words, the admiral gently slapped the side of the Rayeth's face, then pulled her hand back in disgust and wiped the mucus off with a handkerchief.

"That's why we are hiring you," the admiral continued.

The Rayeth jerked in his restraints, a low growl emanating from its throat. His white eyes flashed at Jyn, and she saw accusation and rage there. He was being tortured for the information that Jyn was going to give the Empire.

"Now, now," the admiral admonished, and an interrogation droid zoomed into view. The Rayeth whimpered, but his hate-filled eyes bored into Jyn.

Admiral Rocwyn turned to Jyn. "You asked about payment," she said in a cool voice. "I think we've come to an understanding."

"Yes," Jyn whispered. Her payment was her freedom. Her payment was to escape the fate of this Rayeth.

The Imperial presence on Five Points station had been something of a joke, if Jyn was honest. Commander Solange had sullied herself, her rank, and her authority by entering the gambling halls. This new admiral, however, had reinstated the terror and subservience the Empire demanded, merely by her presence.

How does the Empire keep finding such horrible people? Jyn wondered, looking at the emaciated body of the Rayeth.

"This particular partisan group is rather obtusely antihuman," the admiral continued, her gaze sliding over to Jyn. "We have paid a contact to recommend you highly, and they have made an exception for you."

"I have worked with groups like that before," Jyn said. She tried hard to focus on the admiral's impartial gaze, not on the Rayeth watching, listening.

The admiral raised a brow. "No doubt." The words were delivered as an insult, and inexplicably, Jyn felt her cheeks reddening.

The admiral waved her hand in a dismissive gesture. "Take care of the details," she said to Commander Solange, dismissing them.

Commander Solange turned immediately and headed out of the room. Jyn hesitated only a moment, then followed on her heels.

"Now, where were we?" the admiral asked the Rayeth just before the door slid shut. Jyn could hear the Rayeth's screams through the walls. They chased her down the hall, and they still rang in her ears as Commander Solange led Jyn back to her office to go over the final details of the assignment.

CHAPTER FORTY-FIVE_

It was surprisingly easy to join the partisan group. Jyn was given the name of a contact and the ship's slip number. She went to the ship, a midsized XOI cruiser, and introduced herself as Liana Hallik. When the captain of the XOI pressed her, she added the name of her contact and that she'd worked with Risi Amps before his arrest. Jyn easily pointed out some of the ways she'd already worked with the group, altering logs.

"I like that," the leader of a group, a Devaronian female named Blue, said. "You've worked with us before, but kept your tongue so silent we didn't even know it."

"More like Risi kept his tongue quiet because he didn't want me asking for a bigger cut by going directly to you," Jyn said.

Blue smiled. "Risi spoke the universal language of credits," she said. "You and I, I think, speak another tongue." She threw an arm around Jyn's shoulders, her downy fur tickling the back of Jyn's neck.

Jyn shook her head. "I just want to get paid," she

said. Her stomach churned. She was caught between the Empire and a rebel group, and she *hated* it.

Blue's group operated throughout the Five Points system, with a few runs beyond into neighboring solar systems. Despite the ship's size, the crew was small— Blue, Jyn, a pair of Ma'cella brothers, an older Krish pilot, and a mechanic whose species Jyn couldn't identify and was too shy to ask. It was odd at first for Jyn to be the only human, but she soon fell into a fairly easy comradery with the group.

"You work quick," Blue commented as Jyn uploaded a new manifest and set of clearance codes for the ship after the first week of flight. The ship had done nothing major, just a few legitimate cargo runs. Blue wanted to keep everything on the up and up after Risi Amp's arrest, just in case.

"Thanks," Jyn said.

"I'm thinking we'll head to Watassay next," she continued, taking a sip of caf from her thermal canteen.

"Okay," Jyn said.

"But I don't want it to look like we went to Watassay," she said. "Can the manifest say Hirara instead?"

"Sure," Jyn reached for her code replicator. She paused. It didn't matter. The Imperial tracking code had already been uploaded in the ship's mainframe; Admiral Rocwyn knew exactly where the ship was going and where it had been. But if Blue was taking her to the headquarters, Jyn's participation with the group would be over sooner rather than later. "What's on Watassay?" she asked.

"A job," Blue said simply.

❖

Watassay was surrounded by an Imperial blockade. "Time to see if those clearance codes of yours work, girl," said Shawburn, the pilot of Blue's ship.

"They'll work," Jyn said confidently. *In part because they've got a true Imperial tag.*

There was tense silence as the ship was scanned, then docking clearance flashed over their comm screen.

"Good work," Blue said in a soft voice, dropping a big hand on Jyn's shoulder and giving it a comforting squeeze.

The job, it turned out, was unloading the crates that had been in storage on the freighter. Each crate was full of foodstuffs—not very appetizing, but a full round of nutrients and easily distributable to the locals.

"Thank you, thank you," the man who accepted the delivery kept saying. His cheeks were hollowed, and he had a gaunt look about him.

Blue had the crew work as quickly as possible, unloading and helping with the distribution in a small makeshift town. They were back in the air as soon as possible.

"What was wrong with them?" Jyn asked.

"What do you mean?" Blue countered.

"The people. They looked like they were starving."

The Krish pilot looked at Jyn with wide eyes. "Because they *were*," she said. "Why do you think we were bringing them food?"

Jyn frowned down at the table.

"The Empire wants that part of Watassay for their own resources, so they're trying to starve them out," Blue said. "They've cut them off from importing any food. That was the first shipment they've had in a standard month. Dwindun said they'd been softening tree bark to fill their bellies. The foodstuffs we gave them should help."

Jyn felt something in her heart, a stabbing sensation, like a knife twisting. She looked down at the code replicator in her hand. She had already infected the ship with the Empire's tracker. It was done. There was no going back.

And why can't they just help themselves? Jyn thought savagely. How many times had the Empire done this sort of thing, forcing a company out of business, taking over an area? *They could have just left.* They didn't need Blue. They needed to leave. If there was one lesson Jyn had learned, it was simply this: whenever the Empire or the rebellion showed up at your door, the best thing you could do was run.

That evening, Jyn took a viewscreen uploaded with old holodramas and curled up on the bench behind the table. The day's mission had struck a chord with everyone, and it was quiet on board the ship.

She felt Shawburn's eyes watching her. "What?" she asked, looking up from the viewer.

Shawburn smiled wistfully. "You remind me of Bardbee," she said.

The name, strangely, seemed a little familiar to Jyn. "Who is Bardbee?" she asked.

"He was a member of our crew. Got captured on Uchinao, after a mission went sour. He used to lay on that bench after missions, just like you're doing. Well, not *just* like. He was a Rayeth—long and slender, with these membranes. . . ."

Shawburn kept reminiscing, but Jyn felt sick to her stomach. She knew Bardbee.

"Anyway, we've not heard from him since his arrest," Shawburn said.

Jyn had heard from him. Jyn had heard his screams.

Burta, the ship's mechanic, was watching Jyn and Shawburn as well, looking up from a spare catalyzer she'd been working on. "Don't think you're taking Bardbee's place," she growled.

"I don't," Jyn said quietly.

"She's not," Shawburn said in a louder voice. "'Sides, Bardbee didn't work codes. We hired 'em out. Liana's got a right to be here."

Jyn internally cringed; Shawburn was sticking up for her, and she didn't even know her real name.

Burta rolled her eyes. Black oil stained her lavender skin as she rubbed a spot on her forehead. "That's what all humans think," she muttered.

Shawburn turned back to Jyn. "Don't mind her," she grumbled. "That one has it in for any humans."

"I don't see any Krish in the Empire," Burta shot back. "Or any Devaronians or anyone else."

"I don't work for—I'm not Imperial," Jyn sputtered weakly.

"No one's saying you are," Shawburn said, shooting Burta a dark look.

"I have wondered," Burta said as if Jyn hadn't spoken, "what this galaxy would be like without humans. Would the Krish have left their homeworld?" she said, jerking her head toward the pilot. "Would I have been on a ship soaring through space?"

"Other species have interstellar travel," Jyn protested. "That didn't just come from humans. The humans never would have figured it out if not for—"

Burta cut her off. "That's not what I mean. I mean"—she sighed heavily—"humans *spread*."

"Spread?"

"They're never happy. They're always moving. Spreading out. Taking new planets. Every 'settlement,' every colony, every outpost in the Outer Rim—it's always humans, isn't it? It's always humans spreading across the galaxy, leeching away at the people and the plants and the animals and the worlds. And now there's the Empire and the rebels, and while other species are a part of it, at the core it's just more humans."

"Some people," Jyn said, "would consider this a skill. Humans adapt. Got mountains? Build ridgecrawlers. Too much water? Build scub-subs. An ice planet? Use radiated igurts. People adapt."

"Yes," Burta said, "but should they? Either humans adapt, or they force the planet to adapt to them. This is *not* normal."

This was not an issue Jyn had ever truly considered before. She thought of her family. Her father mining crystals and working with the Empire until the planets could give him no more. But on the other hand, her mother trying to protect planets with legacy status, researching the B'ankor refuge on Coruscant.

And there was beauty out there, too. Jyn ignored it, but if it hadn't been for her parents, she never would have seen the crystal caves of Alpinn. She wouldn't have stood on the island in Wrea and seen the meteors shower down as bits from the asteroid belt broke off and fell to the planet. She wouldn't have gone to Skuhl and tasted bunn or seen a bulba. Or kissed Hadder.

"There are other species all across the galaxy," Jyn protested. "I couldn't even count all the different species on Coruscant—"

Burta waved her hand. "The exception, not the rule. Every species has the rare freak that wants to explore, to abandon their homeworld."

"Including you?"

Burta looked sad for a moment. "Including me."

CHAPTER FORTY-SIX_

Blue took on two more legitimate jobs before restocking with foodstuffs on Satotai for another supply run to Watassay. Jyn was starting to doubt they'd ever go to their secret base, the headquarters that apparently connected Blue's group to a wider network, one the Empire wanted to take down.

She was starting to like working with Blue and the rest of the crew . . . and she *hated* that. The more she fell into a friendship with them, the more acutely aware Jyn was of the futility of it all. She had already infected the ship with a tracker code. Every time they passed an Imperial checkpoint or made it through a blockade, Blue beamed at Jyn, and Jyn knew that Admiral Rocwyn was logging the ship's location.

It wasn't that she felt Blue was making the right choice by subverting the Empire. She just liked Blue and her crew as people. If she could convince them to do something other than undermine the Empire, to leave this system and quit dabbling in insurgencies, Jyn would happily join them.

The day before they reached Watassay, Blue knocked on Jyn's door.

"You've not been with us that long," she said, "and the crew likes working with you."

"Not Burta," Jyn said.

Blue laughed. "Burta likes you well enough for a human," she said. "Don't worry. She's coming around."

She shouldn't, Jyn thought.

"Anyway, after this mission, we're going off-system. There are other people we work with, other partisans. I want you to meet the rest of them. I think you'll like what we're doing."

Jyn's heart sank. So. She was finally being taken to the main base. It was over. But she liked Blue enough to want to be honest.

"Blue," she said slowly, "I don't understand you. You have a ship; you have a crew. Why are you trying to take on the Empire all on your own?"

Blue leaned in conspiratorially. "Who says I'm alone?"

Damn, Jyn thought. "Look, Blue, I like you. But I'm not here for some bigger mission or ideals or anything like that. I care about getting paid. I don't want to get involved in anything bigger. I have seen how bad things can be. I don't want to be a part of that."

"Liana, you saw Watassay. You saw what a difference we made."

"I saw people who should have given up their claims on a mine and gotten off-world a long time ago," Jyn snapped. "The best thing you can do right now is give up whatever group you're in and quit making Imperial enemies." *Or rebel allies,* she thought.

Blue stared at her for several long moments. "I don't believe that," she said. "And I don't believe you believe that."

"You're wrong," Jyn promised.

Blue smiled. "We'll see."

Blue shut the door behind her, and Jyn stared at it silently for a long time. *I tried,* Jyn thought. Blue was a good person.

Too bad she was a rebel.

"I'm always nervous, seeing Star Destroyers like that," Shawburn said, glaring at the blockade surrounding Watassay. "They ain't natural, ships that big."

"Don't be nervous," Blue said from the copilot's seat. "Liana has us covered." She looked over her shoulder and shot Jyn a smile.

Jyn swallowed. She would be so happy when she could quit being in the middle of two groups she hated. It was almost over. And then, even if it took every credit she had, Jyn was leaving the Five Points system.

"Uploading our clearance codes and manifest now," Shawburn said.

"They've locked a tractor beam on us," Blue said, her voice growing tense.

"The codes ain't working this time." Burta glowered at Jyn.

"They should," Jyn said, surprised.

"They're just doing a deeper scan," Blue said, cutting through the tension. "They're still going to accept Liana's codes."

After several uneasy moments, Shawburn said, "Codes cleared."

Jyn let out a whoosh of breath. Burta glared at her.

"Tractor beam still locked," Blue said.

"The Star Destroyer is hailing us directly," Shawburn added.

A steady beeping filled the control room.

"We should answer it," Shawburn said.

Beep. Beep. Beep.

"We should," Blue agreed. But she hesitated a moment longer before answering the incoming holo.

"Admiral Rocwyn from the Star Destroyer *Authority*," the admiral said in a crisp voice. "This ship has been identified as part of a partisan group working to undermine the Empire."

"How did they know?" Shawburn asked in a voice that broke Jyn's heart.

"Prepare for boarding. Do not attempt to resist." The admiral's voice cut out abruptly.

"How *did* they know?" Burta snarled, cutting her eyes to Jyn.

"Settle," Blue ordered. "We know nothing now. They don't have proof. Our docs will check out." She shot Jyn a brief smile. "You two with me," she said to Burta and Jyn after giving Shawburn the order to unlock the port.

The three were silent as they clomped down the metal hallway to the transport tube. Blue stood very straight, her eyes on the port as it opened and two stormtroopers marched onto her ship. It was taking everything in her to show courage, Jyn could tell.

A pair of Imperial officers followed the stormtroopers, then Admiral Rocwyn and two more troopers. They lined up in a curve around Blue, Burta, and Jyn.

"Secure the ship," the admiral said languidly, and three of the stormtroopers filed out.

"Admiral," Blue said, not a hint of quaver in her voice, "our docs are in order. We are a legitimate operation freighting cargo throughout the system. We pay our fees, and—"

The admiral cut her off with a bored wave of her hand. "You're all under arrest for conspiring against the Empire." She did not even deign to look Blue in the face as she said it.

Before Blue could protest, the fourth stormtrooper stepped forward, slapping the Devaronian in cuffs.

"Hey!" Burta bellowed. The stormtrooper blasted her, and she dropped to the ground. Blue cried out, but the blast had been set to stun. The stormtrooper cuffed Burta before she could wake up.

And Jyn just stood there.

The stormtrooper approached with a third set of cuffs. "No," Jyn said, stepping back and shaking her head.

Blue narrowed her eyes.

"Her too," Admiral Rocwyn said idly.

"No!" Jyn said louder, jerking away from the stormtrooper.

"How did you find us out?" Blue snarled, wrenching against her cuffs.

The admiral smiled, her lips curving up slowly, maliciously.

"How?" Blue shouted. The other three stormtroopers marched back to the port, the rest of the crew cuffed, their heads low.

"That disgusting Rayeth gave you up before he died," Admiral Rocwyn said. "But even if he hadn't, Liana was kind enough to plant a tracker on you. We know everything. As captain, you'll be executed for your treason." She stated this in a mild, matter-of-fact tone that brooked no argument. "The others . . ." She shrugged.

"Traitor!" Blue screamed at Jyn.

"I tried to tell you," Jyn said. Her eyes moved to Blue, and she saw only fury and distrust in the Devaronian's gaze.

"You didn't try that hard," Blue snarled. There was such pure rage in Blue's eyes that Jyn flinched. But there was something else there that she recognized, too, that reminded her of Saw. He'd had that same fury.

And Jyn realized with a shock, she had once burned with belief, too. Her heart thudded in her chest, hollow.

"Her as well," Admiral Rocwyn said in an irritated voice, flicking her hand at Jyn. "Hurry up."

"I did what you said!" Jyn said, whirling around to face the admiral. She was aware—and ashamed—of the plea in her voice, of the way the crew of the XOI stood witness to her treachery.

"Do you think that protects you?" Admiral Rocwyn said, feigning confusion. "Don't be stupid, girl. You're a petty criminal at best. We have no further need of you. And besides," she added, shrugging, "if I do, I know exactly where I'll be able to find you."

As Jyn stood there in shock, the stormtrooper finally clasped one of her wrists in a cuff.

"In one of the Empire's glorious labor camps," the admiral finished.

Blind panic surged in Jyn. As the stormtrooper reached for her other wrist, she swung around wildly, slamming her fist painfully into his helmet.

"Come peacefully," the stormtrooper ordered.

"Like hell I will," Jyn snarled. She kicked out, low, sweeping the stormtrooper to the ground. Another attacked her, twisting her cuffed arm painfully behind her, but Jyn wrenched free, pushing him away. Something primal within her roared in her blood, and she fought against the stormtroopers viciously, far more desperately than she'd ever fought before. She felt certain that fate had finally caught up with her, that if she didn't escape now, she never would.

But it did no good.

With the help of a stun prod and a sharp kick in her ribs, a stormtrooper dragged Jyn, cuffed, over to the wall, forcing her to stand beside Blue as the admiral strolled back to her Star Destroyer and the troopers prepared to put them in the brig.

Jyn stared at the metal floor, her eyes stinging. She could tell that Blue was watching her, and she dared to look up at the Devaronian, over to Shawburn. They had accepted her. They had wanted her to be a part of their movement, their cause. They had put their hope in her hands.

And she had thrown it away.

For *nothing*. In the end, she hadn't helped Blue or the cause or even herself. She had only wanted to escape this life, and now she was being crushed by it.

If I was going to go out like this anyway, Jyn thought as the troopers led her to the brig, *it should have been for more than nothing.*

IMPERIAL DETENTION CENTER & LABOR CAMP LEG-817

LOCATION: Wobani

PRISONER: Liana Hallik, #6295A

CRIMES: Forgery of Imperial Documents, Resisting Arrest, Aggravated Assault, Possession of Unsanctioned Weapon (two counts)

MONTH 05_

Her trial had been a joke. Admiral Rocwyn had passed down her sentence with barely a glance in Jyn's direction. Jyn had not been permitted to speak for herself or to defend her crimes of forgery and resisting arrest. When she tried to protest that she had been committing forgery for the Empire and had been resisting an unfair arrest, Commander Solange had panicked, suggesting that the admiral fit Jyn with a muzz regulator. The cold steel wrapped around her head, covering her mouth, and Jyn had not been allowed to speak another word until after the admiral had passed judgment and sentenced her to the LEG-817 prison camp on Wobani.

She had two bits of luck. The first was that Admiral Rocwyn believed her scandocs were legitimate and that Jyn's real name was Liana Hallik. The second was that when they scanned her for weapons, the stormtroopers in charge of inspecting Jyn had thought her necklace was a worthless piece of glass.

As she'd been led away, Jyn had wondered if she could effectively fight back. The muzz regulator around her mouth bit into the thin skin of her skull, and the binders on her wrists were heavy and unbreakable. When she tried to jerk away from the stormtroopers holding her elbows, their grip tightened, and one of them warned he had a stun prod in his other hand. He sparked it in front of her, and Jyn did not need a second warning. She did not see Blue or the others. She never saw any of them again. She liked to pretend that they had escaped, somehow. But she never really believed it.

And then Jyn had been put on the prison transport ship and taken to Wobani, and the warden had led her to her cell.

And there had been no more chances to escape.

After Zorahda died, Jyn had time to think. Of Akshaya, who believed that the giant Empire would never bother with ants like her. Of her father, who had chosen the Empire because he had known, even that long before, that there was no real choice. Of Blue, who had chosen to fight, who had believed *that* was the only option.

The only thing Jyn knew for sure was that her mother had believed hope was the most important thing in the universe, and Jyn had none of that left.

◈

"I'm going to escape," her new cellmate, a Mirialan said. Her smooth, pale yellow skin and the pattern of blackish-blue diamonds across her face stood out in the dim light.

"That's nice," Jyn said in a tired voice.

"I'm going to," Yalla said again, her voice starting to rise from a whisper. "You can help."

"I just want to sleep." Jyn rolled over in her cubby.

The Mirialan made a disgusted noise deep in her throat. "How can you just accept this?" she hissed in the dark.

Because, Jyn thought, *this is all there is.*

"What are you?" Yalla said after enough time had passed that Jyn had dared to hope the conversation was over.

"Human?" Jyn replied in the darkness, not sure of Yalla's question.

"No, I mean—were you a rebel? Why are you here on Wobani?"

Jyn turned around, her mattress emitting a puff

of musty air as her body shifted on it. She could see Yalla's big azure eyes in the dim light, watching her.

Was Jyn a rebel? Not really. And she'd even worked *for* the Empire, not against it.

But when it mattered—when Hadder and Akshaya had been threatened, when Jyn found herself on a slave ship—when it mattered, Jyn had chosen her side instinctively. She had chosen to fight. Was that enough to make her a rebel?

Yalla was waiting for her answer.

Jyn turned back to the wall.

⬥

Yalla was part of an influx of new prisoners. She knew others at Wobani, a network of people from planets in the Mirial system. A small rebellious militia group. The Empire had separated the group across different prisons, but it hadn't done a good enough job. Yalla made contact with other prisoners, brief coded exchanges.

And every night, Yalla glared at Jyn with contempt. "You could do so much more," she hissed, disappointed. "We could overtake the entire prison. There aren't that many guards. The prison is overcrowded."

Jyn ignored her.

But she noticed who Yalla spoke to, and how. She noticed the laser pick she pinched from the work detail, and where she hid it under her mattress. She noticed the way Yalla grew more and more jumpy, waiting for some message.

Yalla reminded Jyn of Saw. He had said once that one person could turn the tide of war with nothing more than a pointed stick. She had thought, then, that he had believed in her and her ability to do such marvels. She knew now she wasn't that kind of person. But Yalla might have been.

And then the moment came. Yalla's group waited until the hour before work detail started. An alarm blared from the level below and above them, and Yalla jumped up, throwing her mattress aside and pulling out the laser pick and a large impact hammer drill that Jyn had somehow missed earlier.

"It's time," Yalla said, a fierceness in her voice that the prison hadn't been able to stamp out. "You in or out?"

Impossibly, the door to their cell swung open. Jyn stared at it, shocked.

Before she could answer, Yalla thrust the impact hammer drill into Jyn's open hands. "Come on!" she yelled, racing out of the room, laser pick held high.

She had made it about six meters past the door when blaster fire rang out. Two short bursts, and Jyn watched as Yalla's body crumpled. The stormtroopers swarmed the hall, a pair racing into Jyn's open cell.

"She has a weapon!" one stormtrooper said.

Jyn dropped the blasting hammer on the ground, her eyes wide, her hands shooting into the air.

She had a new cellmate after that. She didn't know what species Nail was, and Nail wasn't the type to share a friendly conversation with. She was short, tentacles obscuring her mouth, with gelatinous eyes and long fingers. And she hated Jyn for no discernable reason.

Still, Jyn appreciated her new cellmate.

She didn't make Jyn hope for more.

IMPERIAL DETENTION CENTER & LABOR CAMP LEG-817

LOCATION: Wobani

PRISONER: Liana Hallik, #6295A

CRIMES: Forgery of Imperial Documents, Resisting Arrest, Aggravated Assault, Possession of Unsanctioned Weapon (two counts), Escape from Custody

MONTH 06_

Hope, Jyn had found, was by far the most dangerous thing in a prison. It made people do stupid things. It made them believe there was life outside the walls.

And furthermore, hope *hurt*.

It was a physical, painful ache, deep inside her chest. Jyn felt it eating away at her lungs when she coughed from the dust on the rare days she was given farm duty. It gnawed at her belly when the ration cubes didn't satisfy the hunger. It burned her throat when the stormtroopers didn't bother refilling their filtration canteens. It stung at her eyes every night before she passed out from exhaustion.

There were ants in the cell. No doubt drawn by

Nail's stench. Jyn's cellmate was proving difficult; she had even threatened to kill Jyn. One more thing for her to survive.

Jyn watched the ants, marching up the wall and through the corner where it met with the ceiling. There was nothing for them to eat there, but still they marched. Jyn placed her hand against the wall, directly in the ants' path, and they adjusted course, curving around the edge of her fingers.

The ants reminded her of Akshaya, and Akshaya reminded her of Hadder, and Hadder reminded her of just how much she had lost.

She curled into herself, her hand dropping from the wall to the leather cord around her neck. They hadn't taken her necklace. She had been certain they would, but they hadn't. She still had this one link to her mother, her past.

It wouldn't be hard to die. She saw death every day on Wobani. It was just a matter of putting down one's tools, refusing to work. And then a stormtrooper came and held a blaster up, and it was over.

Simple.

Jyn felt as if her chest were filled with ash. But there was one ember still remaining, flickering orange and red, refusing to die.

Jyn clutched her kyber crystal, the hard edges digging into the callouses on her palms. Her mother had given the crystal to her because she had expected Jyn to survive. To live.

To not give up hope.

◈

The alarm for the work shift sounded. Jyn stood. Her cellmate stood. They waited by the door. If they were lucky, they'd be selected for farm work.

They were lucky.

When the doors slid open, they held their wrists up, waiting for a stormtrooper to put their shackles on. Jyn didn't flinch as the heavy metal restraints closed over her wrists, the light on the base blinking from green to red. She and her cellmate filed in behind the others. They marched, their feet beating out a steady rhythm that shook the walls. Jyn knew what to do—follow her orders. She knew what to say—nothing. But she also watched. Her eyes flicked left and right, seeing the stormtrooper, the other prisoners, the walls. She was waiting.

For an opportunity.

◈

The prison transport tank was not comfortable. It wasn't meant to be. Each prisoner was given a small, hard metal seat that folded down from the wall. Beams provided barriers between the seats, and the aisle was large enough for the stormtroopers to constantly patrol. Jyn pushed down her seat awkwardly with her cuffed hands and slid into it. A stormtrooper came up behind her and used the magnalocks to connect the center of her cuffs to the metal chair.

It was surprisingly cold on Wobani. The cold crept through the transport tank's walls and air vents. It seeped into her bones. She flexed her fingers. The gloves they gave the workers did little to protect from cold; they were only meant to keep the skin on their palms so they could work longer. Jyn thought of the synthskin gloves she'd inherited from Maia, and a pang of sorrow bit into her.

Across from her, Jyn's cellmate stared down at the floor. Her long mouth tentacles, reddish-brown and drooping, fluttered nervously. Jyn leaned back. The Aqualish in the group chittered angrily at the rough way the stormtrooper clipped his binders to the seat; they dug into his wrists painfully.

The prison tank's engine warmed up and heaved into motion. It bumped along the muddy, unpaved road, jostling the prisoners.

And then Jyn felt a different sort of lurch.

Her head jerked to the big gray door at the end of the aisle. There was a glow behind it, like the rising sun, peeking through the cracks around the frame.

And then the door blew off.

The stormtrooper who had rushed forward was blown back from the blast, his body prone in the aisle. Jyn jerked up, cursing her restraints silently, her eyes wide. A group of humans rushed onto the transport, a tall man with dark hair and stubble on his chin at the front of the line. While two other men took defensive stances with their blasters, his gaze moved quickly around the cabin. He was clearly looking for someone specific.

Her.

EPILOGUE_

Jyn breathed deeply, relishing the scent of fresh air and plants from outside, mingling with the smell of fuel and the burning tang of jet juice inside.

"Come on," the leader of her escape said, motioning her forward.

"What *is* this?" she asked, rushing to keep up.

"This is the Rebellion," he said simply.

She stared in wonder as she was led past a hangar filled with X- and Y-wings, past people talking excitedly, past droids rushing by. Her eyes drank in the glimpse of the outside world she could see through the hangar door: lush greenery, low mountains, and a stone-stepped ziggurat rising through the jungle. She was led farther into the base. The atmosphere shifted; the flyboys weren't there, making jokes and regaling each other with their exploits. This part of the base was solemn, dark. Her entourage stopped outside a door. She remembered Idryssa and Xosad and their hints that something big was happening, that an alliance was forming. She had no idea that it was *this* big, this organized.

This real.

Her entourage stopped in front of a door, and Jyn tentatively stepped inside the room. The command center, she realized. Green light boards glowed with strategies and maps. The people huddled together in the room spoke in low voices, urgency and worry seeping from their tones.

When the door closed behind her, silence pervaded the room.

Two men—generals—stared at Jyn. The older one seemed to judge her with his eyes, and clearly found her lacking. But Jyn wasn't watching him. Her eyes were on the woman who stood in front of one of the light boards. She wore all white, with a heavy pair of silver chains hanging from her shoulders and a beautiful necklace weighing down her neck. Her short hair was immaculately styled, and her eyes cut across the dim room, straight to Jyn's.

Jyn pretended not to know her, but she did. Anyone with access to the HoloNet knew this woman. Mon Mothma, exiled senator and presumed leader of the Rebellion.

The rumors were right, she thought. Her gaze flicked over to another man she recognized from the HoloNet: Bail Organa.

There was movement to Mon Mothma's left, and a captain emerged from the shadows. He had dark air and eyes that crinkled pleasantly even though his expression was grave. There was something about him that reminded her of . . . she couldn't quite place it. But he had a familiar sort of face, one she immediately wanted to trust. He looked like the kind of man who always got a laugh out of someone. Jyn couldn't take her eyes off him. Part of her wondered if he wanted to laugh at her. Part of her wondered if she'd just forgotten the way people's faces should be. There wasn't laughter on Wobani.

"Be seated." Mon Mothma's cool, even voice demanded attention.

Jyn sank into her seat slowly, nervously. Wary.

One of the generals leveled his gaze at Jyn. "You're currently calling yourself . . ." He checked his file. "Liana Hallik. Is that correct?"

Jyn's heart ramped up. She felt trapped. Exposed. Confused.

The general looked down at his file again, smug. "Possession of unsanctioned weapons, forgery of Imperial documents, aggravated assault, escape from custody, resisting arrest . . ." He met Jyn's eyes. "Imagine if the Imperial authorities had found out who you really were. Jyn Erso."

The world bottomed out at the sound of her real name.

He knew. Her gaze flicked around to the others in the room. *They* all *knew.*

The general was eating it up. "That's your given name, is it not? Jyn Erso? Daughter of Galen Erso." He paused. "A known Imperial collaborator in weapons development."

"I have no father," Jyn said, her words strong with the conviction she put behind them.

Mon Mothma spoke softly, her voice sad, or maybe just tired. "A girl raised to be a soldier."

Jyn turned her gaze to Mon Mothma. Did she expect Jyn to be sad that Saw had taught her how to fight? How to survive?

But she didn't get her first lesson from Saw. Jyn looked at Mon Mothma's pitying gaze, but she didn't see her. She saw her parents, fleeing Coruscant, running away for their freedom from the Empire. They had settled on Lah'mu, but her mother had never quite given up the idea that they were still running. When the Empire came, Jyn's father had surrendered easily. Far too easily. But her mother . . . her mother had fought.

Papa had told Mama to run.

She hadn't.

The Empire had told her to stand down, to go quietly.

She hadn't.

Jyn looked up, glaring at the rebels around her. Who were they to judge? They didn't know the smell of rain on dirt mixed with blood and blaster fire. They couldn't identify stormtrooper boots by sound alone.

They didn't wake up with the nightmares of Jyn's past, the choices that haunted her.

Had it been easy for them, black and white as a stormtrooper's armor, when they chose to rebel against the Empire?

Mon Mothma and the others stated their case, giving the reason they wanted Jyn's help. The ghosts of her past mocked her.

She could never escape her father's long shadow.

She thought of Blue, of Hadder, of Saw, of her mother.

Of her father, walking away with the man in the long white cape.

They were asking her to find her father. To find him and uncover the weapon he had helped make. It was Saw's old mission, fully realized.

Jyn could feel the kyber crystal necklace around her throat. She remembered the moment when her mother gave her that necklace, minutes before she was killed.

But she could remember further back, when her father had given her mother the crystal. They had been on Coruscant then. Her mother had been uneasy unhappy, but her father had relished the funding from the Empire, the chance to follow his dreams deep into his research of the mysterious kyber crystals.

"This," Papa had said, holding up a small kyber crystal after inspecting it in the crystalline spectrometer, "is so much more than a rock."

"Really?" Her mother had laughed at him. "It looks like a rock to me."

Papa shook his head. "That's what makes kyber crystals so special," he said. "They seem like innocent little stones. But they can harness so much more power than you would think. Their history is marred with legend, but the fact remains—they have the potential to change the whole galaxy."

"One little rock," Mom had said, wrapping her arms around him. "And there's a crack in it."

Papa quickly wrapped wire around the clear crystal, threaded it with a cord, and slipped the kyber over Mom's head. He kissed her, a quick little peck, and said, "You never know. Something small and broken really can be powerful."

The last thing Papa had said to Jyn was to trust him. The last thing Mama had said was to trust the Force.

She wasn't sure she could do either of those things, but for the first time since she was eight years old, she was willing to try.

Jyn swallowed. She looked out at the faces of the people around her. Expectant. She recognized something in their expressions that she had never expected to see again.

Hope.

She had thought her hope had died on Wobani. Snuffed out like a flame deprived of oxygen. Before Zorahda had killed herself, Jyn had nothing to help her with, not even lies. But seeing these people, the way they still believed they had a chance—a chance hinged on *her*—rekindled that spark inside her heart that she had thought died long before.

She wouldn't go down again for doing nothing.

They were giving her a chance. It wouldn't change what had happened in the past. But maybe it would help change the future.

"Yes," she said firmly. "I'll do it."